Falling for a Fake Cowboy

VARGAS RANCH PREQUEL

Karen Baney

desert life
media

Falling for a Fake Cowboy (Vargas Ranch Prequel)
By Karen Baney

Cover Design by Karen Baney

Copyright © 2025 by Karen Baney

Publisher:
Desert Life Media, LLC
Gilbert, AZ 85295

www.karenbaney.com

Printed in the United States of America

ISBN-978-1-960217-59-2

With regard to the works of man,
by the word of your lips
I have avoided the ways of the violent.
My steps have held fast to your paths;
my feet have not slipped.

Psalms 17:4-5 ESV

1

"MORNING, AUNT GRETA!" Cara Hollis breezed through the back door of *The Lariat*, her aunt's western bistro nestled in Wickenburg, Arizona. The familiar aroma of bacon grease clung to the air — so familiar, yet something she dreamed of changing. Aunt Greta had taken over from Cara's grandparents fifteen years ago, keeping the place just as it had always been.

Cara rounded the counter and reached for the coffee urn. As she pulled back on the toggle, the rich, dark brew streamed into her travel mug, its tantalizing scent stirring her senses. Someday, maybe Aunt Greta would finally let her modernize the place.

The vinyl seats had been patched so many times they resembled a quilt, the mismatched creamers, the unchanged menu — Cara had a hundred ideas that would transform the restaurant into a modern western café with French bistro charm, all without touching the beloved dishes.

"You're out early." Aunt Greta flicked her wrist to check her watch.

Cara took a sip of coffee and nodded. "Headed over to Vargas Ranch."

"Taking pictures?"

Greta busied herself refilling the creamers before straightening the sugar packets and cup sleeves. The sleeves had been one of Cara's few victories. She held back a grin.

Change took time. Usually more than she had patience for.

"That, and Catalina Vargas hired me to redecorate the casitas, dining hall, and office."

Aunt Greta smiled, tossing her long gray braid over her shoulder. As she absently wiped down the plastic-covered menus, pride flickered in her eyes.

"I'm so proud of you. Have fun!"

Cara hugged her aunt, warmth blooming in her chest at those words. She admired Greta's fierce independence and hoped her own choices would lead her down a similar path of self-sufficiency and self-respect.

With her coffee mug securely nestled in the cup holder, Cara backed out of the lot, excitement bubbling in her veins as the first golden rays of morning kissed the horizon.

The half-hour drive to the ranch stole her breath as the sky blazed with orange and pink streaks. She pulled off to the side of the dirt road, antsy with the creative rush that often propelled her to snap photos of God's amazing creation.

She flung her door open. The cooler morning air tickled her lungs. Cool was a relative term. After all, it was May in Arizona. In another hour, the sun would sizzle the skin off her arms. Right now? It was tolerable.

Cara hopped out of her luxury SUV, camera in hand. Then she hiked up the slope of Vargas Wash. The vantage point gave her a perfect angle to catch the sunlight casting highlights and shadows over Dalton Peak.

She raised her camera and looked through the viewfinder, lightly pressing the button so the light meter could assess the perfect setting. After shooting several pictures, she flipped the settings to her preferences and took more.

"Watch out!"

A deep male voice warned. The words barely registered before an animal barreled into her from behind, knocking her off balance.

Her backside hit the ground first, sending a shockwave of pain pulsing through her low back. She tucked her expensive camera to her chest as her other arm extended forward, bracing for the fall. Her face landed in the sandy dirt bottom of the wadi, a good ten yards below where she'd been standing.

Before she could even blink, a sloppy wet tongue stroked her face, coating it in some nasty-smelling dog slobber. She swiped her arm across her face and sputtered when the mix of dirt and slobber ended up on her lips. Bitter. Ew.

"Get off!"

The dog clearly didn't understand English because it placed its dusty paws on her stomach, barking in her face, its wiggling butt perched in the air. At least the dog thought they were playing a game.

"Goldie! Heel!"

The dog, presumably Goldie, rubbed her face on Cara's chest and neck before slobbering all over her again. Gross.

"Heel!" the male voice exclaimed. Firmer this time, as if he had to work up to that level of correction.

A frustrated groan echoed nearby. Probably the dog's owner.

Cara wedged her arm between herself and the dirty, kiss-happy dog. She shoved with all her might, finally dislodging the mutt from her body. She sat up, using her foot to keep it away from her abdomen, then glanced at her camera. Ugh. Fine silt coated her very pricey lens.

"Goldie!"

"Does she know that's her name?!" Cara snapped, failing to keep the frustration from her voice.

The squeak of saddle leather sounded behind her. The distinct smell of horse hung heavy in the air. Rapid thuds closed the distance. A spray of more silt flew in her face. Could her morning get any worse?

A shadow fell over her in the shape of a cowboy hat and broad shoulders.

"I'm so sorry."

The cowboy's deep voice sent a wave of shivers through

her. A large, calloused hand reached toward the dog's collar, lifting the rather heavy beast away from Cara as if it weighed nothing.

"You need to listen to me," he scolded the dog, voice firm but weary, like he knew it was a losing battle.

Cara snorted, slinging the camera strap over her neck where it should have been. She brushed her hands together, wiping the bits of dirt from her skin, then ran her fingers through her hair to loosen the grit. She had to be a ghastly sight.

The cowboy loomed in front of her, startling her. Green eyes. Too distracting. Heat bloomed on her face.

"Are you okay?"

Her gaze dropped to his hand. Strong. Calloused. Rough in a way that shouldn't be appealing. A bolt of energy surged between them, an awareness that made her pulse skip and her breath catch. She'd never felt anything quite like it—this immediate, noticeable reaction to a complete stranger.

She tugged herself to her feet, sending her camera crashing into his chest. A very broad, sturdy chest. Warm beneath her palm. She gulped as he rubbed his fingers over the spot, his eyes never leaving hers.

Cara tore her gaze away. She was still on a schedule. Important things to do. Ogling a green-eyed cowboy shouldn't be one of them.

As heat warmed her face, she swatted at the dirt clinging to her pants and the front of her blouse. All hope of presenting a professional image in her meeting with Catalina Vargas was long gone.

"I'm, uh. Ugh."

"Is it broken?"

Cara's eyes snapped up to those ridiculous green eyes again. This time she noticed his tanned face, angular jaw, and perfectly handsome chin dimple. Bet that was a pain to shave.

"My hand's fine."

"No. Your camera." An edge tinged his voice. Worry?

She let out an exasperated sigh. "I don't think so. I'll probably have to send it off for professional cleaning."

"Let me know the cost for that. I'll cover it."

Cara snorted at the too-good-looking-for-his-own-good cowboy.

"I can replace it if it's broken." He stepped closer with conviction.

Her eyes traveled from his old brown hat to his cheap shirt, fraying at the cuffs, to his scuffed, well-worn boots that were past due for resoling.

"It's a four thousand dollar lens."

The cowboy choked and beat his fisted hand against his chest, eyes rounding like wagon wheels. She held back a snicker at the imagery her mind conjured.

"Um. Well. Let's hope the cleaning works."

"Maybe if you spent some money on obedience classes, it would be cheaper. Now, if you'll excuse me. I have a meeting to get to."

With her parting barb, Cara straightened her back and marched away from the dumbfounded cowboy and his un-disciplined dog. Not fast enough to miss his muttered snark. Something about cowboys being forgiving of bad manners.

She fought back the sting of tears as she set her filthy camera on the seat next to the camera bag. The last thing she needed was sand working its way into the bag. She hoped she didn't have to replace the lens. It was her first purchase from her own wages instead of her trust fund, which brought her a sense of pride.

She drove the rest of the way to the resort office at Vargas Guest Ranch and Resort. Maybe she would get a few amazing shots off the SD card. She could always hope.

Cara pulled her mussed hair back with a ponytail holder from her purse, grabbed her work tote from the back seat, squared her shoulders, and entered the resort's business office.

"Cara! *Buenos días!*" Catalina Vargas greeted her warmly in her lyrical accent.

"Morning."

"Right this way."

She followed the short middle-aged woman into an office and sat in a guest chair. Cara retrieved her tablet from her bag and loaded the rendering of her vision to transform the resort's casitas, dining hall, and front office.

Cara held the tablet as Catalina sat next to her. She swiped through the images, pleased by Catalina's delighted squeals.

"*Muy bueno!* You've captured the history with a modern feel."

"Thank you."

"If you want to head over to the Cholla Casita to get started, our new handyman, Sawyer, should be there."

Cara thanked Catalina. After they settled a few administrative details, she walked over to the casita, eager to begin her largest interior design job since she started her business a year ago. Landing this account meant everything—and another step in her journey to independence from her family's toxic influence.

SAWYER TRIED TO hold on to his frustration as he watched the sassy photographer walk away. But the stubborn curve of a smile tugged at one side of his mouth against his will. Goldie jumped up, paws landing on his chest. Her pink tongue slathered his neck with sticky dog kisses, breaking down every last wall he'd tried to keep intact.

"Doggone it, dog."

He should be mad. He wanted to be mad. Instead, he scratched her neck on both sides, his fingers tangling in the silky fur he had worked so hard to clean. She gazed up at him with those golden-brown eyes, unburdened by past mistakes, unshaken by his flaws. No judgment. No conditions. Just unfiltered loyalty.

With a sigh, he pushed her off him, but it was pointless. His heart had already melted. Forgiveness came easily with Goldie. Easier than it ever had with himself.

Sawyer swung into his saddle and squeezed his knees to nudge his horse forward. He whistled, and Goldie trotted beside him, tongue lolling to the side like she hadn't just knocked a woman flat on her face.

His gut twisted. He hadn't even asked her name. How could he make this right if he didn't even know who she was? She'd looked at him like he was delusional when he offered to pay for the camera. Four thousand dollars. He definitely didn't have four grand.

Nothing in his possession was truly his own. Not the horse, not the truck, not even the clothes on his back. Everything had been given to him. Not earned. Not chosen. Just handed over in the quiet agreement that he needed saving. The photographer had seen through him instantly. One look at his frayed shirt and worn boots, and she'd known he was broke.

Sawyer sighed. The money disappeared fast between changing his identity and taking in the stray golden retriever. Only two people in the world knew his birth name. And it had to stay that way. One slip, one wrong word, one question that dug too deep and everything would unravel. He needed to make sure no one looked too closely.

Sawyer drove over to the casita, Goldie panting happily in the passenger seat beside him.

He still couldn't believe Tres Vargas gave him a job. No questions asked. A lifeline. That's what this was. But trust like that had never come easy for him. He knew the world had a way of snatching away good things just when he started to believe they might last.

He had so few useful skills. One foster family owned horses, so he learned to ride and work with them for two years. Then they shipped him off to another family. No explanation why. Between his handyman skills and that minor experience with horses, Tres must have decided Sawyer had enough ability to be worth the chance.

When Dalton, Tres' son and the ranch manager, had said they included room and board, Sawyer had felt his composure crack for just a moment before he pulled himself together. Stretching his last twenty bucks for two more weeks? Impossible. They also welcomed Goldie—as long as Sawyer kept her current on her vaccinations and paid for her food and grooming. Another small kindness. Another debt he had no way of repaying.

At least grooming her hadn't been a problem. When he first found her, her fur had been a matted, dirty tangle. Six bucks at the dollar store. Dog shampoo, a brush, a bag of food, and a beach towel. Not much, but enough to give her a fresh start. He'd spent hours bathing and brushing her, untangling her knots as if undoing a small part of the damage life had done to both of them. By the time the brown faded, revealing her golden coat beneath, he knew. Goldie. She was his now. His first real responsibility. His first real friend.

He planned to take her to a vet as soon as he received his first paycheck, make sure she had all her shots, get her taken care of like she deserved. He would do this right. Even if the rest of his life felt like it barely held together with borrowed time and second chances.

As he lugged his toolbox toward the Cholla Casita, Goldie bounded beside him, radiating pure joy while Sawyer carried his invisible burden. In the few days he had known her, she lifted his spirits, gave him hope that, at thirty years old, he might finally get the break he needed to turn his life around for good.

A young woman named Renata waited for him on the rustic porch, her smile warm and professional. She introduced herself as a cousin who worked in the front office.

"The interior designer may stop by to look at the place." She handed him a neatly typed list. "The painting and plumbing supplies are in this closet. Drywall sheets, tape, and mud are in the workshop by the bunkhouse. Help yourself to what you need."

Sawyer scanned the list, noting the detailed work orders. Professional. Organized. Nothing like the haphazard jobs he'd done before.

"Cara will purchase the furniture, decor, and finishes. She'll have it delivered in the next few days. Will this keep you busy until then?"

"I'll stop in the office if I finish early."

"Actually, let me get your number so you can text me instead." She pulled out her phone, thumb poised to enter his contact.

Heat crept up his neck. A phone wasn't gonna happen until payday. "Don't have one yet."

Her smile faltered slightly. "Oh. Well, I'll drop off a loaner phone for you soon."

He nodded his thanks as she left, but unease coiled tight in his gut. Another act of kindness. Another open hand extended in trust. He should be grateful. But mostly, it unsettled him. People had helped before. But the moment they saw him for what he really was, the kindness faded. Then they sent him away. Always sent him away.

Sawyer turned back to the casita, shifting his focus. The morning sun streamed through dust-covered windows, illuminating a space that had seen better days. The kitchenette appliances looked about ten years old, though still functional. Plain white instead of modern stainless steel. The granite countertop had to be from the late nineties, showing chips along the edges and water stains near the sink.

He ran his hand along the worn surface, already envisioning the transformation. Soon, high-end clients would lounge on designer furniture. But first, he would strip away years of wear and tear with his bare hands. People who had roots would come here, stay for a week, and go home to real lives, real families, real stability. Something he never had.

The thought of the photographer—Cara, Renata had called her—flashed through his mind. She clearly came from money, judging by that expensive camera and luxury SUV. Yet something in her eyes when she'd looked at him... not just annoyance at his dog's antics, but recognition. Like she'd seen something worth noticing.

He shook his head, pushing the thought aside. Women like that didn't notice men like him. Not in any way that mattered.

By lunchtime, Sawyer had repaired the plumbing under both sinks and demoed most of the shower tile. The repetitive motions of prying and scraping helped quiet his restless thoughts.

He had just decided it was time for his lunch break when a sound from the front entrance caught his attention.

"Get down!"

That familiar feminine voice—frustrated, slightly breathless. His shoulders tensed before he even looked up. He already knew who it was.

Goldie's happy whines confirmed his suspicion.

Sawyer groaned. Great. Just what he needed. Another reminder of how fast this woman could knock him off balance—literally.

2

CARA PUSHED THE door open to the Cholla Casita, only to be greeted by the slobber monster from earlier that morning.

"Get down!" She groused, shoving the golden retriever off her, trying—and failing—to preserve what little dignity she had left.

The same too-handsome-for-his-own-good cowboy from this morning clamped his calloused, warm hand around the dog's collar, murmuring something low under his breath. He was apologizing, she supposed. Not in words. But in that subtle way men like him probably handled every-thing—action over explanation.

She glanced down at her blouse and groaned. Seriously? A jagged rip stretched across the fabric, exposing far more skin than she was comfortable with. Fantastic. She looked like she'd barely survived a back alley brawl with nothing but a very enthusiastic dog as her attacker.

Tomorrow, she was dressing like a cowgirl. Especially if this man's menace of a dog planned to maul her every time they interacted. And judging by the sledgehammer in his other hand, they'd be interacting a lot.

She folded her arms, trying not to look rattled. "You must be Sawyer, the handyman."

Cara cringed inwardly at the slightly hostile edge to her voice. He didn't deserve her full frustration. Well, he kinda did, but her parents had taught her better.

Sawyer wrangled the rowdy dog into the bathroom and shut the door, effectively sentencing Goldie to temporary exile. Yelps and scratching sounds let them know the dog didn't care for the new arrangement.

He held out his hand for a shake. "Sawyer Fullerton."

She hesitated for half a second before reaching for his hand. Strong. Warm. Rougher than she expected. That momentary contact sent an unwelcome jolt through her chest, settling somewhere far too distracting. The callouses on his palm told stories of hard work, of labor her soft hands had never known.

She forced herself to focus. "Cara Hollis, the interior designer."

"And photographer."

Her cheeks flushed. Great. He remembered. She glanced away. "Um. That's a side gig."

When she looked at him again, his too-sharp gaze flickered downward, and he lifted a brow.

"Don't suppose you have another shirt stashed in your car."

She glanced down again, then sucked in a sharp breath. Wonderful. That big gash exposed her stomach and — oh, no — possibly part of her lacey bra. Heat surged to her face, neck — everywhere. She clutched the two halves together, wishing she could vanish into thin air.

"No."

Sawyer strode over to a stained snap-front shirt balled up on the kitchen countertop. Oh no. He wouldn't dare. He sniffed it before thrusting it toward her. "Want to borrow mine?"

She stilled. The heat in her face intensified. Her eyes darted around, as if another shirt might magically appear in the empty casita. It didn't.

Cara huffed, extended her hand, and snatched the offered shirt. The fabric was warm from his touch, soft cotton worn smooth by countless washings.

"You can change in the bedroom while I tie up Goldie outside."

"Isn't it too hot?"

"Naw. She's used to being outside. 'Sides, the porch offers plenty of shade, and there's a water bowl for her."

Cara scurried to the bedroom and closed the door, wasting no time shedding her shredded designer silk blouse. The contrast struck her—her expensive top versus his work shirt, both bearing the evidence of their very different lives.

Sliding her arms into his shirt, she sighed. It swam on her. The shoulder seam hung halfway to her elbows. Instead of tucking the long ends into her dress slacks, she tied it in a knot just below her waist.

His scent clung to the fabric, warm and masculine, with hints of honest sweat and something indefinably him. The intimacy of wearing his clothes, of being wrapped in something that had touched his skin, sent her pulse racing in ways that had nothing to do with the Arizona heat.

Not a hug, Cara. A shirt.

But her body didn't seem to understand the difference. She shook off the ridiculous thought, but the awareness lingered.

Still, tomorrow jeans.

When Cara opened the bedroom door, Sawyer cracked a cocky grin, showing off cheek dimples that matched the one on his chin. Of course, he had dimples. Of course.

"You look good in my shirt, even if it'd go better with jeans."

Her breath hitched, just for a moment, before she exhaled sharply, shaking her head. Yeah. Tomorrow jeans.

Sawyer turned his attention to the backsplash he'd been demoing in the bathroom, and the rhythmic *thunk* of his mallet against tile resumed. Cara blinked, arms crossing instinctively as she leaned against the doorway. Sawyer Fullerton—professional handyman—was pummeling the outdated tile like he was settling a personal score with it.

The muscles in his forearms tensed with each impact, the controlled power behind his swings almost impressive. Almost.

She arched a brow. "Is that... your actual process? Or do you just wrestle tile into submission?"

He didn't even pause his demolition, just threw her a quick, amused glance and, of course, a dimple popped out with it. Annoying.

"Depends." His voice carried the faintest rasp, like he'd been working long enough for exhaustion to creep in but not enough to slow him down. "Sometimes I negotiate. But this tile wasn't interested in peace talks."

Cara snorted despite herself. "Right. So instead of using a chisel, you went full barbarian on it?"

Whack. Crack. Another section crumbled beneath his unconventional method, sending a spray of crushed tile everywhere. At least she wouldn't have to clean up that mess.

Sawyer lifted a brow. "Would you rather I hand it a resignation letter and let it leave on its own?"

She shook her head, biting back a smile. "I'm just saying. There are actual tools for this kind of thing. Precise ones. Modern ones."

"This works just fine."

Sawyer laughed, the sound unexpectedly rich, and wiped sweat from his forehead with the back of his hand. The movement drew her gaze just for a second. Too steady. Too effortless. Too... male.

She cleared her throat, reclaiming her focus. "How about we just use the right tool instead?"

Sawyer tossed the mallet onto the countertop with a shrug, the weight of it landing with a dull *thud*. "If it means keeping the peace, I'll allow it."

Cara exhaled, shaking her head as he set aside his questionable demo tools, choosing the few she pointed to from his well-worn toolbox. At least that meant fewer broken walls.

She cleared her throat, hesitating for half a second. "You have a measuring tape handy?"

Sawyer unclipped an ancient metal one from his belt and handed it to her. She stared at the battered relic in disbelief. Was this thing older than the casita? She pulled out a few inches, watching it wobble dangerously, as if one more tug might be its final act.

"Nevermind. I'll grab my laser one from my car."

Sawyer chuckled, clipping it back onto his belt. "Gotta admit, I admire the dedication to your fancy tools."

"They're efficient."

"So is my crowbar."

Cara rolled her eyes, already heading for the door. This man!

"You eat lunch yet?" Sawyer asked as she stepped outside.

Cara shook her head, already prepared to decline whatever half-baked offer he had.

"Let me drive you over to the dining hall."

"No, that's alright. I'm not hungry."

As if on cue, her stomach betrayed her, letting out a grumble loud enough to rival his demolition work from earlier. Sawyer lifted one eyebrow, clearly holding back a smirk.

"Come on. I'll leave Goldie here. We can grab some sandwiches to go if you're in a hurry."

Cara sighed, following him toward the beat-up old Ford out front. She blinked at the faded powder-blue and white two-tone color scheme. This truck had clearly survived decades of the Arizona sun and who knew what else. The truck itself could be a classic if someone invested in restoration.

When he pressed the button on the passenger handle, he had to yank hard to get the door open. The hinges protested with a rusty squeal that made her wince.

While she climbed in, he dug around in his toolbox in the bed and came back with a can of WD-40. He sprayed the stuff on the door hinges, leaving a chemical haze that made her eyes water. He opened and closed the door a few times, testing the results.

"Perfect."

Cara squinted through the lingering fumes. Yeah. Perfect.

He tossed the can back in his toolbox and climbed behind the wheel. The engine refused to turn over on the first try, ground uselessly on the second, but thankfully fired on the third attempt with a coughing, sputtering protest.

The torn seams on the seats exposed yellowed foam that had definitely seen better days. The truck vibrated, jerked, and sputtered as Sawyer shifted it into reverse.

"Roll down the window. No AC."

Cara snapped her gaze to him. It was May. In Arizona. He had to be kidding. Sawyer was not kidding. He cranked down his window like it was the most normal thing in the world, while Cara sat there absorbing the pure insanity of this situation.

Well, at least it was his shirt she would sweat in. The thought sent warmth to her cheeks. She shifted uncomfortably, rolling the window down just far enough to let the stifling air crawl through. Close quarters. No airflow. His scent still surrounding her from the borrowed shirt.

Nope. Not ideal.

Sawyer drove in easy silence, one hand on the wheel, the other drumming idly against the worn dashboard. Casual. Comfortable. The kind of guy who could ignore the heat, ignore the discomfort—like he was built for survival. Cara, on the other hand? She was wilting.

When he pulled into a spot behind the dining hall, he pointed toward a walkway.

"If your car is out front, that path will take you there. You want turkey, roast beef, or a salad?"

Cara had no idea why his gravel-tinged voice made that simple question sound far more interesting than it was.

"Roast beef is fine."

Great. Her voice squeaked. Actually squeaked!

Sawyer nodded and hopped out of his truck, leaving it running. Cara figured he didn't dare risk that it wouldn't start again. She could not imagine owning such an unreliable vehicle. Her Porsche had never failed to start, never left her stranded, never required creative problem-solving just to get from point A to point B.

He opened the passenger door for her, and she slid down from the seat, her hand brushing briefly against his as she steadied herself. The contact was brief but electric, sending warmth shooting up her arm. Sawyer didn't react at all. Figures.

"I'll meet you back at the casita," she said. "I'll just drive my car over."

"'Kay."

He ducked into the back door of the dining hall.

Cara sat in her SUV with the AC blasting for a few minutes, letting the frigid air wash away the heat and confusion of the last hour. Yeah. Who owned a vehicle without AC in Arizona in the summer? Once she felt human again, she drove over to the casita and parked in the spot farther away from the door, figuring Sawyer might need easy access to his truck while he worked.

Then she grabbed her tote full of design tools, including a laser measuring device — you know, the modern kind.

By the time Sawyer returned with the sandwiches, she had already logged the measurements for the kitchen and bathroom countertops, the square footage for the backsplash tile in both rooms, and the shower tile dimensions. She even had time to study the casita and snap pictures with her smartphone.

The old Spanish floor tile felt classic southwest to her. She considered keeping it. With the right decor, she could modernize the space without replacing everything. That would certainly reduce costs, too.

When Sawyer entered the casita, that familiar awareness spread through her—anticipation and something she couldn't quite name. She really needed to get a grip.

3

SAWYER SNAGGED TWO bags of roast beef sandwiches and two bottles of water. Cara Hollis struck him as someone who didn't drink soda, too refined for it. That feeling solidified when he parked his on-its-last-leg truck next to her fancy Porsche SUV. His truck looked like it had barely survived a war. Hers? Pristine. Untouched by time.

A thought from his old life came unbidden. She, or more accurately, her vehicle, would have been a mark. With the right codes and equipment, he could unlock the Porsche in six seconds flat. Plenty of time to pull away unnoticed. His fingers twitched. Old instincts, muscle memory wired into him. Some habits never fully faded.

Sawyer exhaled sharply. Not anymore. He wasn't that man anymore. Didn't even have the same name. Changing it had been necessary. One more wall between his past and the future he was trying to build. He didn't have to steal to put food in his belly. Didn't have to prove himself to so-called friends. Didn't have to be the guy people feared, the one who always had an escape route mapped out. Now? He was just trying to figure out how to be someone worth keeping.

Sawyer grabbed the bags of food and bottles of water, pausing in the doorway. Cara sat across the room, scanning blueprints, the arch of her brow furrowed in deep concentration. Dust motes danced in the afternoon light streaming through the windows, settling on everything like a fine coating of the desert itself.

After seeing her car, other signs of money stood out now. The ruined silk blouse, expensive enough that most people wouldn't wear it to work on a ranch. The way she held herself, a posture that screamed finishing school and privilege. Cara Hollis came from money.

She was a beautiful woman. Long, glossy brown hair, high cheekbones, soft skin. Those nutmeg-colored eyes snapped up, meeting his as he scrutinized her.

Sawyer cleared his throat, ambling toward her, his boots clopping on the tile floor. He had to admit, cowboy boots were a lot more comfortable than he had imagined. "Your lunch, m'lady."

Cara snorted, but a sweet smile stretched across her full red lips. Kissable lips. Sawyer shook off the thought, faster than necessary. He needed to focus on rebuilding his life. Not on some gorgeous interior designer who looked way too good in his shirt.

He cleared his throat, dropping the bags of food onto the counter and handing her a water bottle. When she accepted it, her fingers brushed his.

Electricity as fierce as touching a live wire jolted through his entire being. His mind went completely blank for a few seconds. Breath held. Static crawling up his spine. His fingers tingled long after the contact broke, and the way she'd looked at him when it happened, that brief widening of her eyes, the slight catch in her breath, told him she'd felt it too. That knowledge settled somewhere dangerous in his chest, a complication he couldn't afford.

Then his stomach growled, reminding him it was well past noon. Good. A distraction. Sawyer took it.

"You didn't start demoing the floor, did you?"

Sawyer shook his head as he bit off a chunk of the sandwich, leaning back against the edge of the counter.

"I'm thinking about keeping it."

Cara's voice held certainty, her eyes scanning the worn

tile like she could already see its transformation. Then she looked up at him through her long lashes, sending his heart slamming against his chest. Sawyer chewed slower, hoping she would keep talking. Keep describing her vision, keep pulling him into something beyond the next job, beyond survival.

"We could hire professional tile and grout cleaners. Patch any grout that may have chipped out."

He swallowed the bite in his mouth. "Haven't seen any yet."

Her nutmeg eyes sparkled with excitement, like the idea clicked perfectly into place in her mind. "Can't you just picture it? Modern tan furniture in the great room. Rustic wood side tables. Lamps with creamy shades and wrought iron stands. Bright paintings or photography on the walls. Touches of turquoise pottery sprinkled throughout."

Sawyer swallowed, the bite of food sitting heavier in his mouth. It wasn't just her words. It was the way she lit up when she talked about it. The enthusiasm lifting her voice, the way her hands moved, as if the space was already shaping itself into something alive beneath her fingertips. She loved her job, and somehow, that lifted his mood too.

This was what passion looked like when it wasn't twisted by desperation or survival. Clean. Honest. Beautiful.

He quickly downed a third of his water, ignoring the dryness in his throat.

"With modern curtains and an airy sheer, I know I can make the old flooring work."

Sawyer could picture it now. "Stainless appliances?"

"Of course. Maybe black stainless."

Sawyer turned his attention back to his food, biting down to ground himself, to shake off the strange pull of their easy conversation. He had been away for five years. Long enough that things like modern kitchens felt foreign. On the surface, five years didn't sound like a long time. But everything had changed. He wasn't the same man. And yet something about her made him feel like he could catch up. Like maybe the future wasn't so far away.

"I'm thinking about a light quartz for the counter." Cara tapped her fingers absently against her water bottle, still focused on her thoughts. "Although that could stain. Maybe black quartz would be more practical. I'll have to look around."

Sawyer finished his meal and forced himself to make an excuse to get back to work. Even though he would have rather sat and talked to her all afternoon. The Vargases were paying him good money. He would earn every penny and prove that he wouldn't waste his second chance.

Cara packed up her things, slipping her tablet into her tote before turning toward him. "I'll return your shirt in the morning."

Sawyer nodded. He hoped so. Given he only owned one other besides the few white undershirts. And given that she looked far too good in his shirt.

Once Cara left, Sawyer untied Goldie and let her back inside. She curled up on the cool tile, her soft exhale settling into sleep almost instantly. Yeah. He was glad the dog found him. Her companionship might be the thing to help him finally let go of his dark past.

Sawyer grabbed the sledgehammer, tapping it against the underside of the kitchen countertop edges. The hollow thunk echoed through the empty space as he tested for weak spots. If he could keep it in one piece, Tres Vargas could donate it to a charity. Once the granite loosened from the cabinets, he texted Renata on the borrowed phone, letting her know he'd need help carrying it out. She texted back that someone would come by within the next half hour.

While Sawyer waited, he carefully dismantled the upper cabinets, the screws squeaking as they came free from wood that had expanded and contracted through countless desert seasons. He set them outside, sweat beading on his forehead despite the shade.

Just as he finished, a black dually rumbled up in front of the casita, its diesel engine growling before cutting off. Two tall, broad-shouldered cowboys exited the vehicle.

Sawyer stilled for half a second, clocking their similar features. The Vargas bloodline, unmistakable. One carried an easy, confident swagger, all bold energy and commanding presence. The other moved slower, more deliberate, quiet in a way that felt intentional rather than hesitant. Brothers with contrasting styles, but both radiating the kind of belonging Sawyer had never known.

Sawyer adjusted his stance, instinct making him analyze before engaging. Stay under the radar. Keep interactions brief, neutral.

"Rennie said you need help."

The larger cowboy introduced himself as Derin Vargas. Sawyer kept his nod short, calculated. Enough to acknowledge without encouraging a deeper exchange.

His brother, Dylan, offered his hand for a shake but said nothing. Sawyer grasped his hand firmly, holding it for half a second longer than necessary. Strong. Steady. No need for words. That, he appreciated.

He motioned them inside. "Got a granite countertop piece in good condition that can be donated."

Between the three of them, they hauled the heavy slab outside, their boots scraping against the tile as they maneuvered the unwieldy piece. Sawyer's shoulders burned from the weight, but the work felt good. Honest strain, honest sweat. Then Derin and Dylan brought out the smaller piece, setting it down carefully against the exterior wall.

Dylan crouched down, running his hand gently over Goldie's fur. "Good girl."

Goldie rewarded him with a soft lick, her tail barely wagging, more of a quiet acceptance than her usual wild enthusiasm. Sawyer tilted his head, watching. Huh. Seemed like the only person she ever jumped on was Cara. That was… interesting.

"I'll have Papi send someone over to pick up the donations next week. Just stack everything over here," Derin said.

Sawyer kept his expression neutral, only nodding after a short beat. It took him a second to realize "Papi" meant Tres. When his brain caught up, he simply grunted in agreement, keeping the exchange brief. He thanked the brothers as they climbed back into the massive pickup truck, pulling away with the ease of men who belonged to the land they worked on.

The quiet settled back in, leaving only the low hum of the desert heat and the soft shuffle of Goldie's paws as she stretched out nearby. Sawyer exhaled, rolling his shoulders as he surveyed the nearly gutted kitchen.

By the end of the day, he had stripped the space down to the drywall. A clean slate. Tomorrow, he'd repair and patch it, then demo whatever Cara wanted gone before moving on to the other small casita.

He turned in a slow circle, taking in the fruit of his labor, letting the feeling settle deep in his chest. No shame. Just work done. Honest work that created something instead of destroying it. Pride. Not the kind that made a man reckless. The kind that made him want to do it all again tomorrow.

Sawyer whistled for Goldie to follow him out. She jumped onto the truck seat, settling in as he climbed behind the wheel. Despite the soreness in his muscles, there was something settling about the way this day ended. Yeah. He could get used to this feeling.

4

CARA PARKED HER SUV in front of the duplex she rented and darted up the stairs to her front door. The heat pressed against her skin, heavy and suffocating even in the afternoon air. After unlocking the door, she stepped inside, immediately stripping off Sawyer's checkered shirt and tossing it onto the washer before hurrying down the hall to change into a sundress.

The lighter fabric was a relief, instantly cooling her overheated skin as she gathered a small load of laundry. She hesitated for a second before tossing Sawyer's worn shirt in, running her fingers briefly over the frayed seams and soft cotton worn thin by countless washings.

A quiet awareness settled over her. He had little. The observation wasn't judgment, just fact. The way he'd looked when she mentioned the four-thousand-dollar lens, the careful way he'd offered his only spare shirt, the truck that barely ran. She'd make sure this came back to him in perfect condition.

The contrast struck her as she started the washer. Her duplex was modest by her family's standards, but it was still more than most people had. Clean, comfortable, hers by choice rather than necessity. Sawyer's circumstances felt different. Harder earned, more precarious.

She left herself a sticky note to dry the clothes later before flicking off the lights and locking the door behind her.

Phoenix's eclectic furniture district sprawled over an hour away, but Cara barely noticed the long drive. She loved hunting for the right pieces, the ones that pulled a space together with invisible threads of color and texture. As soon as she entered the massive showroom, fluorescent lights buzzing overhead, her eyes landed on the perfect tan suede sofa and loveseat with rustic nailhead trim.

She trailed her fingers over the soft texture, imagining the warmth they'd bring to the casita. The fabric felt substantial under her touch, well-made and inviting. They were exactly what she pictured, comfortable yet striking. After checking the dimensions against her notes, she grinned. Perfect fit.

Flagging down a sales associate, she pointed out several other furniture pieces she wanted to purchase. He jotted down the tag numbers while Cara roamed the store, handpicking details. A weathered wood coffee table with genuine character marks, rich iron lamps that would cast soft glows against earthy tones. Each piece would tell part of the story she was creating.

With the purchases finalized, she paid and scheduled the delivery for next week, grateful for the company card the Vargases had provided. The freedom to choose quality pieces without checking her own bank balance left her feeling both liberated and slightly guilty. She'd grown up with that luxury, but working with her own money had taught her its true value.

Cara drove to a few boutique decor shops next, picking out pottery with authentic imperfections, hand-thrown vases, and small accent pieces that would bring depth to the space. By the time her trunk was full, ceramic pieces wrapped carefully in tissue paper, the only thing she hadn't purchased was artwork for the walls.

She knew exactly what she wanted. Large prints of scenes she had captured on the ranch over the years. Catalina had already approved the idea, and Cara was relieved.

The thought of her photography gracing those walls made the project feel personal, not just a job. It would also highlight the natural beauty of the Vargas Guest Ranch property, creating a connection between the interior space and the landscape beyond.

Back at home, she tossed the laundry in the dryer, the familiar tumbling sound filling the small space. She made a quick dinner of leftover pasta, eating standing at the kitchen counter while mentally reviewing tomorrow's schedule.

She reflected on the day, on the satisfaction of seeing the casita's design come together piece by piece. Interior design gave her stability and income, but photography remained her passion. The creative freedom it offered, the independence it symbolized, had been hard-earned through years of proving herself capable.

That lens represented more than just equipment. It was her declaration of independence from her trust fund, her proof that she could succeed on her own terms.

After eating, Cara settled at the kitchen bar and carefully removed her expensive lens from the camera body, holding it downward to prevent any remaining dust from sneaking inside the delicate mechanisms. She extracted the SD card and set it aside, then grabbed a can of compressed air, the cold metal familiar in her hands.

The first gentle burst sent a small puff of dust floating out. Barely anything. Maybe she wouldn't need professional cleaning after all.

Dare she hope?

She brushed the plastic casing of the lens with slow, precise movements, each stroke deliberate and careful. The routine was meditative, almost therapeutic after the stress of the morning. When she removed the UV filter, deep scratches caught the light, evidence of how much damage it had absorbed in its final act of protection.

She tossed it without hesitation, grateful it had done its job so well.

The lens cleaner swept over the glass in steady, methodical circles before she affixed a new UV filter and snapped the lens back onto the camera body with a satisfying click. Anxiety coiled in her stomach as she inserted a fresh SD card and carried the camera into her bedroom.

With every light blazing, harsh and clinical, she pointed the camera at the stark white closet door and snapped a dozen test shots. The familiar weight of the camera in her hands was reassuring, the mechanical sounds of the shutter a language she understood completely.

Her stomach twisted as she loaded the images onto her computer, each file transferring with agonizing slowness.

She zoomed in on the first image, pixel by pixel.

So far, so good.

Three images later, she still couldn't find any trace of dust or scratches. The glass was pristine, the focus sharp and true. She exhaled, the tightness in her chest finally easing.

Thank goodness.

Replacing the lens would have been more than a financial blow. It symbolized something deeper than photography. It was a tangible reminder of her break from her parents' control, of the independence she had carved out for herself one careful choice at a time.

Cara stowed her equipment in her camera bag, swept away the remnants of dust from the counter, and folded the warm laundry. The scent of fabric softener mixed with the lingering trace of Sawyer's cologne from his shirt.

When she set his clean shirt into her tote bag for work, she paused, fingertips lingering on the soft cotton.

She'd make sure to let him know she had cleaned the camera and lens without any extra expense. The relief would matter to him, she was certain. Just as his concern for her equipment had mattered more than she'd expected. Such a small gesture, but it revealed something about his character that the expensive suits and polished manners of her family never could.

THE NEXT AFTERNOON at the Sedona Casita, Sawyer installed the tile in the casita's bathroom. He liked the earthy neutrals Cara had picked out, hints of warm tones in the backsplash complementing the rust-colored Spanish tile flooring. The twelve-by-twenty-four-inch wall tiles for the shower brightened the space, their cream base color accented by stone-like brown striations. It was subtle. Refined. Not flashy. And it worked.

He took extra time to vary the pattern, laying the tiles out in the empty great room first before snapping a picture and sending it to Cara for approval. The thinset mortar's sharp scent filled the small space as Sawyer secured the last row in place, his knees aching from hours crouched on the hard floor.

"Knock! Knock!"

A grin tugged at his lips. He wiped his hands on a rag and stepped into the great room, catching sight of Cara near the entryway.

"Great timing. Just finished the shower tile. Still need to install the fixtures."

Her eyes lit, curiosity sparking in them instantly. "Ooo. Can I see?"

The glow in her expression hit something deep in him, something soft that he wasn't used to feeling. Grinning, he stepped aside, motioning her in. Cara gasped, her fingers grazing the frame of the bathroom doorway as she took in the design.

"This looks so good! Even better than the picture you sent." She shifted, tilting her head slightly, inspecting the details. "I love how you flipped the pattern here. Nice touch."

Sawyer cleared his throat, but his chest puffed slightly at

the praise. No one ever complimented him for honest work. It felt different. Good.

He grabbed the shower head and brushed past her, holding it in place. "What do you think?"

She leaned in, inspecting it from an angle. "It's going to look even better than I imagined."

Sawyer set the fixture on the counter and joined her back in the great room, stuffing his hands into his pockets. "When do the new cabinets come in?"

"They should deliver them this afternoon." Cara sighed, pushing a loose strand of hair behind her ear. "The counter-top will be here early next week. Hopefully not on the same day as the furniture."

She set her tote bag down near the short wall, then reached inside, pulling out a bag and handing it to him. Sawyer took it without thinking, then froze when she spoke.

"It's your shirt. I hope you don't mind. I washed it."

He stilled. Warmth spread through his chest, unexpected and unfamiliar. People didn't do things like this for him. They didn't spare a thought for whether he had a clean shirt. Didn't notice, didn't care. And yet here she was, acting like it was no big deal, handing him something that meant he wouldn't have to scrub it himself tonight just to have something to wear tomorrow.

The simple kindness hit deeper than it should have. She'd taken his work shirt, his only spare, and cared for it like it mattered. Like he mattered.

Sawyer cleared his throat, trying to school his reaction. "Thanks."

Cara flicked her wrist casually, her tone light. "It was nothing. I had other laundry anyway."

Nothing. Except it wasn't nothing to him. He carefully laid the shirt next to his toolbox, making sure he wouldn't forget it later. The fabric felt softer than before, smelled like her detergent instead of his own sweat and dust.

She rocked slightly on her heels, eyeing the surrounding

space. "Where's Goldie? I kinda miss being dropped to the ground without warning."

Sawyer chuckled, shaking his head. "Left her at the bunkhouse this morning. Didn't know if she'd get underfoot while I tiled."

Cara grinned, amusement flashing in her nutmeg eyes. "Probably a smart move. She'd find a way to add paw prints to the grout."

Before Sawyer could respond, she perked up slightly, her tone shifting to something more casual. "Oh! I cleaned my camera and lens."

Her voice held the slightest note of relief, and Sawyer felt his own breath leave him louder than expected. Thank goodness. He didn't have the money to replace a lens. Didn't even have the money to get it professionally cleaned. She must have known that.

He glanced at her, but she was already moving back toward the door, shifting the tote bag onto her shoulder. "Anyway, text me when the cabinets come in."

"Do you want me to install them without you?"

Cara tapped a finger against her chin, considering. "I think that would be fine. There's really only one way they fit. But if you want a second set of eyes, I'm happy to stop by."

Sawyer nodded, biting back a smile. She would stop by anyway. He had a feeling about that.

A few minutes later, Cara left, so Sawyer cleaned up the grouting tools and sponges, the bucket of murky water sloshing as he carried it outside. Then he installed the bathroom fixtures, the metallic clink of fittings echoing in the tiled space.

Another project completed. As Sawyer cleaned up his tools, his fingers brushed against the soft fabric of his freshly laundered shirt. Such a simple thing—washing someone else's clothes. But it had been so long since anyone had shown him that kind of quiet care. The gesture settled somewhere deep in his chest, a warmth he wasn't quite ready to name.

5

IT WAS NEARING dinnertime, so Sawyer headed over to the bunkhouse to let Goldie out before driving to the dining hall. He appreciated how the Vargases had built all the employee and equipment buildings away from the resort, obscured by a large berm of dirt with desert plants and gravel. The separation provided a sense of privacy, something he'd come to value.

When he parked in the back, he turned off the rickety old truck and followed a few cowboys he recognized from the bunkhouse inside. The dining hall buzzed with low conversation and the scrape of silverware against plates. They all stood in the buffet line, grabbing plates and making their selections. Tonight's menu included a savory beef roast, roasted potatoes, carrots, biscuits, and a salad.

While most of the cowboys skipped the salad, Sawyer didn't. It had been years since he had seen fresh produce, much less had the opportunity to eat it. The food here tasted ten times better than the meals he'd endured for the last five years.

He took a seat at a large community table next to Dylan Vargas. Another brother sat across from him and introduced himself as Devon. Dalton Vargas stood when everyone had full plates. Around the table, the other men quickly followed suit, so Sawyer joined them, not wanting to stand out. Then, every man bowed his head. Sawyer angled his downward but kept his eyes open. The last five years had taught him to be careful about such things.

"Lord Jesus, we thank You for keeping us safe today. We ask for Your blessing over this food and over the new faces around the table."

Then, as one, all the men spoke in unison. "We do not deviate from Your plan. Amen."

Sawyer stiffened. What on earth?

He was the last to sit, hesitating as the words settled in the surrounding space. His grip tightened around his fork as he dug into his meal, willing the food to ground him in something tangible, something he understood.

Across the table, Devon glanced up, catching the shift in his expression. "It's our family's motto. My great-grandfather started the tradition when he built this place back in 1952. It comes from Psalm 17:4-5."

Sawyer listened as Devon recited the verses smoothly, like it had been ingrained in him from birth. "With regard to the works of man, by the word of Your lips I have avoided the ways of the violent. My steps have held fast to Your paths; my feet have not slipped."

The words landed heavier than Sawyer expected. Avoided the ways of the violent. Held fast to Your paths. Feet have not slipped.

His chest tightened, his mind racing. Whose words made it possible to avoid violence? If he'd known that years ago, would his life have looked different? What were the paths they held fast to? How could he avoid the men hunting him now? Was it even possible to keep from slipping up again, to hold on to this second chance?

The questions multiplied faster than he could process them. Clearly, the Vargas brothers understood something he didn't. Should he ask Dalton? Maybe not. He was the ranch manager, and Sawyer had learned, painfully, that drawing attention from authority was a mistake. That meant Derin, the foreman, wasn't an option either.

His gaze flicked to Devon. Maybe he could explain it. Or was he even old enough to understand it all? From what Sawyer had heard around the bunkhouse, Devon was barely twenty-one. At thirty, Sawyer figured he had lived significantly more life than the young man. And yet Devon spoke like a man who understood something Sawyer didn't.

After he finished eating, Sawyer excused himself and drove back to the bunkhouse to pick up Goldie. Then he steered his truck down a private ranch road, the quiet hum of the engine filling the space between his thoughts.

When he found a good spot, he parked and hopped out, clipping Goldie's leash onto her collar. The pair walked along the dirt trail in the fading sunlight. The sky stretched wide above them in hues of deep orange and violet. Goldie seemed content to sniff the edges of the path until Sawyer picked up his pace, forcing her to trot beside him.

But even as his feet moved forward, his mind stayed caught on dinner. The Vargas family knew what they were about. They understood something, a secret almost, that he didn't. Would they be open to sharing it with him?

A gravelly voice sounded off to his right, pulling him from his thoughts. "Good evening."

Sawyer froze, instinct kicking in before his rational mind caught up. An older man shuffled forward, his shoulders hunched slightly, his gait slow but purposeful.

"Saw you park down the way as I was about to turn around and head home. Thought I would meet you first."

Sawyer studied him briefly, then moved closer, sensing no threat in his aging frame, the deliberate way he carried himself. "Sawyer Fullerton." He extended his hand.

The old man grasped it firmly, his grip steady despite the gnarled edges of time. "Nice to meet you. I'm Dalton Vargas, Junior. Padre to the boys. Junior to everyone else."

Sawyer cocked an eyebrow. "Tres' father."

"Ah."

Junior glanced down at Goldie, who had moved closer

to investigate the newcomer. "Who's this?"

He held out a hand, letting Goldie sniff before giving her a gentle scratch behind the ears.

"Goldie. I found her right before I started working here."

"Pretty dog."

Silence stretched between them, comfortable rather than awkward. Sawyer weighed his options. Ask the man his questions, or turn around and head back to the truck. Junior beat him to it.

"Maybe you can help me. Seems I walked farther than I intended. Could I trouble you for a ride back to the ranch house?"

"Of course."

As they made their way back, Junior's voice came easy. "You must be the new handyman I've heard so much about."

Sawyer's gut clenched. Sweat prickled along his back. He'd tried to fly well under the radar, hoping to stay out of trouble. What had he done to draw attention?

Junior chuckled. "Catalina loves the work you and Cara have done in the casita."

Sawyer exhaled loudly, relief settling deep in his chest. "Good to know."

When they reached the truck, Sawyer opened the passenger door and Goldie jumped in. Junior climbed in after, moving slower, settling into the seat as Sawyer rounded to the driver's side. It took a few tries to start the old truck, but thankfully, Junior said nothing about its reluctance.

Instead, he ran a gnarled hand over the dash, his expression briefly distant. "Had a truck like this a long time ago. Seems in decent shape for her age."

Sawyer chuckled. "Yeah, she's an oldie."

A thought rooted itself in his mind, sudden and unshakable. The questions from dinner pressed against his chest, demanding answers he didn't know how to find.

"Junior, you know the family motto, right?"

Junior's reply came without hesitation. "We do not deviate from Your plan."

Sawyer gripped the steering wheel, his thoughts racing before he could stop them. "Yeah, but what does it mean? Whose plan is it? How do you know what it is?"

Junior grinned, angled toward him. "It's the Lord's plan. And we know what it is when we seek Him and read His word."

Sawyer hesitated. The words felt too big, too absolute. "Is it... Could I learn about it?"

He bit the inside of his lip, unsure why he'd asked, why he suddenly wanted to know. But something in Junior's weathered face invited the question, made it feel safe.

Junior's gaze softened. "Son, it's for everyone who wants to know it."

A pause. Then Sawyer asked the only thing that mattered. "Where do I start?"

Junior's reply was simple. "You have a Bible?"

Sawyer shook his head. "No, sir."

Junior nodded, like he had expected that answer. "Well, if you aren't in a hurry, when you drop me off, I'll get you one. Then you read it. Start with the book of Matthew. I'll bookmark it for you. And any of my grandsons would be happy to answer your questions. So would I."

Sawyer pulled up to the massive ranch house, keeping the truck idling while Junior stepped out. Minutes later, he returned with a worn, thick book, placing it carefully in Sawyer's hands. The leather cover was soft from years of handling, the pages edged in gold.

Sawyer felt bad instantly. "How much do I owe you for it?"

Junior waved off the question. "Not a penny. You keep it."

He flipped to the bookmark in Matthew, pointing at the first verse. "Start here. Don't worry, the list of names doesn't go on too long. You can skim those for now."

Sawyer let out a breath. The weight of the book in his hands felt significant, like he was holding something precious. "Thank you."

Junior smiled. "You're welcome to join us for cowboy church on Sunday, too. Might answer some of those burning questions for you."

Sawyer thanked him again before driving back to the bunkhouse with Goldie. The Bible sat on the seat beside him, its presence both comforting and intimidating.

When he sat down on his bunk, he flipped open the book, scanning the first few chapters. A special baby. His parents. A man named Joseph, who married a pregnant woman because an angel told him to. A plot to kill the baby named Jesus. A guy named John, preaching about repentance.

He didn't know what it all meant. But if Junior said the answers were in here, Sawyer would keep reading. Maybe in time, he'd make sense of it all.

6

***

Toward the end of the following week, Cara drove slowly down the gravel path to the casita just past noon. She had texted Sawyer earlier, asking him to meet her here to help unload the furniture that would be delivered in the next hour.

As she turned onto the drive, her breath caught.

Sawyer leaned back against the weathered wall of the casita, one booted foot propped against the wood, causing his knee to pull his jeans taut. He wore a white v-neck t-shirt, the sun catching against his tanned skin, the fabric outlining the lean strength in his frame. His cowboy hat tipped low, casting a shadow over his face, while a single shaft of sunlight illuminated his straight leg and arm as he bent slightly forward to scratch Goldie's head.

The dog's golden coat shimmered, her eyes adoring, locked onto her human with a devotion Cara knew would make the perfect shot.

She shifted her car into park, lowering her window, her heart hammering. Perfect subject. Perfect lighting.

She reached for her phone, nerves tingling through her fingers as she framed the shot. She took several pictures, capturing the broad slope of his shoulders, the shadowed edge of his jaw, the casual way his thumb hooked in a belt loop. The faded metal of his vintage buckle caught the sunlight, his worn but sturdy boots grounding him in place like they had always belonged there.

Extreme satisfaction filled her chest, and everything else faded away.

Then he lifted his head. And she snapped the picture at the exact second his eyes rounded.

Never one to take just one shot, her fingers tapped three times in quick succession. Her instructor's voice echoed in her head. *Storage space is cheap. The moment is priceless.*

The instant his forehead wrinkled, deep V cutting into his brow, Cara shoved her phone into her purse and parked closer to the building, reeling in the giddy energy that pulsed through her veins. She smiled from the safety of her vehicle, hoping he hadn't noticed.

Goldie barked sharply, lunging forward. But she didn't make it far before Sawyer clamped down on her collar, hooking her securely to the lead.

Then he turned. And strode toward her. His entire posture shifted, his muscles tightening like a coil ready to snap.

Cara squared her shoulders, pushing away the unease creeping down her spine.

"You can't take pictures of me."

The edge in his voice threw her off. "Huh?"

She punched the button to close her window, gathering her things, suddenly acutely aware of his stance. Wide. Unmoving. Fisted hands propped aggressively on his hips.

She eased the door open, stepping out to her full height, but the weight of his stare had her throat tightening.

"You can't photograph me." His jaw flexed. "It's not safe."

Cara lifted a brow, crossing her arms over her chest. "Safe? What does that even mean?"

Sawyer stretched out a hand, palm facing upward. "Let me see your phone."

Her glare snapped to his hand, confidence faltering slightly. "No. Most of the pictures I took don't even show your face."

His lips pressed into a line. "It's my body. I have the right to refuse."

She exhaled sharply, frustration creeping in. "Why are you making such a big deal out of this?"

Even without reviewing them, she knew she had captured something incredible. These weren't just photos — they were art. Moments frozen in time she wouldn't get back.

Sawyer stepped forward, his movements controlled, deliberate. "Hand it over or find someone else to help you."

Her jaw tightened. "It's your job to help me."

Goldie growled from her spot on the porch, a quiet but forceful warning. Sawyer barely acknowledged it.

"I'm serious, Cara. It's dangerous for you and for me if those pictures get out."

She locked onto his gaze, searching his expression. And then she saw it. A flash of fear — quick, barely noticeable before he smoothed it out, masking it beneath rigid control.

Her skin prickled.

Cara unlocked her phone, shoulders drooping slightly as she handed it over. She swallowed down her disappointment as he swiped through the photos, his fingers moving too fast, too determined, presumably deleting them all.

If she was lucky, they had already synced to the cloud. Except the ones showing his face.

She tapped her foot against the concrete, waiting.

When Sawyer thrust the phone back, she snatched it from his grip and dropped it into her purse. "Satisfied?"

His frown deepened as he yanked his brown cowboy hat from his head, running a hand through his hair before plopping it back on. His shoulders lifted, breath held, before he slowly released it.

When his features finally softened, he straightened his back. "What do you need help with?"

Cara searched his expression, her own emotions still simmering beneath the surface. "I have some decor in the back that we can leave in there until after they deliver the furniture. While we're waiting, I'd like to iron and hang the curtains. Rods and hardware are in the back seat."

She half-expected him to refuse. But instead, he nodded, shifting toward the SUV.

Neither of them addressed what had just happened. And Cara couldn't shake the feeling that she had just stumbled onto something far bigger than she understood.

Sawyer opened the back door and loaded his arms full of the curtain rods, moving with efficiency, as if eager to bury the tension between them beneath the weight of work.

Cara grabbed the packages of curtains, sheers, and the iron, nudging the back door closed with her hip before stepping inside, nearly colliding with Sawyer.

His warm hands clasped her upper arms, steadying her easily, his grip firm but gentle. Silly flutters danced in her belly as she inhaled the crisp scent of his aftershave, the subtle spice of cedar and something darker that she couldn't quite place.

Goodness. Those green eyes could make a girl blush.

A sharp bark behind her. Loud. Eager. Familiar.

Cara's breath hitched, dread prickling along her spine. No. Not again.

She barely had time to tense before heavy paws launched into her back, a full-force collision that sealed her fate. Goldie!

Sawyer wasn't ready for the impact and they tumbled to the floor, Cara landing squarely on top of him. The curtains and iron spilled from her grasp, scattering around them like discarded thoughts.

For a heartbeat, neither of them moved.

Sawyer's hands had found her lower back, holding her with a stillness that sent warmth radiating through her skin, her chest pressed against his. Heat seared her face as her eyes locked onto his, her breath coming faster than she intended. She caught his gaze as it dropped to her lips, the moment stretching, shifting.

For half a second, her treacherous mind wandered. What would it be like to kiss the mysterious cowboy handyman? Would he taste like the desert heat and quiet strength? Would he hesitate, or would his grip tighten, pulling her closer instead of letting go?

Her pulse kicked, the air between them thick, charged with something she wasn't prepared to name.

Then Sawyer exhaled sharply, the rough sound cutting through the silence, like he was forcing something back into place. His grip loosened, and Cara snapped back to reality, the sudden absence of movement shattering the spell.

She pushed up, clearing her throat, fingers shaking slightly as she quickly reached for the scattered curtains, avoiding his gaze as she sat back on her heels.

Goldie wagged her tail, entirely pleased with herself, as if she had orchestrated the moment on purpose. Cara shot the dog a half-hearted glare, but her pulse was still unsteady, her fingers fidgeting with the fabric in her lap.

Sawyer sat up slowly, rolling his shoulders before tugging his hat firmly back into place, looking anywhere but at her.

"What do you need help with, again?" Sawyer asked, his voice only slightly strained.

Cara hesitated. Just for a beat.

She lifted her gaze to his, her stomach still tight, knotted with something unresolved. "Curtains. Hanging them."

He nodded, standing to his full height.

Neither of them addressed what had just happened. But as Cara gathered the fallen fabric, her fingers brushing absently over the creases, she knew they both felt it.

And if this kept happening, if the moments kept stretching, kept pulling them toward something neither of them had asked for, eventually they'd have to figure out what to do about it.

ALL THE AIR left Sawyer's lungs as his back hit the tile floor. Cold seeped through his shirt, sharp against his skin, while warmth spread through him—heat, contact, Cara. Whatever she had been carrying lay scattered beside them, forgotten.

Instinctively, his arms wrapped around her, hands flattening against her back, catching her weight before he even had time to process what had happened. Gravity pressed her against his chest, her softness molding into his frame, her jeans-clad legs entwined with his.

And then Sawyer drank her in, every feature too close, too vivid, too tempting. Nutmeg eyes, wide with shock before softening into something more unreadable. Translucent freckles, delicate dusting across the tops of her cheeks. And her mouth. Full. Pink. Entirely kissable.

And boy, did he want to kiss those lips, to lose himself in this woman, in the charged, lingering space between them. For a second, he wondered if he shifted just slightly, would she let him?

Then a loud diesel engine rumbled outside, shattering the moment. Reality came crashing back, slicing clean through whatever had just passed between them.

Sawyer's arms fell away, hands dropping against the chilly tile, forcing distance where he wasn't entirely sure he wanted it.

"Are you okay?" His voice was rougher than he expected, edged with something he didn't want to name.

Cara scrambled upright, palms bracing on either side of him before she pushed off, transitioning into a crouch, then onto her feet. The loss of her warmth allowed him to breathe easier—but his arms still ached to hold her again. He should not allow himself to think like this.

"I... Fine." Her breathy answer triggered a slow smile across his face. She had felt it, too. That was almost worse.

Sawyer pushed onto his elbows, waiting for her to say something, anything—

"Wipe that smirk off your face and go make sure your dog won't damage the furniture or the delivery people."

His grin deepened, some of the tension unraveling in her exasperated tone. "Yes, ma'am."

Sawyer stood and exited the casita, but Goldie was already waiting for him outside. The dog grinned, tail wagging with far too much enthusiasm. Like she had planned the whole thing. Evil dog. She'd get an extra helping of kibbles tonight—an unspoken reward for her matchmaking schemes.

He grabbed Goldie's collar, unclipping the lead from the front railing and coiling it neatly before rounding to the back porch. There, he secured her to heavy patio furniture, making sure she couldn't unleash any more mischievous plans today. Not that she wouldn't try again tomorrow.

When Sawyer joined Cara at the front of the casita, she had already set the curtains, sheers, and iron on the quartz counter, organizing everything with effortless precision. She directed the delivery men, pointing out where each larger furniture piece belonged. The moment she confirmed that the entire load belonged in this casita, Sawyer grabbed the smaller items from the truck, working quickly to get everything inside.

Before long, the delivery men left, the space falling into quiet as Sawyer removed the packaging from the smaller furniture while Cara smoothed out the curtains with measured strokes of the iron.

He sorted through the curtain rods, noting the different styles. "Where do you want each of these?"

Cara joined him, tucking a loose strand of hair behind her ear before gesturing to the rods. "Oh, these two are for the bedroom. The rest go into the great room. This one—"

She clasped a sleek, smaller rod, holding it up briefly. " — is for the kitchen window. I'll set it on the counter."

Sawyer nodded, retrieving his stepladder from the back of his truck before pre-drilling the holes for the anchors. Cara worked beside him, threading a cream sheer onto the smaller rod, the fabric delicate against her fingers.

When she handed it over, he accepted it without a word, the silence between them companionable, filled only by the quiet hum of work. He hung the sheer onto the inner bracket, adjusting it briefly before reaching for the larger rod as she passed it to him next.

With easy rhythm, they fell into sync, moving between tasks fluidly. Sawyer installed brackets. Cara perfected the drapes, smoothing mustard-colored fabric between her fingers before fussing over the folds, ensuring every detail sat just right. Neither rushed. Neither hesitated. Just steady work, like they'd done this a hundred times before.

While they worked, the passage Sawyer had read from Junior's Bible kept circling in his mind, refusing to settle. Maybe. No. It might be worth a shot to ask Cara. She was a captive audience, after all.

"What do you know about Jesus?"

Cara's hands froze, the iron suspended mid-motion. "Some." She hesitated, then glanced at him. "Was there something specific you wanted to know?"

Sawyer finished tightening a bracket, still wrestling with the confusion wedged deep in his chest. "Why did his dad, Joseph, listen to the angel who told him to marry the pregnant lady?"

It didn't make sense. He couldn't imagine himself doing something like that.

Cara paused, turning the words over. "He grew up knowing God, I guess. So, he knew to listen to the angel."

Sawyer installed the next set of brackets, the simple mechanics of drilling the screws offering a sliver of clarity where his thoughts felt muddled. "What's the big deal about

Jesus?" His voice dipped slightly heavier now. "Why did God go through so much trouble to make sure Joseph kept him safe as a baby?"

When Cara faced him, her features slackened, something unreadable flickering across her expression. Then a quiet smile. She shifted slightly, fully turning toward him now, her hands settling against the counter.

"Where are these questions coming from?"

Sawyer hesitated. He couldn't lie, but admitting it felt... Raw. "Junior gave me a Bible and told me to read Matthew, but I don't understand it."

Too late, he realized he should have weighed admitting that. But the need to understand felt more important than saving face.

Cara's cheeks puffed slightly before she blew out a noisy breath, her casual ease making the moment feel less intimidating than it should. "Have you ever gone to church?"

Sawyer shook his head, his throat tightening slightly. His heart squeezed. Maybe he should have just kept his mouth shut.

Cara shifted slightly, her tone softening. "God wants to have a relationship with every person. But we sin — meaning we break all of His rules. So He sent Jesus, His Son, to die for our sins. Because He did this, anyone who believes can have a relationship with God."

Sawyer rubbed his temples, still grappling with the weight of what all that meant. But he appreciated she had tried to explain.

"Listen, Sawyer, it can take time to wrap your head around all of this." She handed him another sheer curtain, waiting until he took it before she continued. "I'm still trying to understand it, too. I only started going to church a few years ago when I moved out here."

She let out a small laugh, shaking her head slightly. "Keep reading Matthew. I think it'll answer some of your questions. And if you go to cowboy church with the others, the pastor teaches about the things in the Bible."

She met his gaze, gentler now. "I'm happy to answer questions, too. If I know the answers."

Sawyer dropped the sheer onto the bracket, his fingers lingering against the silky fabric a beat longer than necessary. So many questions swirled, but Cara's advice was solid. He would take it. And maybe, eventually, he'd make sense of all this.

They worked silently, each movement deliberate, until every remaining window was perfectly dressed.

"Alright. All we need now is the decor from my SUV."

Sawyer followed her outside, falling into step beside her as they made several trips, carrying box after box into the casita. His arms ached slightly by the time they set down the last load, but he barely noticed.

"You need help with any of this?"

Cara nudged open a box, surveying the contents. "Can I borrow the stepladder?"

"Of course."

"Then I'm good. I can hang the artwork myself."

Sawyer's stomach tightened. Tres Vargas would expect him to handle it, not leave her alone with the task. "If you show me where you want them, I can hang them."

Cara waved him off lightly, dismissive but not unkind. "Really, it's fine. I'm a bit of a perfectionist."

He fought the instinct to push back, forcing a tone he hoped sounded casual. "Okay. I'll swing by later to pick up the stepladder. When do you have furniture coming for the other small casita?"

Cara shifted her weight slightly, glancing toward the space they had just set up. "Next week. I decided on a unique look for each one."

Sawyer studied the room, his gaze sweeping over the carefully placed pieces. Even without the final touches, the space felt welcoming. He nodded, the words leaving him before he could second-guess them. "This looks really nice,

Cara."

Pink bloomed on the apples of her cheeks. "Thanks."

Sawyer ducked his head, exiting before his nerves could get the best of him. She got to him in ways he couldn't shake. But he needed to stop thinking about her. She was a distraction. And distractions were dangerous.

7

GOLDIE BARKED FROM the back patio, tail wagging enthusiastically when she spotted him. Sawyer untied her, leading her toward the other small casita. Once inside, he filled her water bowl, watching as she lapped up the water for a solid minute, before flopping down onto the cool tile, entirely satisfied. Her simple companionship had a way of calming him, grounding him in something familiar.

Still, Sawyer didn't linger. He grabbed his ladder from the truck, along with drop cloths and painting supplies, preparing for another set of measured tasks—ones that didn't leave room for wandering thoughts.

The cream-colored paint he had applied earlier to the main room had dried perfectly. Now, he laid out the drop cloths, methodically taped off the bedroom edges, and began painting, refining his process with every brushstroke. With each casita, his method improved, cutting down time.

Good. Because tomorrow, he'd move on to the large six-room casitas, starting with demolition.

Sawyer scanned the freshly painted walls one last time, a profound sense of satisfaction settling in his chest. Work he could understand. Work had no complications.

By the time Sawyer cleaned up and stowed his supplies, the sun had dipped low, streaking amber and deep violet across the sky. He hurried back to the bunkhouse, dropped off Goldie, and opted not to shower. No time.

He arrived at the dining hall just as the kitchen staff began pulling up the chafing dishes.

"Just under the wire, Sawyer," the chef teased, wiping his hands on a rag. "Grab a to-go box and fill it up. We'll wait another minute."

"Thanks."

Sawyer moved quickly down the line, stuffing large piles of comfort food into the big container. He doubted he'd eat it all tonight, but after years of meals that barely qualified as food, he wasn't leaving anything behind.

The chef came behind him, picking up each dish as he went. Sawyer thanked him again before leaving, setting the container and plastic silverware on the passenger seat as he drove back to the bunkhouse. After dropping his food onto the table, Sawyer fed Goldie, then grabbed a soda from the fridge and sat down alone in the kitchen.

His fingers hovered over his meal for a few seconds. After watching Dalton Vargas bless every meal in the dining hall, it seemed disrespectful to the family not to do the same, even when alone. Then, he bowed his head. He offered a prayer—the first one he had ever said for a meal.

"Missed you at supper."

A hand slapped his shoulder, jerking him from the moment. Sawyer swallowed his bite of fried chicken, savoring the chef's cooking.

Derin stood beside him, grinning faintly, before sitting down across the table. "I was finishing up the painting in the Ocotillo Casita."

"Make sure you log your time."

Sawyer's spine stiffened at the shift in tone. "We don't pay overtime during the off-season, like now, so be sure to take off early tomorrow."

A slow tightness coiled in his chest. Mistake. He dipped his head. "Yes, sir."

Derin chuckled. "I think you're older than me, so no 'sir' needed."

Sawyer forced a strained smile, nodding just enough to end the conversation. As soon as Derin left, he focused back on his food, mind spinning. He needed to remember he wasn't in prison anymore. Derin was the ranch foreman, not a guard. Not the warden. People on the outside didn't talk like he had.

Goldie rubbed against his leg, a silent reminder that she understood him. He reached down, scratching her head, then shoveled a few more bites of mashed potatoes and gravy into his mouth before tossing the plastic silverware into the trash. He stored the rest of his food in the fridge, marking it with his name, then grabbed Goldie's leash. Her tail wagged so hard her entire back end wiggled from side to side.

Sawyer clipped it on, and they headed out, following their usual evening path along the trail used by those staying in the bunkhouse and nearby women's housing.

The stars dotted the inky black sky. The temperature had dropped slightly, but not enough to call it cool. Still over a hundred degrees. Goldie didn't mind. Best Sawyer could tell she had lived on the streets for a while before he found her — always comfortable outside, always keenly aware of her surroundings. He made sure she had shade during the worst of the day, or he brought her inside with him.

Once the busy season started, though, he wasn't sure how much flexibility he'd have. Not a problem for tonight. A problem for another day.

As they neared the bunkhouse, his gaze snagged on a couple. After a few seconds, he recognized Derin. Janessa, the office manager, pressed against him, shifting in a way that looked like she had just tried to kiss him.

Sawyer's mind stumbled over the sight. Wasn't she Dalton's girlfriend?

A few heated words passed between them before Derin stormed away. Janessa turned — and spotted him immediately. Her gaze hardened before she strolled directly toward him, her movements controlled, calculated. She stopped, her eyes narrowing sharply.

"If you so much as breathe a word about this, I'll get you fired."

Sawyer swallowed. Rumors followed her. And he believed them now. She would absolutely live up to the threat.

He nodded, then hurried inside the bunkhouse, forcing his expression neutral, unreadable. Would she trust him to keep her secret? Did it even matter? This job meant everything to him. He couldn't lose it. Especially not over accidentally seeing something he wasn't supposed to.

Yeah. That would be just his luck if history repeated itself.

CARA FLIPPED ON the lights, her duplex illuminating in soft, familiar warmth.

It wasn't grand or sprawling, like the estate she had grown up in. No marble staircases, no imported chandeliers, no rooms designed more for appearances than actual living.

It was quaint, practical, intentional.

And it fit her better.

Here, every corner felt lived in, every detail chosen, every space hers. Not some curated display of wealth and status.

The mansion had been too much, too suffocating, a place where expectations clung to every square inch like dust that never truly settled.

This duplex? It was freedom. A space she could breathe in, exist in, shape however she wanted. Without oversight, without obligations, without the pressure to be anything but herself.

She set her things on the kitchen table, exhaling as she moved to the refrigerator to pour herself an iced tea. The cool, refreshing beverage hit the back of her throat as she drank deeply, ice clinking softly against the glass. She kicked off her boots, letting them thud against the hardwood floor before nudging them toward the coat closet with her foot. Far less careful than her mother would have liked.

In her bedroom, she changed into loose shorts and a tank top, the cotton soft against her overheated skin. The house felt cooler now, the air conditioning finally winning its battle against the desert heat.

Her quick meal was nothing special. Leftover grilled chicken and vegetables, eaten standing at the kitchen counter. But it was hers, something simple and filling.

That alone made it a luxury.

Growing up, meals were five-course affairs, prepared by private chefs with ingredients sourced from places she couldn't even pronounce as a child. Everything was excess. Everything was presentation.

She had spent years rejecting that world.

And yet, if she hadn't walked away, if she still lived under her parents' control, she would have a different wardrobe, a different home, a different car.

The Porsche SUV parked outside was the last relic of that life. It was paid off, free and clear, so she kept it. But sometimes she wondered if she finally let it go, would it feel like cutting the last string between her and them?

Shaking off the thought, Cara settled at the kitchen table with her laptop, bringing up her photo folder linked to her phone. The wooden surface was smooth beneath her forearms as she leaned forward, excitement building.

She blinked.

Sawyer hadn't deleted all the photos. In fact, most of them were still there. Only the ones of his face were gone.

Huh.

Her fingers flashed across the trackpad as she opened her photo editing software, excitement bubbling to life as she studied each picture. They were even better than she had hoped. The full-length shot of Sawyer with Goldie stole her breath. A true work of art. The sheer natural composition, the rugged lines of Sawyer's stance, the adoration in Goldie's eyes. She didn't even need post-production.

It was perfect.

She moved it to her special folder, the one reserved for pictures she planned to print, mat, and frame.

Maybe one day, Aunt Greta would let her redesign the restaurant, bringing fresh life into the space. If she had her way, she would use this photo and others like it as artwork on the walls. Maybe, if she was lucky, she could convince Aunt Greta to list them for sale, giving her an actual start in the world of professional photography. It was the most she could hope for. Starting her own gallery, her real dream, was unlikely.

At least not without dipping into her trust fund.

And that she refused to do.

Her parents' money came with strings. And strings with them? Always meant control.

Cara pushed the thoughts aside, losing herself in the careful sorting of Sawyer's photos. Her fingers flew across the keyboard, selecting favorites, running them through different filters, adjusting contrasts just enough to enhance what was already naturally stunning. The laptop's fan hummed quietly as it processed each edit.

Eventually, she opened the trash folder and scanned the ones he had deleted.

There was one she absolutely loved. His green eyes sparkled, just like they did when he flirted with her. It must have been the moment he noticed her taking the photos. She restored it, cropped it down to just his face, then saved it to her phone as his contact photo.

She could have sold it, used it in an exhibit. Artistically, it was exceptional. But she respected his request.

At least she wouldn't use it for anything other than her own personal reference.

Yawning, Cara shut down her laptop and padded down the short hallway to her bedroom. She curled up beneath the cotton sheets, her phone resting against her palm. Her thumb brushed absentmindedly across Sawyer's face on the screen. Despite her embarrassment over falling on him, she couldn't help remembering how good it felt to be close to him. How his eyes had looked into hers, with that rare moment of charged silence between them. The lightning zinging between them, subtle, but undeniable.

She had dated a few guys over the years. None of them affected her like Sawyer. Most were upper-class associates of her father, close to her age, polished, predictable. Only one had ever interested her enough for a second date. He had been charming, effortlessly so. For six months, she thought they had shared something real.

She had been wrong.

A single tear slipped down her cheek, the memory still raw even though it had happened five years ago. The betrayal had cut deeper than her parents' constant criticism, maybe because she'd chosen to trust him.

Cara shook her head, refusing to dwell on past relationships. She had moved on. She had built her own life, free from her parents' influence.

And Sawyer?

A giggle slipped out. Her parents would hate him. Too down-to-earth. Too poor.

That first week, he switched between the shirt he'd loaned her and one other. The next week, after payday, he wore a new one for a couple of days, then went right back to the worn-out ones. As for his jeans, she was fairly certain at least one pair had been a recent purchase.

She scoffed at herself. Who was she to judge? She'd been born into a world where money never ran out.

If not for her family, her wardrobe would look thinner, her assets smaller, her lifestyle less effortless.

Interior design paid well enough, but the fewer recurring bills she had, the sooner she could afford to rent a gallery or studio. A space of her own, where she could sell her photography on her own terms.

Cara traced Sawyer's face on the photo, the phone screen warm against her fingertip. She liked him. His smile. His demeanor. His humor.

If only she could figure out the mystery behind his refusal to be photographed.

What had he said?

It's dangerous.

Why? What was he afraid of? Better yet, who was he afraid of?

She yawned again, her eyelids growing heavy. The phone slipped from her fingers onto the mattress beside her. It was late. Best to leave the mystery for another day.

8

"SAWYER, THERE'S SOMEONE at the resort office to see you. Says he's your parole officer."

Dalton's voice came through the earpiece, measured but firm. "Papi will meet you there."

Sawyer cleared his throat, forcing himself to sound normal. "Alright. Be there shortly."

In the four weeks since starting at Vargas Ranch, he had settled into a rhythm, a life that felt steady, predictable. His solitary job gave him room to adjust, time to get used to the outside world without constantly looking over his shoulder. He worked hard, staying busy with each project.

After finishing the Ocotillo Casita, he moved on to the six-bedroom Sedona Casita, knocking out the kitchen last week and beginning work on the main bedroom suite yesterday.

His evenings were quiet. He read his Bible, walked his dog, and occasionally met Junior along the trail near the family's ranch house. The old man never hesitated to answer his questions, never minded the heat, never treated Sawyer like he had something to prove. In those moments, Sawyer had begun to see him as both a mentor and a friend, something he hadn't expected.

But now, out of nowhere, his parole officer was here.

His stomach tightened, familiar anxiety crawling up his spine. He ran a hand through his hair, pushing out a simple prayer.

Not knowing how long he'd be gone, he closed the can of paint, washed the roller, and scrubbed his hands cleaner than necessary. Then, pulling a snap-front shirt over his white t-shirt, he was relieved he had picked one of his newer ones today. Showing up in something ratty didn't seem wise.

After grabbing Goldie from the back patio, he drove toward the resort office, gripping the wheel tighter than usual. He hoped bringing his dog wouldn't cause problems. He had already wasted too much time cleaning up and couldn't leave her in the truck, not with the heat pushing past a hundred degrees.

Pulling into the lot, Tres Vargas hopped out of his truck, waving him down before holding open one of the glass double doors.

"We can use Cat's office. I thought I told them to come to the house, but this will do. We will meet over there next time."

"Thanks," Sawyer said, stepping inside. The air conditioning hit him immediately, a stark contrast to the desert heat.

Janessa poked her head out of her office partway down the hallway, eyes narrowing, sharp and suspicious. That couldn't be good.

Renata stood behind the tall front desk, her computer monitor glowing as she offered a kind smile. "I can take Goldie for you. I'll see she gets some water, too."

Sawyer nodded, handing over the leash. "Thanks."

He followed Tres down the hallway toward Catalina's office at the end, his neck muscles tensing with each step. Catalina Vargas's lyrical Mexican accent floated toward them just as Tres held the door open for Sawyer.

Stepping over the threshold into the spacious office, his stomach twisted.

Sawyer recognized the shorter, balding man immediately. Jerry's familiar, gruff face was etched with disdain, his suspicious brown eyes already dissecting him, searching for weakness. The sight made his gut churn, though he willed himself to keep his expression neutral.

Jerry extended his hand for a shake, a gesture Sawyer still wasn't entirely comfortable with. His palm was slick with sweat, so he quickly wiped it on his pant leg before gripping Jerry's hand firmly.

"Good to see you again," Jerry said.

Sawyer's gaze locked onto his. "Jerry."

He let the name sit between them before Tres stepped forward to shake Jerry's hand. Catalina excused herself, closing the door quietly behind her, leaving them in the suddenly suffocating space.

For the next half hour, Jerry grilled him about his job, his answers coming faster, sharper, as his defensiveness rose. Hadn't he done everything right since leaving prison? Hadn't he worked hard, stayed out of trouble?

Jerry handed him a folded paper, sliding it across the polished desk surface. "You'll need to go here for the random drug test. Either this afternoon or tomorrow."

Sawyer's fingers fisted slightly as he glanced at Tres. "I promised to finish painting the main suite in the Sedona Casita by tomorrow afternoon. Cara has furniture coming Friday."

Tres gave him a sympathetic smile, a rare note of reassurance in a room that felt claustrophobic with judgment. "I'll talk to Dalton to get you some help. After the tour, you might as well take care of the drug test."

Sawyer swallowed. "Yes, sir."

He hated not keeping his word to Cara. More than that, he had looked forward to seeing her smile at him, her nutmeg eyes shimmering with excitement over the finished space. The thought of letting her down made his chest ache in a way he hadn't expected.

Tres must have read his unease. "Don't worry. We'll

make sure everything is ready for Cara."

Sawyer nodded grimly, unsure if he could trust Tres to follow through.

They stood, Tres offering to drive them to the bunkhouse after Jerry completed his inspection of Sawyer's truck.

Six months left. Six more months of forced reminders of his past, of Jerry's looming presence, of everything he wanted to forget.

At the bunkhouse, Sawyer showed Jerry his narrow bunk, the thin mattress and sparse belongings that comprised his entire world. The communal space felt exposed under Jerry's scrutiny.

Thankfully, they let him bring Goldie, so he asked her to lie down on her bed in the corner. For once, she listened without hesitation, sensing the tension crackling through the air.

Jerry lifted the mattress, searched through his belongings, but found nothing, as Sawyer expected. The drug test would prove it again.

Next, they drove to the Sedona Casita, the truck's air conditioning struggling against three bodies and the blazing afternoon sun.

Sawyer's lunch threatened to revolt the second he spotted Cara's SUV parked out front. He checked his phone. No text.

"Hey, Jerry," Tres asked, "can we give Sawyer a minute to talk with the interior designer?"

Jerry scoffed. "And give him time to hide something? I don't think so."

Sawyer's shoulders tensed, muscles coiling tight. He didn't want Cara's trust in him to wane.

Tres tried again. "Alright. Can you be discreet? She doesn't know about Sawyer's past, and he deserves some privacy if he's expected to turn his life around."

Jerry snorted, killing Sawyer's hope entirely. "Looks like she drives a fancy SUV. Kinda like the ones you used to steal."

The words hit like a physical blow, shame burning through Sawyer's chest. He kept his mouth shut, forcing himself to stay calm as he climbed out of the truck's backseat. He hated that Cara was about to find out. Just when he thought they were connecting.

"Hey, Sawyer!" Cara called, slinging the strap of her bag over her shoulder, her smile easy. "I just came by to remeasure the owner's suite. Feeling a little paranoid about how much furniture I ordered."

"Hey. Tres asked me to see him, so I had to leave."

"No worries. I'll see you Friday. Painting will be done by then, right?"

"Yup."

He tried to sound confident, but the words felt shaky. Losing half a day made it unlikely, but Tres had promised him help.

"See you later!"

She turned toward her car, never suspecting anything, never questioning Jerry's presence here, saving him from the embarrassment of her learning he had been in prison.

Relief and guilt warred in his chest as he watched her drive away.

Tres led Jerry inside the casita, and Sawyer followed, his boots heavy against the Spanish tile flooring. The familiar scent of fresh paint and new grout filled the air, reminders of honest work that felt threatened by Jerry's presence.

Jerry inspected each of the six bedrooms, great room, kitchen, and bathrooms, dragging out the process as long as possible. He opened every cabinet door, checked behind every fixture, his methodical search turning Sawyer's sanctuary of honest work into a crime scene. But he found nothing. Only wasted another hour and a half of Sawyer's time.

Climbing into the back of Tres's truck, Sawyer forced himself to be patient. The vinyl seat stuck to his back through his shirt. Changing his life would take time, more time than the four weeks he had already spent learning this new version of himself.

He would do it, though. Junior believed in him, and since Junior was the first real friend he'd ever made, Sawyer trusted the old man. Junior even reminded him he could pray.

The idea of talking to God still felt foreign, but he did it anyway, praying about the situation, thanking God for keeping Cara from finding out about his past.

When Tres stopped the truck outside the resort office, Jerry offered a curt nod. "Positive inspection. Don't let me down with the drug test."

Sawyer wouldn't. Nor would he let Jerry's guilt trip take root in his heart.

Instead, he headed for his truck, pointed it toward Wickenburg, and drove. Intent on getting the drug test finished as soon as possible.

One more hurdle. One more step toward proving that he could be redeemed.

9

CARA LOVED HOW the owner's suite in the Sedona Casita turned out. As promised, Sawyer had completed the painting in time for it to dry before the furniture arrived, making the space come together.

In the month since she had first met him, she had learned to trust him completely. When Sawyer said a job would be done, it was done. If he discovered an issue, he reached out right away, never leaving her scrambling for solutions or last-minute adjustments.

She depended on him more with each project, and she appreciated his input just as much as his reliability. Like that morning, when he had suggested altering her closet design. A small adjustment, but one that made the space more functional and surprisingly elegant.

"Looks good," Sawyer said as he secured the last shelf, setting his drill aside before wiping his hands together. Then, those gorgeous green eyes landed on her.

"Thanks to you."

He snorted. "I made one tiny suggestion. You created all this."

With a quick sweep of his arm, he motioned toward the bedroom, the carefully styled retreat she had designed. "A welcoming escape."

She was about to respond, maybe tease him about how his suggestions were always spot on.

Suddenly, her phone blared the theme song from *Frozen*. Ugh. Livvy.

Cara instinctively winced, swiping to answer as she offered Sawyer an apologetic shrug before slipping into the nearest smaller bedroom for privacy. She closed the door behind her, leaning against the cool painted surface.

"Hi, Livvy."

Her sister's voice brightened instantly. "Hey, big sis. Please tell me you're coming to Mother's party tonight."

Cara clenched her teeth, willing herself to stay polite. She had received and deliberately ignored the invitation to her mother's ridiculous summer affair. The woman's idea of an evening gathering differed vastly from Cara's own preferences. Extravagant. Pretentious. Full of people she had spent years trying to distance herself from.

Her free hand pressed against her stomach, where familiar knots were already forming.

"Wasn't planning on it."

"Come on. There's going to be a big announcement, and it would mean the world to the family if you came."

The petulant whine grated on Cara's nerves, pressing at her already-thin patience. "What kind of big announcement?"

Livvy hummed, clearly enjoying the upper hand. "The only way to find out is if you attend."

Cara frowned, her mood worsening by the second. She really wasn't in the right headspace to attend alone or to deal with Livvy's games. The thought of walking into that house, facing all those perfectly dressed people who would look right through her, made her chest tighten.

She needed an ally.

"Cara, please. I'm asking for a personal favor."

That was new. Cara's neck tingled, a warning creeping over her skin. Livvy never pushed like this. It must be more important than she was letting on.

Cara exhaled sharply. "Fine. How many people will be

there?"

"Oh, only sixty of our closest friends and family."

Cara closed her eyes, suppressing the urge to groan. The familiar anxiety crawled up her spine, reminding her of every other family gathering where she'd felt like an outsider in her own home.

"Be sure to bring a date. You-know-who will be there. I'd die of embarrassment for you if you showed up stag."

And just like that, her stomach sank. Ugh. If he was going to be there, then showing up alone wasn't an option. Livvy was right about one thing, she couldn't walk into that world without someone at her side. But where would she find a date with fancy enough duds to fit in with her family?

The panic started small, then built. She needed someone who could hold his own in that environment, someone who wouldn't be intimidated by her family's wealth and judgment.

"Fine. I won't make any promises."

"Cara—"

She rolled her eyes, cutting off Livvy's next inevitable plea. "Bye, Livvy."

She hung up before her sister could launch into further conniving.

Cara took a slow, steadying breath, her heart still racing from the call. She pressed her palms against the door behind her, letting the cool wood ground her for a moment. The frustration mixed with something deeper, that old ache of never being quite enough for her family.

When she finally stepped out, she found Sawyer standing just outside the doorway, his expression curious but concerned. Had he heard any of that? Her cheeks heated at the thought.

"Hey. Everything okay?"

Her shoulders slumped under the weight of it all. "No."

His brows drew together slightly, but there was no push, no demand for an explanation. Just the unwavering offer. "What can I do to help?"

The simple question, asked without hesitation, made something inside her chest loosen. Here was someone who actually wanted to help, not manipulate or judge.

Cara met his steady gaze, her mind whirring as she studied him from head to toe. Maybe... A wild idea began to take shape. It might just work.

SAWYER RESISTED THE urge to step back as Cara's gaze moved over him, slow and unapologetically calculating. Not admiring. Assessing. Which, oddly, left a flicker of disappointment threading through his chest.

It wasn't the charged looks they had traded in the past, those moments when attraction zinged between them, igniting something they both carefully ignored. This was different. Deliberate, measured, layered with purpose he wasn't privy to.

Cara was plotting something. It had to do with that phone call from her sister, the one that had drawn her brows together in a deep V, followed by an exasperated sigh. A sound that had triggered an irrational instinct in him to fix whatever had gone wrong for her.

Now she was looking at him as if he might be the solution.

"What is it?"

She hesitated for just a breath. "How tall are you?"

His frown deepened instantly. "Six foot even."

The second her eyes lit with excitement, something shifted. The way her attention stayed on him, weighing something in silence, assessing him as though she had already chosen him for whatever scheme she had just built in her mind. It had his blood beating out a slow, anticipatory rhythm.

She had chosen him. The realization settled deep in his chest, warm and unfamiliar. No one ever chose him. Not for anything that mattered.

"It might just work. You're about the same build."

Caution flared, but there was something satisfying in her tone, smooth and confident with the assurance that he was exactly what she needed for whatever this was. When was the last time someone had needed him? Really needed him, not just his labor or his silence, but him specifically? Not the old him, but Sawyer?

"Same build? What are you talking about?"

"What time are you clocking out today?"

Sawyer checked his cheap pay-as-you-go phone, brows pulling together. "An hour."

Cara made a face. "Eh. That's gonna be cutting it close."

Without hesitation, she scrolled through her phone, tapped the screen, and suddenly Dalton's voice filtered through the speaker.

"Hi, Cara."

"Hey, Dalton. Can Sawyer leave an hour early today? I need his help on a special project."

"Yeah. If he's okay with it, then I'm good with it."

Sawyer blinked, thrown. She'd just arranged his schedule as if it were nothing. Like she had every right to rearrange his life.

She flashed him a slow, confident smile, hanging up before he could protest. That smile carried expectation, not hesitation. She knew exactly what she was doing.

"I don't suppose you own a fancy suit?"

His stomach dropped. He had no use for one, certainly not with his finances stretched thin from starting over. The reminder of how little he had, how different their worlds were, stung more than it should have.

"Ah, no."

She didn't seem the least bit concerned. "No worries. I'm sure Jorge has something that will fit you."

Before he could argue, she grabbed his hand, fingers sliding against his too naturally, too easily. Her grip was firm but light, guiding him toward whatever came next without hesitation.

"Find someone to watch Goldie tonight. You're coming with me."

Sawyer sent a quick text to Devon, who agreed to feed and water Goldie, even volunteering to take her for a walk. Somehow, he already knew this was going to take longer than expected.

"When will I be back?"

Cara laughed, fingers tapping idly against the steering wheel. "Maybe not until tomorrow morning."

His unease spiked. "And what am I doing?" In his old life, plans that lasted until dawn never ended well. But sitting here with Cara, her confidence radiating through the car, maybe this time would be different.

She glanced sideways, her smile carrying just enough amusement to keep him guessing. "You'll see."

Before he could press for more, she dialed a number.

The voice on the other end boomed enthusiastically, stretching her name like taffy. "Miss Caraaaa! I thought you forgot about me."

"Jorge, no one could ever forget you."

"Are you going tonight?"

"Maybe. Probably. It depends on you."

"Mmm. Who am I dressing? Spill."

Sawyer could almost picture Jorge clapping his hands together and jumping up and down.

"Do you have something about Carson's size? Say in a navy pinstripe?"

Words like navy pinstripe only fit one type of party — a fancy one. The kind where people like him didn't belong.

Jorge hummed dramatically. "Meet me at the guest house in an hour."

Guest house?

"What size shoe does your man wear?"

Cara glanced at him, pulling to a stop in front of her quaint duplex. Sawyer cleared his throat, his pulse kicking up. "Eleven."

Jorge gasped theatrically. "Ooo. His voice is divine. Measurements?"

Sawyer growled low, shooting Cara a pointed look, but she only smirked, entirely unconcerned. Yeah, she was doing this on purpose. Having fun with him.

"Just tell him," she said, still ridiculously at ease.

Sawyer complied, though still annoyed.

Jorge laughed, delighted. "See you soon."

The line went dead.

Sawyer stared ahead, the weight of what he had just agreed to settling into his stomach.

"Where are we going?"

Cara laughed, not answering. Instead, she shifted in her seat, turned slightly toward him, still smirking.

"You'll see. I just need to run in to grab a few things. I'll leave the AC on for you."

Then she swung the car door open, disappearing inside the duplex.

Sawyer exhaled, letting himself take in the vehicle for the first time. The immaculate interior of the six-year-old Porsche SUV gleamed under the soft overhead light. Buttery leather seats, polished wood trim, technology that responded to the lightest touch. He could recite the stats from memory, the engine size, the horsepower, even where they sourced the leather for the seats.

He had always loved cars. But in his previous line of work, details had mattered for a different reason.

Running a calloused hand over the pristine dashboard, he traced the fine craftsmanship, feeling something unsettling slip through his ribs. The contrast between his rough hands and the luxury surrounding him was stark, a reminder of how far he'd fallen and how far he still had to climb.

Yeah. It was a vehicle he would have boosted back then.

The back door opened, interrupting his dark thoughts, and Cara dropped a pair of strappy four-inch sandals onto the seat. A garment bag followed, shielding whatever dress she had chosen. Judging by the designer name, it had cost a pretty penny.

Probably fit her to perfection, too.

A half-smile tugged at his mouth. He would see her in the dress soon enough.

Unless he missed his guess, they were headed to a cocktail party. An event where people would look at him and know he didn't belong, even in a borrowed suit.

His brow furrowed slightly, suspicion building fast. "Are they gonna mind I didn't have time to shave?"

Cara's smile turned secretive, like she enjoyed having the upper hand. "Jorge will take care of everything."

His gut twisted. Wasn't too sure he liked the sound of that.

10

FROM THE PASSENGER seat, Sawyer recognized the road immediately as one of the few ways into Paradise Valley, where multi-million-dollar homes stretched across the desert landscape, each more extravagant than the last.

Professional football players, C-suite executives and their trophy wives, tech moguls—those were the kind of people who lived here.

He had been right about Cara coming from money.

His jaw slackened slightly as she buzzed down a long driveway, heading toward a building so massive, it dwarfed the small casitas, dining hall, and office combined at Vargas Guest Ranch and Resort.

Then, just before reaching the main estate, she veered right, turning down a road flanked by two towering hedges, perfectly manicured, leading toward a smaller building, but still bigger than anything Sawyer had ever lived in.

When she cut the engine, Sawyer glanced down at his paint-stained jeans and snap-front shirt.

He definitely didn't belong here.

"Hello!"

Jorge's voice sang through the air as he opened Cara's door, air-kissing each of her cheeks with practiced ease before walking toward Sawyer.

His eyes raked over him, assessing, appraising, calculating. Heat rose to Sawyer's face.

"Hmm. You'll do. This way."

Cara flashed Jorge a smile. "Thanks, Jorge. Text me when he's ready."

Then she slid behind the wheel of her car, driving away — leaving Sawyer no choice but to follow.

Stepping inside the guest house, Sawyer's breath hitched briefly.

An ornate crystal chandelier hung overhead, its bright light bouncing off polished tile, illuminating the windowless entrance with dazzling precision.

Straight ahead, a massive great room opened up, a wall of glass doors revealing a perfectly manicured lawn stretching toward a mountain, the view so pristine, it barely seemed real.

"I brought three options of everything," Jorge said briskly, leading Sawyer past the living space toward an enormous owner's suite.

Sawyer fought the urge to gape at the surroundings, keeping his expression carefully neutral even as he scanned the room.

A king-size bed sat in the center, framed by an expensive wooden headboard and footboard, the glass windows offering yet another flawless view of the landscape.

Jorge snapped his fingers, pulling Sawyer's attention to the three very expensive suits hanging in pristine condition.

"I'm thinking the Versace."

He held one up, eyes narrowing before shaking his head decisively. "Um. No. The Armani."

He took a step back, examining. "Yes, yes. The Armani."

Sawyer kept his face carefully controlled, but his gut twisted unexpectedly.

He had been around plenty of rich people before prison. Stealing high-end cars was easier when their owners trusted you. Or when you worked as a valet.

Playing the part had been necessary and he had done it convincingly.

Now? The thought unnerved him in a way it never had before.

"You a painter or something?" Jorge asked, waving a hand toward the splotches on Sawyer's jeans. "You don't strike me as the artist type."

Former car thief turned handyman didn't exactly fit in Paradise Valley's guest house. Not that Sawyer had any intention of divulging that to Jorge.

He grunted. "I'm in construction."

Jorge's face screwed up slightly, narrowing his eyes before exhaling dramatically.

With a sweeping motion, he gestured toward the audaciously appointed bathroom. "Shower is all yours. There's a shaving kit, Cara's favorite cologne, and—well—fresh everything. I'll be in the great room when you finish. Leave the jacket off so I can style your hair."

Jorge breezed out, closing the double doors behind him with a casual flick of his wrist.

Sawyer exhaled, staring at the impeccably designed bathroom for a beat before shaking himself free of his hesitation.

He shaved. He showered.

And he pulled on the expensive suit, adjusting the perfectly tailored fabric.

If the old him could see himself now? He'd be freaking out over his good fortune to have landed in the middle of such a party, surrounded by money, power, and influence.

Sawyer's hand shook slightly as he buttoned the silver dress shirt, smoothing the fabric with his palm.

Wonder what cars the guests drove. He'd love to see them.

Sawyer envisioned Junior Vargas's wizened face, hearing the old man's words as if he were standing beside him.

The difference between his old life and new, Junior had explained it before.

And this? This must be one of those times of testing.

The tempting fruit—pricey cars, wealth, indulgence—called to him.

Junior would tell him to pray for strength.

So that's exactly what he did.

As he entered the great room, Jorge nodded his approval, then motioned for Sawyer to sit in a chair, the smooth confidence in his movements stark against Sawyer's unease.

Jorge palmed the hair product over Sawyer's head, sculpting, smoothing, styling—transforming.

"I wish Cara had mentioned you were a cowboy. I don't get to style very many, and you would slay everyone in an ivory hat and brown boots."

Ignoring the pout in Jorge's tone, Sawyer shrugged into the Armani jacket, the tailored fit surprising him.

"Cara is good at that. Figured your size right."

Jorge tucked a business card inside the pocket, smoothing the shoulders with practiced ease.

"Call me if you need my services again. Any friend of Cara's is a friend of mine."

As Jorge spun toward the door, Sawyer asked, "How do I get the suit back to you?"

Jorge laughed. "You don't. It's yours. Courtesy of Mr. Hollis."

Sawyer frowned. Cara wasn't married, was she?

"Her father. Enjoy your evening."

Then, with a breezy departure, the stylist was gone, taking the unused suits with him.

Sawyer moved toward the full-length mirror in the foyer, pausing as he blinked hard, barely recognizing the reflection staring back.

Angling his shoulders one way, then the next, he noted the sharp lines, the flawless fit.

Sleek. Sophisticated in a masculine way.

He would surely slay some guests at this party.

But there was only one guest he cared about.

No one would ever believe he had lived in an orange

jumpsuit for the past five years—or that this new suit cost more than he would earn in a month.

The distinct sound of a purring engine came from outside.

Sawyer turned toward the driveway, stepping forward just in time to see it happen.

One very long, silky leg peeked out from the open driver's side door.

His heart raced faster than a Maserati GT2.

And then—Cara.

When she stepped away from the car, his mouth went dry.

She tossed him the keys, but he didn't even attempt to catch them.

Instead, they clattered to the ground, scraping against the stone floor of the portico as he studied her dress.

The navy fabric, covered in silvery swirls, shimmered in the light. A modest high neckline framed her toned shoulders, while the hemline rested a few inches above her knees, showcasing her shapely legs. Four-inch heels added to the effect, highlighting the curve of her calves.

She had swept her long brown hair into an elegant updo, exposing the soft skin of her regal neck.

Sawyer wondered—

What would it feel like to press his lips against it?

"Dropped something."

Cara shot the comment over her shoulder, barely breaking stride.

And then she turned, showing him her back.

For all the modesty of the neckline, the dress plunged low at the back, revealing the elegant line of her delicate spine. More skin than he'd seen in a long time.

His jaw dropped, then he shook off a dozen wayward thoughts, forcing himself back into composure.

Clearing his throat, he bent low to retrieve the keys, tossing his handyman clothes into the trunk before sliding into the driver's seat.

He ran a hand over the leather steering wheel, gripping the shifter in the center console, grounding himself in something familiar — something he understood.

Then, finally, he turned to her, voice steady.

"Where to?"

THE RICH TIMBRE in Sawyer's voice confirmed what Cara suspected — he liked her dress. That thought sent a wave of delight through her as she resisted the urge to fan herself. Jorge had outdone himself. Sawyer looked every bit the part of an elite socialite, the Armani suit perfectly draping his broad shoulders in the most appealing way.

She smiled as he revved the engine, admiring how his suit complemented her dress, just as she had planned. They looked like a well-coordinated couple. Carson would hate that.

"Follow the driveway to the end, then make a right toward the house," she said.

Sawyer's grip on the steering wheel remained easy, but his tone carried a sharper edge. "How do you know these people?"

A giggle bubbled up before she could stop it. Strange, considering how much she disliked spending time here or admitting her connection to the residents. She must be more flustered than she realized.

"It's my parents' home."

Sawyer choked briefly, his reaction swift before recovering. "You live here?"

"No. My controlling parents do. I live in that comfy duplex in Wickenburg."

His gaze flicked toward her, brows furrowing. "Why are you remodeling a ranch resort in the middle of nowhere when you could live here?"

Her pulse faltered for half a second before she forced out the answer, firm and final. "You know that saying about money and happiness? It's true. I'm a thousand times more content in our small town, designing beautiful, inviting spaces, than I ever was under their roof."

Silence stretched between them for a moment before he asked, "What are their names?"

She exhaled slowly before answering. "Peter and Gail Hollis."

As they pulled into the curved drive, slowing near the grand entrance of the estate, his voice was quieter. "The tech mogul."

She sighed. "I see you've heard of him."

"Who hasn't?"

The valet reached for the door handle, but Cara held up a finger, signaling she needed a moment. She turned slightly, angling toward Sawyer.

"My parents aren't like they appear in the media," she said, pressing back the rising tide of hurt. "They are shallow and all about appearances."

Sawyer studied her carefully. "Then why did you bring me?"

"I needed a date."

He snorted. "Somehow, I doubt you've ever had trouble finding a date. Why me, the poor resort handyman?"

She hesitated only briefly. "I trust you, okay? I needed just one person at this awful event I could count on. That's you."

Sawyer rubbed a hand over his clean-shaven jaw, the scent of her favorite cologne catching in the air between them. She had picked it for him intentionally, knowing it would bring some comfort.

"I hope I don't disappoint you," he said.

Cara placed a hand on his forearm, a simple gesture of reassurance, but the heat between them passed instantly, searing her skin. She nearly pulled back, startled by the intensity of it. Maybe she had brought him because she found him insanely attractive too.

But he didn't need to know that. And she couldn't face Carson alone.

She tapped on the window, and the valet immediately opened her door, offering his hand. Cara slid from the leather seat, tucking her clutch under her arm as the warm evening air settled over her.

When Sawyer joined her, he casually looped his arm around her waist, resting his palm against the fabric of her dress. The contact sent a surge of electricity through her, startling her with its intensity.

"And do I call them by their first names or go more formal?" he asked.

Cara huffed. "Depends. Do you want to get on their good side?"

He glanced down at her. "Do you want me to? I'm here to support you, apparently."

She let out a breath, knowing that if Sawyer played his part right, it would make things easier—at least on the surface. "Just call them Mr. and Mrs. Hollis unless they instruct you otherwise."

"Got it. Anything else I should know?"

Cara considered telling him about Carson but pushed the thought aside. No way did she want to bring that up. "I don't think so."

She let Sawyer guide her into the massive house that had been her childhood home, forcing herself to steady her breathing. Painful memories bubbled to the surface with each step.

Money could buy many things—exquisite furnishings, breathtaking architecture, lavish parties—but it had never bought her real friends or true love. Nor had it ever secured the approval or affection of her parents.

She had spent the first twenty-two years of her life trying to make them proud. Trying, failing, trying again. Nothing was ever good enough.

At twenty-three, she had finally left.

Her interior design degree had been a point of contention, something they abhorred rather than celebrated. So, she had moved to Wickenburg to stay with Aunt Greta until she earned enough for her own place.

Aunt Greta had taken her to church, talked to her about freedom in Christ, and helped her understand that love didn't have to be earned, only accepted.

Before her twenty-fourth birthday, she had found the love of her Savior.

It should have been enough.

But standing here five years later, facing the walls that had witnessed years of rejection, she couldn't stop the deep, aching loneliness from creeping in.

Across the room, Cara's gaze landed on her mother just as Mother's eyes narrowed slightly.

Then, without a word, she turned away.

A sharp pain struck Cara's chest—too familiar, too predictable.

That was exactly why she hadn't wanted to come. A person could only take so much rejection from the people who were supposed to love them unconditionally.

Beside her, Sawyer gasped, pulling her attention back to him. She glanced up, startled by the expression on his face, the way his gaze flickered between her and the room around them.

Despite his slobbery dog, his meager wardrobe, and his seemingly unremarkable job, Cara liked him. Trusted him. There was something so disarming, so authentic about him. Something that pulled at her, even when she didn't understand why.

If she wasn't careful, she might let him in.

And that would give him the power to wound her just like everyone else had—everyone except Aunt Greta.

11

SAWYER FOLLOWED CARA through a twenty-foot glass and wrought iron door, the sheer scale of the entrance setting the tone for what lay beyond. Everything about the mansion screamed money, endless, effortless, unapologetic wealth.

His breath hitched slightly as his gaze landed on the grand staircase curving up to a balcony overlooking the entryway. A man in a dark gray tux sat poised at a black grand piano, the polished surface gleaming under the chandelier's glow as he played some stirring classical piece.

Overhead, gold paint coated the inlays of the dome ceiling. At least, he assumed it was paint. Given the obvious display of wealth, it could very well be real gold leaf.

The European white oak floors gleamed beneath his shoes, and the tall windows stretched toward impossibly high ceilings, their panes separated with precision that spoke of custom craftsmanship.

Sawyer exhaled slowly. "How big is this place?"

Cara barely hesitated. "This building is over ten thousand square feet. The guest house is around four thousand. Father's garage holds a ton of cars. I don't even know how many square feet that is. It puts Jay Leno's collection to shame."

He swallowed, the dryness in his throat refusing to ease. A car collection that put Jay Leno's to shame. His fingers twitched involuntarily, old instincts stirring. The kind of cars he used to boost would be pocket change compared to what Peter Hollis probably kept in that garage.

That earlier connection he had felt with her? It was distant now, buried beneath everything this house represented.

He knew Peter Hollis was a multi-billionaire.

Lest Sawyer forget, he and Cara were from entirely different worlds.

Yet, she trusted him and had called him a friend.

He bit back a snort. If she ever learned about his past, about where he had been, about who he used to be, that trust would vanish. Especially growing up in a place like this.

His boots felt heavy, cemented to the pristine floors, but he pushed forward, trudging a few more steps into the massive entryway.

Cara motioned toward the right wing. "That leads to a stairwell to the basement. It has a library, Father's den, Mother's lady's den, a theater, and a game room with three pool tables, ping-pong, and more."

Sawyer shook his head, staring ahead in quiet disbelief. He had never had his own bedroom growing up. Sometimes not even his own bed. And she spoke about a theater like it was just another room.

Then a sudden shift at his side.

Cara leaned into him, her body going rigid, tension rolling through her frame.

Sawyer inhaled sharply, his gaze snapping to where hers had settled.

A young woman in a bright red dress, dark hair piled high on her head, stood out against a sea of navy, charcoal, and black. Her neckline was low, deliberately revealing, like she had modeled herself after Hollywood's most daring starlets. Nothing about that dress left room for imagination.

His instinct kicked in before his mind could process it.

Sawyer wrapped his arm around Cara, his hand settling

naturally at her waist, grounding her as the woman shuffle-jogged in her high heels toward them. Cara's posture tensed even further, something unreadable shifting beneath the surface.

He was seeing why she needed some moral support tonight.

"CARA! DON'T JUST stand there at the entrance. Come, give me a hug!"

Cara tensed at the cheerful call, forcing an almost friendly tone. "Livvy." She barely managed to keep the bite out of her voice. She added, for Sawyer's benefit, "My sister."

Livvy leaned in, arms barely brushing Cara's back before pulling away. Patronizing affection, more for show than sincerity. Then, effortlessly, she hooked her arm around a man standing beside her, her body pressing too easily, too familiarly into his frame.

Cara's stomach tightened as the man possessively slid his arm around Livvy's waist. She already knew before her gaze even traveled up the length of his sleek, dark gray suit. The second she met his face, her throat constricted.

The nerve. Of them both.

"I'm so glad you made it," Livvy practically purred. "I believe you know my boyfriend."

Cara wanted to gag. Of course, he wouldn't let the dust settle before moving on. She had heard he finally divorced his wife, or more likely, she had divorced him.

Sawyer cleared his throat, his voice cutting through the moment. "Hey, I'm Sawyer. And you are?" He held out his hand toward Carson, steady and polite, but the touch of his other hand against her lower back nearly distracted her from the rage pooling in her chest.

She remembered her manners. Sort of. "Sawyer, meet Carson. Or, as I like to call him, my two-timing ex who failed to tell me he was married."

Carson flashed his best smile, shaking Sawyer's hand while casually stroking Livvy's side, his easy charm disgustingly intact. "Still sexy as always, I see."

Cara scowled, not the least bit surprised by the inappropriate comment. "Careful, Livvy, you'll want to watch this one."

Livvy laughed, but her eyes turned sharp. "Unlike you, dear sister, I have no trouble keeping my man. Maybe if you—"

"Livvy, is it?" Sawyer cut in smoothly.

Livvy scoffed. "Olivia to you." The distraction only lasted a few seconds before her attention snapped back to Cara. "You never told me you're seeing this dreamy man." Then, without hesitation, she placed a palm on Sawyer's chest, fingertips resting far too deliberately against the fine fabric of his suit.

Cara nearly lost it. "Olivia, just stop." Her sharp breath shuddered between them, her rage gathering speed.

Before she could go off on her conniving sister, Sawyer pressed a gentle pressure against her back, guiding her forward with effortless ease. "Darlin', introduce me to your parents." Then, as an afterthought, he added, "Good to meet you, Livvy. Clyde."

Carson bristled instantly. "It's Carson!"

Cara snickered, her temper finally cracking. "You did that on purpose."

Sawyer's smirk barely hid his amusement. "He deserved it. Besides, he looks a good twenty years older than your sister."

"Close. Twenty-two, I think."

Sawyer hummed, his hold still firm against her back. "I'm glad you benched him permanently. He's completely unworthy of you."

Cara's shoulders eased, warmth settling into her chest as Sawyer's words sank in. No one ever stood up for her. Especially not in this house.

"Your parents?"

The peace vanished instantly, tension creeping up her spine like a reflex. Mother's lack of acknowledgment said everything. Disappointment, disapproval, maybe even shame. Cara could feel it without needing a single word spoken. For all her efforts, the little girl inside of her still wondered, was there anything she could do to win her mother's affection? Or was it truly as impossible as it seemed?

Her breath faltered. "Uh, let's mingle for a bit. Mother has a way of finding me in a packed room if she wants to."

Cara wove through the crowd, Sawyer close at her side, his presence a steadying force against the ever-present tension thrumming beneath her skin. At the bar, she ordered a club soda with lime, needing something cool, crisp, grounding. When Sawyer ordered a Coke, her respect for him ticked up a notch. No alcohol. No need to fit in with the excess surrounding them.

They moved deeper into the expansive great room, the familiar space primed for hosting events like this. A stage stood in front of the lanai glass doors, perfectly framing the water fountain and zero-edge pool, the mountain standing tall in the background. Like many of Mother's gatherings, bar-height tables draped in silk dotted the room, every detail polished, intentional, excessive.

Cara walked toward one, setting down her soda before accepting appetizers from a passing server. Sawyer snagged a shrimp cocktail, biting into it without hesitation.

"You seem more at ease than I expected," Cara observed, forcing herself to speak, to act normal, to pretend none of this was suffocating.

Sawyer shrugged, unfazed. "I've been to parties before."

"Yeah, but I'm sure this is different."

His gaze flicked around the room before settling back on her. "You mean more stuffy people full of themselves? That describes all the parties I've been to. Maybe the surroundings are more upscale than I'm used to."

Cara popped a stuffed mushroom into her mouth, chewing slowly before nodding. "Thanks again for being my plus one."

"Anytime. You sure you don't want to say hi to some friends?"

Cara smirked slightly. "Hi."

Sawyer's green eyes sparkled, amusement flickering in their depths. "Glad you consider me a friend."

Heat rose to her face, her hand smoothing absently over the side of her updo, trying to distract herself from the way he looked at her. As she lowered her hand, he caught it gently, holding it for a beat longer than necessary.

"You look amazing. Not a hair out of place."

His words were simple, pure, completely removed from the sickening, loaded compliments Carson used to give her. This felt different. This felt real. Her pulse steadied, warmth settling into places of her heart she didn't realize were still broken.

"What's the deal with your sister?"

Cara exhaled so long her shoulders sagged under the weight of it. "She lives to make my life difficult. I can't believe she's dating Carson."

Sawyer's expression softened, his hold shifting slightly, sending ripples of warmth up her arm. "It was good of you to warn her about Carson."

Cara snorted, bitterness creeping into her voice. "Oh, she knows. Not only did he forget to tell me he was married, he also had a third woman on the side."

Sawyer released her hand, a sharp hiss of air escaping through his gritted teeth. "Ouch."

Then the music stopped.

Father's voice boomed through the speakers, carrying

over the murmurs of the crowd. "Thank you for joining us on this very special occasion."

Cara stiffened, confusion threading through her nerves. "What?" This wasn't a holiday, anniversary, or birthday.

Sawyer's breath warmed her ear, his voice dipping lower. "Everything okay?"

Her throat tightened. "I don't know."

Mother lifted her hand delicately, gesturing forward. "Carson, Livvy."

Cara's pulse stopped. She watched in horror as Carson bent on one knee before Livvy, her father holding the microphone like some grand master of ceremonies, his posture proud, expectant. Carson's voice carried through the room, pledging his undying love, his devotion, and his commitment. Livvy gushed, feigned surprise, an act so smooth it made Cara's stomach turn.

He slid the perfectly sized diamond ring onto her waiting finger, the giant rock catching the spotlight, shimmering like a mockery of every painful mistake Cara had ever made.

Her vision blurred, reality spinning. This. This was why Livvy had wanted her here. To rub it in her face. To make her feel small. Livvy had known Carson was going to propose.

The proverbial knife in her back felt almost real, as if she could actually feel the sharp edge twisting, the wound searing through her chest. She hated her family. Her heart thundered. Her breath caught.

She pushed away from Sawyer, needing space, air, escape. Then she ran. She fought through the crowd, forcing her way toward the front of the house, swimming upstream against the press of bodies, against the weight of the moment crushing down on her.

She couldn't breathe. This could not be happening.

12

SAWYER TURNED TOWARD Cara, watching the color drain from her face at the announcement. She hadn't known. She had no inkling that Carson planned to propose to Livvy, no warning, no chance to prepare for the humiliation, no way to stop the knife twisting in her back.

"Cara." He reached for her, instinct driving him forward.

She shoved past him, barely acknowledging him as she pushed into the crowd, slipping between bodies before he could react.

Sawyer straightened, scanning the room. He was tall, which normally gave him an advantage. Not tonight. The music blared again, amplifying the buzz of voices, the sudden press of bodies all moving toward Carson and Livvy as if drawn by the spectacle. Sawyer's anxiety spiked, his pulse tightening, his breath turning shallow as the space closed in on him.

Then his eyes locked onto a face. His stomach plummeted.

No. She couldn't be here.

The second he realized she spotted him, he dropped his head, averting his gaze fast. Under his breath, he started reciting the verses from Psalms, the ones Junior had drilled into him. "With regard to the works of man, by the word of your lips I have avoided the ways of the violent."

Someone's elbow caught his side, jerking him back to the moment. Sawyer looked up. "Sorry," he muttered, forcing himself to move toward the exit, pulse hammering as she wove through the crowd in his direction.

He kept reciting the verses. "My steps have held fast to your paths."

"Wesley."

Sawyer closed his eyes, the name slicing through him like a blade. Not Sawyer. Not who he was now. Wesley. His breath hitched, the weight of the verse pressing against his ribs as he finished the line almost as a prayer. *My feet have not slipped.*

They hadn't. Yet. But the night was still young. And the parking lot was full of opportunity.

Sierra's presence could ruin everything. She had always been a complication, always too close to Angelo's operation, always right in the thick of things, knowing just enough to be dangerous.

"Miss! I'd like some of those."

Sawyer glanced over his shoulder just as a man waylaid Sierra, stopping her mid-step. His heart kicked hard against his ribs, the relief temporary at best. He picked up his pace, veering toward the paver-lined path around the house, the exit burning in his mind.

Guess Angelo's girl had kept the business running after he and Angelo went to prison. She wouldn't give up her lifestyle, not for anything, not even for a prison sentence that should have thrown her off track. She had grown too comfortable with the money. And now she had spotted him.

And nothing good ever came from running into people from his past.

Sawyer continued around the side of the house, the sharp scent of manicured hedges filling the warm air, his dress shoes crunching softly on the gravel path. At a break in the shrubs, he slipped through, only to hear the soft sounds of crying.

His chest tightened. "Cara?"

He followed the quiet, broken breaths, his pulse steadying only when he spotted her seated on a stone bench nestled in a small alcove, hidden from the main party by towering hedges. Soft lighting from hidden fixtures cast gentle shadows across her face, streaked with tears. Her shoulders drawn in, her elegant composure finally cracked. A sharp ache settled deep in his ribs.

Without hesitation, he sat beside her on the cool stone, wishing Jorge had thought to hand him a pack of tissues or a handkerchief. Instead, he did the only thing that made sense. He tucked her against his side, feeling her body tremble slightly as she turned her face into his chest. His throat closed as he glanced over his shoulder, scanning the narrow opening in the hedge, wondering if Sierra had seen him enter.

The hidden garden felt like sanctuary, but sanctuary could become a trap if the wrong person found it.

Cara's voice was muffled against his suit. "How did you find me?"

Sawyer exhaled. "Dumb luck, I guess."

She snuffled, her soft breath warming his skin, pressing against something in him that he hadn't realized was still raw. Rejection and betrayal—he knew them intimately. They had carved deep canyons throughout his entire life, places no amount of time or distance had ever truly filled. The Vargases had been the first people to see him. To accept him.

He ran his large hand gently over her hair, careful, yet hesitant. Maybe she saw him, too.

It was foolish, and he knew it. They were colleagues, despite the fancy suit that disguised him tonight. They weren't friends, no matter how much she had claimed otherwise earlier. And they certainly weren't a couple. They came from entirely different worlds.

People like him had stolen from people like her and her family. Not for survival, but to fit in with criminals, to feel some twisted sense of camaraderie after years of being on his own. Too bad it had been fake. Cara had never wondered where her next meal would come from, never slept with one eye open, never been forced to choose between stealing or starving. She had everything a person could ever want. He had nothing.

And yet he held her tighter. Ignoring every reason he should run from her, he stayed. However unlikely it might seem, he longed to be her friend. To mean something to her.

Cara let out a breath, barely above a whisper. "Thank you."

She eased away slightly, the warm imprint of her presence fading from his side. Had it not been for the scorching summer heat, he might have missed the loss of it entirely.

Sawyer cleared his throat, his voice rougher than intended. "What do you say we get outta here?" Too much emotion lurked beneath the surface, threatening to pull him under. And Sierra was still out there somewhere, looking for him.

Cara patted her damp cheeks, smoothing away the last traces of her tears. "I'd like that. We could even grab some dinner at the steakhouse back in Wickenburg. It'll be my treat."

Sawyer chuckled, the sound hoarse but genuine. "Let me buy you dinner."

She stood, offering a wan smile, barely there but real enough. "If you insist."

His own grin sharpened. "It's the least I could do since your dad bought me these fine threads."

Her soft laughter wound around his chest, lifting the weight that had been sitting there for far too long. "I guess we're a little overdressed for that place."

Sawyer smirked. "I don't mind if you don't."

"Not at all."

When she looped her arm through his, he led her back toward the valet stand, moving past the luxury vehicles dot-

ting the lot. He spotted the valet, but the man was still retrieving another car, so he turned to Cara. "Find your key?"

They drifted through the parking lot, the shimmering
lineup of Alfa Romeo, Porsche, McLaren, BMW, Bugatti
stretching before them like a billionaire's playground. Each
vehicle represented more money than most people saw in a
lifetime. Chrome gleamed under the estate's landscape
lighting, leather interiors visible through pristine windows,
keys probably left in ignitions by owners who'd never imagined anyone would dare.

His mouth went dry.

My steps have held fast to your paths.

The old him could have made a fortune chopping any of
these cars, stripping them for parts, moving them across
state lines, setting himself up with one last job. Skip town.
Start over. The temptation clawed at him, pressing in,
threatening to drown out everything else. His fingers
twitched, muscle memory kicking in as he calculated entry
points, alarm systems, escape routes.

One McLaren sat with its windows cracked slightly.
Probably worth half a million. He could be inside in thirty
seconds.

"There it is!"

Cara's fingers closed around his, pulling him back,
dragging him toward her Porsche like a lifeline to safety. She
pressed the keys into his palm, her touch solid, grounding.
"You drive."

Sawyer stared at the keys, the weight of them unexpectedly heavy. He held the door, mentally shaking off the
chains threatening to pull him back into his old life. He
didn't want to steal cars. Never had. And certainly not now,
not when he had a second chance to rewrite everything.

Junior had told him once, you can pray anytime, anywhere, for anything. So Sawyer prayed. For strength. For the
ability to step into this car, drive it the way it was meant to
be driven, and leave the Hollis estate without a single glance

backward.

Then, finally, he slid behind the wheel and steered them toward Wickenburg. To his simple, but free, life as the handyman cowboy at the guest ranch and resort.

But as the estate's lights faded in the rearview mirror, unease settled in his gut. Sierra had seen him. She knew where to find him now. And people from his past never brought good news.

He gripped the steering wheel tighter, pushing the worry down. Tomorrow he'd figure out what to do about Sierra. Tonight, he just wanted to take care of Cara.

CARA GAZED OUT the passenger window as Paradise Valley faded in the distance, the luxury estates shrinking behind them, replaced by the expansive stretch of desert. Sawyer navigated onto the freeway, the hum of the tires and the rhythmic flick of the passing streetlights blending into the quiet tension settling in her chest.

Her stomach twisted, her emotions tangled in a mess she couldn't quite unravel. She didn't know whether to be angry, hurt, or simply exhausted. If Livvy went through with the marriage, she'd be in for a lifetime with an unfaithful spouse, bound to a man who had already proved he had no loyalty, no integrity, no shame. No way had Carson changed, especially not after his lewd comment about her.

The bitter truth sat heavy in her ribs, pressing harder the longer she stared at the blur of highway lines streaking past.

Then warmth. Sawyer's hand rested gently on her knee, the simple touch drawing her out of the spiral threatening to consume her. She blinked, pulling herself back to the present. It was Livvy's life. Her choice. She could live however she pleased.

"You okay?" Sawyer's voice was low, careful, measured.

He withdrew his hand, settling it back on the steering wheel, eyes flicking toward her briefly.

Cara exhaled. "I shouldn't let them get to me. I know how they are."

"Carson and Livvy?"

She snorted softly. "And Mother and Father. Mother saw us when we first entered and, with just one look, made it clear she disapproved." The memory stabbed at her, familiar but still painful. She had spent years chasing their approval, clawing for scraps of affection they refused to give.

Sawyer's brow furrowed slightly. "I'm sorry."

She glanced at him, catching the sincere empathy in his expression, the way he wasn't offering hollow reassurances, just understanding. And somehow, that bolstered her more than anything else could.

"Like I said earlier, money can't buy happiness. I gave it all up once I realized nothing I did would ever please them."

Sawyer didn't answer right away, just nodded, absorbing the words like they meant something personal to him, too.

By the time he pulled off the freeway, it only took a few minutes to reach the steakhouse, her sanctuary, a place far removed from her parents' world, simple and warm in a way the Hollis estate never had been.

She loved everything about Wickenburg. Its rich history, the way strangers genuinely smiled and asked about her day, the unspoken sense of community she had never known before moving here. At the church she attended with Aunt Greta, Cara had finally found an amazing group of women, people who honestly cared about her. For the first time in her life, she felt close to others.

Sawyer parked the car, cutting the engine. "Here we are."

He stepped out, opened the back door, and carefully laid his suit coat on the seat. Cara watched as he unfastened the cuffs, then pushed up the sleeves of his expensive dress shirt, baring his forearms, tanned and strong. She held back a cringe, knowing the wrinkles that formed would have scandalized her mother. And for some reason, the thought made her smile.

Cara squared her shoulders, dropping her clutch into the center console. She wasn't her mother. She never would be. She could choose to be kind, to be open, to be different.

Sawyer rounded the SUV, opened her door, and Cara looked up at him, catching the easy grin stretching across his face. The warmth of it caused a swooping feeling in her stomach, something light and unexpected after such a brutal night.

"Thank you."

"Of course."

She tucked her hand in the crook of his arm, letting the old-fashioned gesture steady her. Something about it calmed her, rooted her in something solid.

Inside, the cool air of the steakhouse lobby brushed against her skin, a stark contrast to the thick heat outside. The familiar scents of grilled meat and fresh bread wrapped around her like a comfortable blanket. A hostess greeted them, and since it was nearing eight o'clock, they were seated right away, the dinner rush already fading. Sawyer pulled out her chair, waiting until she settled before taking his own seat across from her. The simple gesture made her feel worthy.

She flicked her gaze up, covertly studying him over the top of the menu. His green eyes looked even brighter than earlier, more at ease now, more comfortable in this smaller-town version of "fancy" than he had been among the billionaires. The silver-gray shirt made his tan seem darker, the subtle lighting in the restaurant sharpening the lines of his jaw, making the dimple in his chin more pronounced.

Then his gaze lifted. He caught her staring. His half-smile appeared, holding just enough mischief to send her pulse into double time.

Cara dropped her gaze back to the menu, cheeks warming with a blush.

Sawyer rested an elbow on the table, voice dipping slightly. "Did I tell you how lovely you look?"

Her breath hitched, her eyes traveling up to meet his again. She shook her head.

"You look beautiful."

Before she could respond, the server arrived, sparing her the mortifying possibility of babbling endlessly. After placing their orders, Sawyer cleared his throat.

"So, why do you live in Wickenburg when your family has more money than they could spend in three lifetimes?"

Cara curled her fingers around her soda glass, the condensation slick beneath her fingertips. She took a slow sip, considering how much to share, how much to admit.

"Living there, nothing I did ever met Mother's expectations. Father hated that I chose an interior design degree instead of business. He expected me to be involved in the family company."

Sawyer frowned slightly. "But you had everything you needed."

Cara straightened her back, the memory of her childhood pressing down on her like a weight she had carried for too long. "Did I?" Her voice was quiet but pointed, cutting into the comfortable ease of the meal.

She paused, letting the question settle between them, knowing he needed to understand the difference between having things and being loved.

"I can count on one hand the number of times my mother hugged me. My life was filled with threats. 'Be quiet or...' I'd lose some privilege or be sent to bed without supper. Anything less than a perfect report card was met with punishment. A hair out of place, poor posture, normal kid behavior, none of it was tolerated."

The words sat heavy, stretching between them in the

dim lighting of the restaurant. She blinked, biting back the stinging at the edges of her eyes. "Like I said earlier, money can't buy happiness."

Sawyer shifted slightly in his chair, his jaw tightening, unreadable thoughts passing through his expression. The server returned with their salads, briefly breaking the tension, offering a small reprieve from the painful memories stirring to the surface.

Cara could still feel the imprint of her mother's rejection, the lack of affection, the cold dismissal, the endless reminders that she had never been enough. Her parents may not have raised a hand against her, but their games and manipulations had left scars that took years to untangle. She didn't want Sawyer to dismiss it. She wanted him to understand.

"Is it any wonder that when I met Carson and he showered me with affectionate words and touches, I became putty in his hands?" Her bitter laugh held no humor. "It shouldn't surprise me that his tactics work on my attention-starved sister."

"Cara—"

She shook her head, cutting him off. "I could never say no to him. Even though I suspected he wasn't faithful. It didn't matter." Her throat burned, and her fingers tightened around the fork in front of her like it was the only thing keeping her steady. "I felt seen. I felt important when I was with him." Her gaze flicked across the restaurant, her voice lowering. "Learning about his wife destroyed me." She swallowed hard. "He used me in a far more painful way than my family ever had. It left me broken."

Sawyer replied gruffly, his voice dipping just enough to reveal something unspoken beneath it. "A life with money and no love is better than a life without either."

Cara stilled, bristling at the words, at the casual dismissal of everything she had just said. A response perched on the tip of her tongue, but Sawyer continued, oblivious to the wound his words had just opened.

"At least you didn't have to worry about having food. They didn't abuse you."

Her breath hitched sharply. She forced herself to exhale slowly. "Not physically." The words were cool, deliberate, sharp enough to cut through the ease they had built in the evening. "But the emotional and mental scars have taken years to unwind." She sighed, willing herself to stay steady. "And a lot of intentional prayer."

Sawyer scowled, his grip tightening around his knife and fork, his movements more forced, deliberate, as he attacked his meal. The reaction struck a nerve. She had hit something raw, something buried deep in his own past, and she wasn't sure if he would let her see it.

Good. She wanted him to understand how much damage her family had done, how staged the tabloid photos and company portraits were, how they painted a false version of a life that had never existed. She had never been loved. Not until Aunt Greta introduced her to a Savior and God who loved her exactly as He had made her.

Their conversation cooled, the words sitting too thick between them. Cara turned her attention to her food, but as much as she wanted to retreat, she felt a gentle nudge in her soul. She should pray for Sawyer. She wasn't sure if he'd ever let God in. But God was in this moment. Unexpected. Tense. Present.

13

ACROSS THE TABLE, Sawyer sawed into the steak, his grip tightening around the knife. The blade screeched as it scraped against the plate, the sound grating, cutting straight through the tight coil of frustration wound deep in his chest. Cara had no idea what she was talking about. Life with money was better. It had to be.

Lack of money was why he had stolen cars, why he had learned the trade, why he had bought into the lie that survival meant taking whatever wasn't given freely. With money, he never went to bed hungry. Never had to scrape for scraps. Never had to endure a day alone and isolated. The thought sat heavy in his mind, a last-ditch effort to hold on to the justification he had once clung to.

Then shame. A slow, merciless wave, washing over him and dragging the truth up from the depths he had tried to bury. That hadn't been true. Not even close. He had felt plenty of loneliness in the gang. Even with a woman on his arm, or in his bed, or whispering sweet promises about a future they both knew would never come.

Angelo never let up. The pressure to make more money was a constant weight, always just sufficient to keep Sawyer shackled, yet never quite adequate to set him free. It had never satisfied Angelo's demands. Even when Sawyer himself had been ready to stop, to step away, to breathe — Angelo had pushed harder.

The truth slammed into him, an impact so sharp it might as well have been a fist to the ribs. Money hadn't bought him happiness. Hadn't bought him love. Not any more than it had for Cara. His throat tightened, his stomach twisting as he swallowed the bite of juicy steak, tasting nothing. The remorse churned deep, a slow, aching burn.

"I'm sorry."

Cara's head snapped up, startled by the sudden confession. "Apology accepted."

Sawyer stared at his plate, picking at his baked potato, not quite sure what he was apologizing for. For brushing off her pain? For assuming wealth meant security? For everything she would never truly understand about his world? He exhaled, forcing himself to keep going. "I've... life has been hard."

Cara snorted softly, dry humor lacing her voice. "Ain't that the truth?"

Sawyer nodded, a ghost of a smile flickering before vanishing as quickly as it had come. Maybe he could trust her with a fraction of the truth. Maybe. The thought was frightening. But still, he plowed ahead.

"I spent my childhood in foster care. I know some kids ended up in good homes. Not me." The words sat thick in the air between them, heavier now, harder to force out. "An—" His throat tightened, the name sticking in his mouth like glass shards. No. He couldn't say it. He couldn't let any part of his old life creep into this new one.

"Andy and I ended up at the same home when we were sixteen. The dad was a harsh man. Got the scars to prove it." His grip closed into a tight fist, but he forced himself to relax. "Andy and I became friends. After one frightening night, Andy made a plan. He and I could survive on our own far better than under that man's roof. Far better than in the system."

Sawyer drew in a deep breath, the memories pressing against his ribs, then let it out slowly, leveling his voice before it could crack. "Anyway. I won't bore you with the details. Life was a different kind of hard on our own." He pushed his plate away, suddenly unable to force another bite down, his forearms resting heavily on the table.

"Tres and Junior Vargas are the first men I've met in my life that treat me well and want nothing from me other than an honest day's work." His voice dipped, something unsteady creeping in. "As weird as it sounds, Junior — the old man — is the closest friend I've ever had."

Cara reached across the table, her fingers resting gently against his arm, her touch warm, grounding, completely unlike anything he had ever known before now. "He is a wonderful man, isn't he?"

Sawyer pursed his lips tight, overwhelmed by the jolt of emotion searing his heart. He nodded, a quick motion, then reached for his soda, taking a long swig to rein himself back in. By the time he set the glass down, he had decided. That was enough transparency for one night.

He shifted the conversation, needing to put some distance between himself and the weight of it. "Why interior design?"

Cara's soft smile lingered for a few seconds, as if she were searching for the right words. Then, slowly, she began telling her story. Sawyer listened to every word, only interrupting briefly to place a dessert order.

"In high school, one teacher assigned us a service project. She said it was important that kids with money understood not everyone was so fortunate. So the teacher signed us up for a Habitat for Humanity project." Her voice softened, threading memories into the present. "We built a house for a family who had nothing. When it was done, it looked so plain. I took my father's credit card and bought pictures for the walls and some decor. When the mother saw it, she cried. She loved how homey I made the place feel. No one had ever done something so special for her."

Cara scooped a bite of cheesecake onto her fork. Sawyer

waited while she swallowed it, then portioned some for himself.

"It was the first time someone besides a teacher praised something I had done. It felt so good to give away a small part of myself and to experience their gratitude."

He pushed the last bite of cheesecake toward her, but she shook her head. So he ate it.

He could see similarities in their lives, the way they both knew what it meant to be overlooked. Different circumstances. Same emotions.

"When I learned I could get a degree in interior design, I decided that's what I wanted to do with my life. And I'm so glad I did. I have a strong creative bent. Aunt Greta says it would have been a shame not to share it with the world."

Sawyer nodded. "She sounds like a smart woman."

"Have you met her?"

"Should I have?"

"She runs *The Lariat*. It's a bistro in town."

Sawyer frowned slightly. "I'm not very familiar with Wickenburg yet."

The server arrived, placing the check between them. Sawyer swiped it before Cara could, ignoring her attempt to claim it instead. He could afford the meal. He had been careful with his paychecks, buying a few new pieces of clothing with each one, making sure his spending stayed low and controlled.

"Thanks for dinner." Cara's genuine smile did something unexpected to him.

"I suppose I should get you back to the ranch."

Sawyer handed her the keys, hesitating. "If you don't mind, I'd like to change back into my clothes before you drop me off."

She barely hesitated. "Yeah. You can change at my place."

The ride back to her home was quiet, the weight of the evening still settling in his chest. When she let him inside,

Sawyer felt his pulse slow, the space unexpectedly comfy, far different from the cold glamour of her parents' mansion. He could picture it—him, sitting on the overstuffed couch with her nestled against his side, a bowl of popcorn in his lap, an action flick playing softly on the modest TV. A quiet life. A normal life.

"The bathroom is the first door on the right."

Sawyer's mouth dried as she stepped past him, heading toward her bedroom. The dress. Her home. His pulse raced, sending his mind down paths it shouldn't go—thoughts about how to spend the night, none of which involved leaving her house or going back to the bunkhouse.

Cara flicked on the bathroom light, the glow cutting sharply through his thoughts. "Here you go."

When she turned to face him, he reeled in his wayward emotions, locked them down, forced himself to remember who he was trying to be. She trusted him. And given everything she had shared at dinner, he wanted to be worthy of her trust. A fleeting night in her arms would only hurt them both. Junior would be disappointed in him if he failed to behave himself. And somehow, that mattered.

Sawyer stepped inside the bathroom, closing the door, then quickly changed out of the fancy suit, slipping into his jeans, T-shirt, and snap-front shirt. He pulled on his boots, the familiar leather grounding him. It was almost as if the western clothing transformed him into someone new, someone more like Junior, like who he wanted to be.

When he stepped into the living room, his gaze traveled over the walls, taking in the absence of her photography. From the few pieces he had seen at the casitas, and the ones she had captured of him with Goldie, her talent exceeded most photographers he had come across. He had expected to see her work mounted, surrounding her in pieces of herself. Instead, she had abstract paintings filling the space.

A few minutes later, Cara joined him, her hair loosely hanging over her shoulders, dressed in baggy shorts and a

T-shirt. Something about the simplicity of her presence made it harder to leave. She smirked lightly. "Ah, there's the cowboy handyman I know. Ready?"

Sawyer rubbed the back of his neck, hesitating. He thrust the suit toward her. "You think you could hang on to this for me?"

She lifted a brow. "Why?"

His throat tightened slightly, but he pressed on. "Doesn't really belong in a bunkhouse, and I don't want anyone thinking I came by it dishonestly."

Cara held his gaze, searching, considering. Finally, she nodded. "Sure. I'll get it cleaned and keep it in my closet."

"Thanks."

By the time she dropped him off, the hour had grown late. Goldie lifted her head, watching as he climbed into bed, her tail thumping against the mattress in a soft rhythm. Out of all the images of Cara that could have stuck with him, he fell asleep to the one where they sat on the couch together, watching a movie, her tucked against his side like she belonged there. And maybe, for a brief moment, he let himself imagine it was real.

CARA WAVED AS Sawyer ducked into the bunkhouse, his silhouette disappearing into the dim lighting of the ranch quarters. Goodness, he had looked amazing at dinner. So polished in that expensive suit. And yet, somehow, when he had changed back into denim and a snap-front shirt, he had looked even better.

Two entirely different personas—cowboy and socialite—both of which he played so convincingly, it was difficult to believe either wasn't his natural state. She never would have fathomed he had lived on the streets. Or that poverty had been his norm.

As she drove back toward Wickenburg, her fingers loosened around the steering wheel, thoughts circling like a slow-moving storm. His phrasing about the suit lingered. Something about not wanting anyone to think he came by it dishonestly. What did it matter what people thought? Sure, it would be odd for a cowboy handyman to own an Armani, but there was something deeper beneath his words—something almost like fear, a tension she hadn't quite placed.

She pulled into her driveway, cutting the engine, pressing her palms against the leather steering wheel before finally climbing out and heading inside. The second she entered her duplex, a long breath escaped her, the weight of the night settling into her bones.

Sawyer Fullerton was a paradox. Foster system. Living on the streets. Perfectly at ease in threadbare clothing and an expensive suit. Gentlemanly. Attentive during her breakdown. A hard worker at the ranch. Polite. And so handsome, he consumed all the oxygen in any space.

Cara set her keys on the counter, fingertips brushing absently against the fabric of his suit, still carrying the lingering scent of his cologne. Without thinking, she pressed it against her face, inhaling the warm, familiar smell, the traces of his presence woven into the threads. Comforting.

She folded it carefully over the edge of the couch, deciding she would take it to the cleaners before storing it in her closet, so it would be ready the next time he needed it. Not if. When. The thought sat heavier than she had expected.

Cara sighed, heading down the hall to her bedroom, pleased he had been her plus one, thankful for the steady presence he had been all evening. As she slid beneath the covers, her mind spiraled, thoughts of Sawyer swirling without pause, winding through fragments of their night together. Until exhaustion finally pulled her under, silencing the storm in her head. For now.

14

THE NEXT DAY, Cara spent the late morning tidying her apartment before pulling her hair into a loose ponytail and sliding into a pair of light shorts and a fitted tee, determined to get to *The Lariat* before the Arizona afternoon heat became unbearable. She drove across town, knowing that even though it was off season, her aunt's bistro would be buzzing with locals.

By the time she arrived at one o'clock, the worst of the rush had passed, leaving behind the steady hum of conversation and the rich scent of fresh-baked bread and roasted coffee lingering in the air. The second she stepped inside, Aunt Greta called her name in greeting, waving her toward the worn bar, its bare edges nicked from decades of use.

Cara slid onto a stool, absently running her fingers over the wood's surface, wondering how many first responders, cowboys, and office workers had sat in this exact spot since her grandparents opened the place in the sixties. The bar top needed stripping, sanding, and refinishing. Or, honestly? Completely replaced.

Aunt Greta placed a steaming cup of coffee in front of her. "You hungry, honey?"

She sighed. "Yeah. Club on sourdough would hit the spot."

"Coming right up."

She took a slow sip, savoring the rich bitterness before

stirring in another pack of sugar, watching the granules dissolve into dark swirls. As she waited, her gaze traveled across the restaurant, absorbing the familiar worn edges of the booths lining the outer walls, their centers faded, their edges tattered, remnants of decades of conversations, first dates, and morning rituals.

It felt less like a modern bistro and more like a diner from the last century, its charm rooted in nostalgia rather than sleek branding. Gen Z might scoff at it—no carefully curated aesthetic, no Instagram-worthy interior. She sighed, picturing a way to bridge past and present. A chalkboard menu wall, sleek white subway tile, a dual espresso station, and a glass pastry case with warm LED lighting. Yellow and red—Aunt Greta's favorite colors, reminiscent of a French bistro, softened with knotty pine accents for a touch of western sophistication.

Now all she had to do was convince Aunt Greta to let her do it. She knew her aunt had been saving for much needed renovations. Maybe a small business loan could bridge the gap. The remodel would pay for itself in no time.

Cara swiveled at the sound of a familiar voice, the vinyl seat sticking to the backs of her legs.

"So, this is *The Lariat*?"

Sawyer stood near the bar, worn cowboy hat in hand, his fingers raking through freshly cut hair—hair she suddenly imagined running her own fingers through. She blinked hard, pushing the thought away. He had chosen new denim, a crisp snap-front shirt, the usual belt and boots, looking every bit the cowboy—the version of him that felt most authentic. Cara realized she was staring.

She cleared her throat. "What are you doing here?"

He winked, dimples etched deep as his grin stretched, sending her pulse ticking up against her will. "A good friend told me I should check it out."

Aunt Greta appeared with Cara's plate, eyebrows raised, curiosity sparking in her expression. "Who's your cowboy?"

Cara rushed to explain before Aunt Greta could get any ideas. "He's not mine, Aunt Greta."

Aunt Greta's sly smile said otherwise. She introduced them quickly, but her aunt was already snatching back her plate, motioning toward a booth. "Let me find you a table. Together."

Cara groaned inwardly, catching the matchmaking look in Aunt Greta's eyes. Still, she followed her to table seven, settling into the booth, coffee close at hand.

"What can I get you, Sawyer?" Aunt Greta asked, handing him a menu.

He skimmed it quickly. "Give me a few?"

"Sure thing."

Aunt Greta disappeared, clearing another table, leaving Cara alone with him again.

"What are you doing here?" She repeated, curiosity nagging at her.

Sawyer leaned back slightly. "I have the day off and thought it was about time I see more of what Wickenburg offers."

Cara grinned. "If it wasn't the middle of a summer day, I would suggest a walk at the Hassayampa River Preserve."

His eyes glinted slightly. "If you joined me, and it wasn't already one-hundred-twelve degrees, I might take you up on it."

Heat spread across her cheeks, far hotter than the desert air outside. She reached for her sandwich. Then stopped. A lifetime of harsh reprimands from her mother echoed in her ears.

Sawyer eyed her closely, brow arching. "What's good here?"

She rolled her eyes. "Everything? I told you my aunt runs the place."

His head tilted slightly, gaze sharp. "Why aren't you eating?"

She hesitated, tucking a loose strand of hair behind her

ear. "Mother would say it's rude to eat in front of someone."

Sawyer snorted, shaking his head. "She's not here. Eat."

Cara finally picked up her sandwich, biting into the corner, savoring the perfect crunch of the toasted sourdough. She loved how Aunt Greta sliced the bread diagonally, keeping her grandparents' tradition alive.

An idea sparked, and she reached for her tablet, fingers moving with purpose as she started sketching. While Sawyer placed his order, she worked through her vision, drawing every detail with careful precision. When she finished, a satisfied smile curved her lips. It was perfect—modern meets classic, tradition meets fresh beginnings.

Sawyer glanced at her tablet. "Whatcha got there?"

Cara lifted her chin proudly. "The design to update this place. If Aunt Greta would ever let me."

SAWYER CHEWED A hunk of the Reuben, the tangy bite of sauerkraut and melted Swiss hitting just right. It had been years since he'd had one. Maybe that's what made it so good. Or maybe it was the company.

He had rolled out of bed later than normal this morning, eager to shake off the restlessness that had settled over him. After a quick haircut, he spent the late morning exploring town, absorbing more of Wickenburg, letting himself sink into a place that still felt unfamiliar but strangely right. Then, driving past *The Lariat's* sign, he remembered Cara's aunt owned the bistro.

He hadn't expected to see her there, but the moment he spotted her sitting at the bar, he couldn't resist spending more time in her orbit. Now, sitting across from her, watching her eyes light up with excitement as she sketched out renovations, Sawyer pointed his pinky finger toward the bar in her drawing.

"What's the plan for the facing?"

Cara didn't hesitate. "I was thinking beadboard."

Sawyer frowned slightly, still chewing his bite, shaking his head before swallowing. "How about tin roofing? Or better yet, some of that material that looks like tin but is shaped like tiles."

Her eyes sparked with interest. "Oh, I love that idea. With a pattern like this?" She sketched semi-circles and simple four-petal floral shapes, filling the front of the bar in her drawing.

Sawyer didn't know what they were officially called, but she had captured his idea perfectly. "Exactly. What were you thinking about the walls over here?"

Her cheeks turned rosy, and her gaze dropped to her uneaten fries. Sawyer polished off the last bite of his sandwich, waiting. She hesitated, then finally admitted, "Until I can raise enough money for an art gallery of my own, I was hoping to display some of my photography. It would add to the restaurant's local feel and provide exposure for my work."

Sawyer leaned forward slightly, dipping a fry in ketchup before pointing it at her. "Like the pictures you took of me?"

Cara picked at a stray piece of lettuce, avoiding his gaze. "Yeah, the one where your face hides in the shadow of your cowboy hat while Goldie looks up at you with the most adoring expression."

Sawyer popped the fry into his mouth, nodding as he chewed. He remembered that picture. It was why he let her keep the ones where his face remained hidden. Because somehow she had seen something in him he still struggled to see in himself.

"Can you show me more of your work?"

She tapped and swiped on her tablet, then turned it toward him. "Here are a few of the Vargas brothers. This one is Derin. He's the quintessential hunky cowboy and the foreman."

Sawyer smirked. "Met him."

Cara giggled, her cheeks blooming red, dipping her head slightly as she laughed at herself. "Oh, duh. You work there."

She flipped through a few more photos — Dalton, Dylan, one wrangler named Adan Franco. From what Sawyer had heard, Adan had been a big pro bull rider a few years ago. That was an interesting part of his new life — the whole rodeo thing. He had never been to one, but it seemed like the cowboys watched rodeo highlights every weekend, right alongside pro football.

The words escaped before he could stop them. "You ever go to a rodeo?"

Cara arched a brow. Sawyer realized too late that she saw him as a cowboy, someone who should have been to one. His neck heated, embarrassment climbing fast, so he shifted gears.

"I think you should hang your photography on this wall. You're already planning chalkboard paint behind the counter, right?"

"Yeah. For the menu."

"The photography would add balance if it took up most of this wall, don't you think? Pack it full of your western landscapes, cowboys, and horses."

Cara bounded out of the booth, moving toward the wall in question, studying it from every angle, then circling back again. Sawyer watched as her eyes lit, brightening her entire face, making it impossible to look away. Something had changed between them last night. Something good. Something he wanted more of.

She slid back into the booth, breaking the moment. Sawyer snagged a few of her fries after she pushed her plate aside, absently wondering if she had any idea how much time he had spent reading about remodeling, design, and home construction over the past five years.

"How long would it take you to fix up this place?"

A piece of fry lodged awkwardly in his throat, prompting a sudden coughing fit. He pounded his chest, taking a swig of his drink as his lungs finally cleared.

Cara half stood, her concern genuine, brows pulled together. "I won't have to Heimlich you, will I?"

Sawyer sucked in a sharp breath, shaking his head. "Nope. I'm good."

"So?"

He wiped his mouth with a napkin, focusing. "I'm pretty busy at the ranch."

Cara wasn't fazed. "That's not what I asked. Let's pretend you aren't busy. How long would it take?"

"Just me?"

She shook her head. "I'd help too. Maybe we could enlist some of those Vargas brothers?"

Sawyer thought it over, adjusting his stance. "Let's say we had you, me, Derin, Adan, and one other man. We could probably demo in a day. Maybe two. Then patch the drywall... You're not moving any monuments, right?"

"You mean the bar? No."

"Yeah, I could handle drywall repair in a day. Painting, more like three days. We'll want to scrub the walls, then apply primer given the age." His fingers stroked his clean-shaven chin, as if searching for something that wasn't there. Surprisingly, his words came out confidently. "I think two weeks tops. Would only need the Vargases for a demolition day. Maybe for installation if we want that to go faster."

Cara's face lit up instantly. "Perfect. Aunt Greta usually takes a week or two off during July, where she shuts down the restaurant. Now all I have to do is convince her to let us remodel it."

Sawyer waved a hand. "Aren't you forgetting a few important details?"

Cara dismissed his concerns without hesitation. "No worries. We'll work it out."

Sawyer watched as she gathered her things, excitement buzzing through her every step. As she hurried out, he let himself admit one truth. Seeing Cara's smile—it was like sunlight breaking through dark clouds. No. Too cliché. Her smile brightened every shadowed corner of his existence, making him feel alive in a way he had never had before. It was better than the adrenaline high of stealing cars. It thrilled him beyond words.

And that's when Sawyer knew that Cara Hollis had pilfered his heart. Hopefully, she wouldn't return it once she learned about his past.

15

CARA PRACTICALLY BUZZED with anticipation as she drove back to her duplex, fingers tapping against the steering wheel as ideas begged to be formalized. She had never been this excited about remodeling *The Lariat*.

Sawyer and she had made a great team before, but sharing her vision with him had elevated the partnership, making it feel like something bigger than just a renovation. She loved, loved, loved his idea of using tin ceiling tiles for the front of the bar. The contrast between them and the knotty pine bar top perfectly captured the balance between classic Western charm and modern elegance.

Sliding onto her couch, she opened a browser window, pulling up images of tin tiles, scanning for the right pattern, the perfect texture. When she found a company selling reclaimed ones, she called immediately, speaking with the rep about availability, pricing, and shipping timelines.

After an hour of gathering sample images and planning materials, she dialed Tres Vargas.

"Afternoon, Cara. What can I do for you?"

"I'm working on a design to update *The Lariat* and I wondered if we could work out a deal for labor?"

"What were you thinking?"

She took a breath. "Well, after Sawyer and I complete the Flagstaff Casita and office, we won't have enough time to complete the dining hall before the Independence Day

Fireworks Show."

"Catalina mentioned that. No worries. As long as you can complete it by the end of August, we should be fine."

"Thanks. So… I'd like to borrow Sawyer for a reno of *The Lariat*."

Tres chuckled, amusement clear in his voice. "What's Greta think of that?"

Cara cringed, thankful Tres couldn't see her expression. "I wanted to make sure the plan was viable before presenting it to her."

"Go on."

She explained Sawyer's estimated timeline, the help she needed, and the labor-for-discount trade she wanted to propose. The line went silent for a moment, and she could almost picture Tres rubbing his chin, considering it.

Finally, he spoke. "Send me the numbers for Sawyer's time and the discount. Let me know more details about what you need from the boys. I'm happy to have them help as a neighborly favor for a few days, as long as they aren't needed for the Fourth of July prep."

Giddiness bubbled up, but she forced herself to keep her tone steady. "I'll get you an email this weekend. Thanks, Tres, for considering it."

"Anytime, Cara."

As soon as she disconnected the call, she dove into the numbers, working out the cost trade-offs. Her profit on the Vargas project would be slimmer, but it meant less out-of-pocket cost for Aunt Greta. She could live with that.

On Monday, Tres Vargas called back, confirming the approval for her plan. Sawyer didn't need her input that afternoon as he focused on touch-ups at the Sedona Casita and started demo on the Flagstaff Casita, so she headed straight to her aunt's home.

Aunt Greta always took Mondays off, making it the perfect time for a proposal. Cara used her key to open the door, calling out to avoid startling her aunt.

"Cara, what brings you by? I was just about to reheat a bowl of leftover chili. Want some?"

Cara shook her head. "No thanks. I wanted to show you my remodeling plan."

Aunt Greta's expression shifted, a shadow passing over her features. "We've been over this before. I can't afford you, and I won't have you working for free."

Cara exhaled, steadying herself. "And I told you, if you can pay for materials, that's enough."

Greta retrieved her chili, settling at the kitchen table. As her aunt prayed over her meal, Cara waited, sending up her own quiet prayer for a peaceful conversation, an open heart.

Once Aunt Greta finished, Cara pressed forward. "I arranged with Tres Vargas for the labor, so the entire project will cost even less. Plus, I won't charge you for my photography if you agree to sell it for a thirty percent commission."

Greta's brow lifted slightly, weighing the deal. "Make it forty, and you have a deal."

Cara smiled. She had been willing to go to forty-five, so forty suited her just fine.

"Show me your design."

She treated it like any other presentation, pulling up professional renderings on her tablet, showing physical samples, laying out options. The moment she mentioned reclaimed tin tiles, Aunt Greta's eyes lit, interest sparking fast. Cara knew she had closed the sale.

Greta leaned back, nodding slowly. "I have to say, you've impressed me. No wonder the Vargases hired you. Your work is amazing. I honestly wouldn't change a thing."

"So, we have a deal?"

"Yes. When can you start?"

"The week of July fourth. It'll take two to three weeks, though we could add finishing touches while the place is open if needed."

Aunt Greta grinned, shaking her head like she still couldn't believe it. "Mom and Pop will love it, too. You should send them pictures as you work on it, a before and after."

Cara straightened, warmth settling in her chest. Her grandparents had retired to Florida, and because of the rift her parents had caused, she had only really gotten to know them since moving to Wickenburg. The mention of them sparked a question that had lingered for years.

"Aunt Greta?" Cara's voice came out softer than intended. "Why did my parents never talk about Mom and Pop? Or you, for that matter? I grew up thinking we didn't have any extended family."

Aunt Greta's expression grew thoughtful, her fingers tracing the rim of her empty chili bowl. "Your father started pulling away when his tech business really took off. Success changed him, made him think he needed to leave his roots behind." She paused, meeting Cara's eyes. "Things got worse after he married your mother. Gail thought his humble beginnings from a small town hurt his image as an elite billionaire."

The words settled heavy between them. Cara had always wondered if there was something fundamentally wrong with her, some reason her mother remained so distant. "So my mother isn't just cold towards me?"

"No, honey." Aunt Greta's voice carried a gentle sadness. "In that department, she's even colder toward me and my parents."

An odd mix of comfort and sorrow washed over Cara. Relief that maybe she wasn't inherently unlovable battled with grief for all the people her mother's icy heart had hurt. Her grandparents, whom she'd fallen completely in love with since moving to Wickenburg despite having missed twenty-four years of knowing them. They sent birthday cards with handwritten notes about how proud they were, called every few weeks just to hear her voice, and asked endless questions about her business and life in Arizona. Her aunt, who had welcomed her with open arms when she'd shown up lost and searching for something she couldn't name.

The renovation would be more than just updates to share with them. It would be proof of who she'd become, evidence of the life she was building in their world. A chance to show them that even though her parents had stolen decades from their relationship, she was here now, rooted in the place they'd raised her father, ready to make up for every lost Christmas morning and missed Sunday dinner.

As she left her aunt's home, something unfamiliar but steady settled inside her. Several pieces of her life were finally coming together. And this time, she was building something that would last.

SAWYER WIPED HIS forehead on his sleeve, the relentless summer heat pressing against his skin, thick and suffocating. One hundred fifteen degrees. Usually, June settled in with triple-digit heat, but this? This was unseasonably brutal.

The resort office buzzed with activity as they prepared to move everything to a temporary location. Cardboard boxes lined the hallway, and the air conditioning struggled against the constant opening of doors as staff carried equipment back and forth.

"Gatorade?"

Sawyer lifted his hand, ready, catching the bottle midair as Derin tossed it toward him. The cap twisted off smoothly, the first sip hitting icy and sharp, a welcome relief against the fire raging outside.

"Why'd we pick the hottest day of the year to move everything out of the office?" Drake, the youngest Vargas brother, whined, kicking at a stray pebble. Still high school age. Still learning the ropes.

Dalton clapped a hand on his shoulder, grinning. "Think

of it as character building."

He hefted another box, muscles straining under the weight. "Besides, we want this done before the Fourth of July Fireworks Show."

"Der, can you toss me one of those?"

"Sure thing, D4."

Sawyer smirked at the nickname. Dalton was the fourth Dalton J. Vargas in the family, after all. He kinda liked it. Judging by Dalton's eye roll, he didn't.

Derin cracked open his own drink, taking a long pull before setting it aside. "Hey, I'm thankful for all the help. This has been on my to-do list for weeks."

Sawyer nodded, wiping sweat from his neck with a bandana. "Me too. This is a lot for one man to move. With half the staff helping, it's going fast."

"I'm just here for the burgers," Drake joked, earning a round of laughter from the group.

The tension eased for a moment, the camaraderie cutting through the oppressive heat and physical strain.

"Sawyer!"

He turned toward the voice, spotting Tres Vargas approaching. The easy banter around him faded as he registered the serious set of Tres's shoulders.

"Yes, sir?"

Tres pulled him aside from the others. Sawyer's pulse ticked up, unease creeping into his chest like ice water despite the blazing heat.

"Your parole officer called."

His stomach dropped, and the Gatorade turned sour in his mouth.

Tres's voice remained steady, but his eyes searched Sawyer's face. "There was a car theft during a party in Paradise Valley last weekend. Fits the pattern from the gang."

His throat went dry, his skin suddenly feeling too tight, too hot. Sweat that had nothing to do with the temperature beaded along his forehead.

"Jerry wanted me to confirm you were nowhere near the area."

The words hung in the air between them, heavy with implication. Sawyer rubbed a shaky hand against the back of his neck, buying himself a moment to think, to breathe.

"Whatever you're about to say, I want you to know we'll deal with it together," Tres said, voice steady as bedrock.

Sawyer swallowed hard, forcing the words out past the tightness in his throat. "Cara took me to her parents' home Friday night as her plus one. They live in Paradise Valley."

Tres blinked, processing. "Cara Hollis?"

"Yeah. Her parents are Peter and Gail Hollis."

Tres's face sobered, all traces of easy camaraderie vanishing. The shift sent ice through Sawyer's veins.

His parole officer wouldn't be asking about his whereabouts through Tres unless something serious had happened. Something that would put an ex-con right back in the crosshairs. And Sierra had been at the Hollis estate that same night... Sawyer's grip tightened on the plastic bottle as the pieces clicked into place. Whatever had gone down Friday, his presence there made him a suspect.

The bitter irony wasn't lost on him. He'd finally started to find his place at the ranch, finally felt like he had a real future ahead of him, and now his past was threatening to destroy it all over again. Even innocent, he knew how this looked. How it would always look.

"Can she vouch for your whereabouts?"

"Yes." The word came out rushed, desperate. "She and I were together most of the night. We drove to and from the event in her car."

Tres nodded slowly, his expression thoughtful. "Alright, I'll let Jerry know."

As he started to turn away, Sawyer grabbed his arm, urgency pressing through his fingers. "Tres, there's something else..."

Tres faced him fully, hooking his thumbs into his belt

loops, waiting with the patience that had become his trademark.

Sawyer's breath hitched. The words felt like glass in his throat. "I saw… Someone from my old gang working as a server for the catering. Name's Sierra Guerra. It's her boyfriend that I testified against."

Tres didn't react right away. One beat. Then two. The silence stretched while he processed this new complication.

"Thanks for being honest. I'll make sure Jerry knows you volunteered the information."

Sawyer exhaled, barely releasing an ounce of the tension coiling inside him. "I think she recognized me."

Tres clapped a hand firmly on Sawyer's shoulder, his grip solid and reassuring. "You have nothing to fear. I'll talk to Cara to confirm your attendance at the party, and I'll handle Jerry."

Sawyer nodded, grateful for the steadiness in Tres's voice, but knowing his past wasn't done haunting him. He hoped Sierra wouldn't pin this on him. He had done nothing wrong. But he knew her. She could twist the truth with ease, could manipulate the cops better than most. And if she found out where he lived… He didn't want to think about that.

"Hey!"

Sawyer pivoted, catching Cara's wave as she approached across the parking lot. Tres stepped forward to intercept her, and Sawyer gulped another mouthful of Gatorade, pretending like his world wasn't unraveling around him.

Then sharp voices edged with tension cut through the afternoon air.

"Someone said they saw you in another man's arms," Dalton growled, voice dangerously low.

Sawyer froze, not wanting to draw attention to himself, but also not wanting to hear this conversation at all. The parking lot suddenly felt too small, too exposed.

Janessa's voice dripped with syrupy reassurance. "Let's be real. I've only got eyes for you, Dalton."

Sawyer watched as she wrapped one arm behind Dalton's neck, slid her other hand up his chest, and caressed his jawline with practiced ease. The diamond ring on her finger caught the light, flashing like a warning sign. Engaged. That was new.

Then she leaned closer, whispered something, kissed him hard, making sure everyone could see it. A performance designed to reassure and manipulate.

Sawyer turned away, remembering the threats she had made before. He didn't know what her game was. All he knew was that he wanted no part of it.

He returned to the office, focusing on transferring file cabinets, the familiar weight of honest work helping to push away everything clouding his mind. The metal drawers scraped against the floor as he and Dylan maneuvered them toward the door.

Then Janessa cornered him.

She appeared at his elbow as he eased a particularly heavy file cabinet onto a dolly, her voice low and sharp. "You better not have told Dalton. You're going to ruin my plan."

Sawyer's jaw clenched, his hands still gripping the dolly's handle. "I said nothing to anyone."

Janessa's eyes narrowed, stepping closer so her voice wouldn't carry. The acid in her tone sent a chill through his skin despite the oppressive heat. "You say anything, and I'll tell your parole officer that you stole the missing car."

His stomach twisted violently, but he forced himself to keep control. "That wasn't me."

"I don't care."

She laughed, tossing her head back like this was all an amusing game, before flashing a cold, knowing smile. "When he comes here to arrest you, Cara will see it and learn you're a convict."

Anger spiked, hotter than the Arizona sun. His grip tightened on the cabinet until his knuckles went white. "Leave Cara out of this."

Janessa's lips curved, triumphant. She'd found his weakness, and she knew it. "Thanks for confirming you like her. I wasn't sure. Now I know."

Her voice turned icy, each word deliberate. "Keep your mouth shut, Sawyer. Last warning."

She spun on her heel, marching away, leaving behind wreckage he wasn't sure how to fix.

Sawyer leaned an arm against the wall, forcing his stomach to settle, refusing to let the bile rise. Women like Janessa and Sierra, they were determined to drag him back. To make redemption impossible.

He lifted his cowboy hat, ran a shaking hand through his cropped hair, feeling the despair lacerate his heart. Just when things were starting to feel stable, the past came clawing back.

Then Junior's words surfaced, cutting through the darkness. Jesus made him right with God. No one—no one—could take that from him. God had rescued him, and that wasn't because Sawyer deserved it, it was because God was good. His job was to trust that. Avoid the ways of the violent. Hold fast.

He exhaled slowly, straightening his shoulders. Then he turned.

Cara stood there. Eyes wide. Face crestfallen.

Sawyer felt the ground shift beneath him. He hoped, desperately, he hadn't lost her trust.

16

"TRES, WHY ARE you asking about the party at my parents' house?"

Cara narrowed her eyes, concern creeping into her voice as the summer sun blazed against her bare arms. The heat pressed uncomfortably close, making her tank top stick to her skin. Sweat beaded along her hairline despite the early hour.

Tres glanced away, rubbing the back of his neck in a way that meant he was working up to something. "Derin mentioned Sawyer came home pretty late last weekend. Just making sure everything's good."

Cara's frown deepened. She stepped into the blessed shade of the portico, the temperature dropping a few degrees as she moved away from the worst of the heat. Her voice lowered instinctively. "Everything's totally fine. After we bounced from the party, he drove me to that steakhouse in Wickenburg—you know, the one with the massive portions? He actually paid for dinner, which was sweet."

She paused, remembering the way he'd looked in that suit she'd picked out for him. "Then he changed out of his fancy clothes, and I drove him back here. I think it was around ten when I dropped him off."

Tres studied her face, his dark eyes weighing something she couldn't read. The silence stretched between them, heavy with unspoken questions. "Thanks, Cara. That lines up with what Derin and Sawyer told me."

His expression remained tight, controlled in a way that made her stomach clench. "Nothing for you to stress about."

As he walked away, Cara's shoulders sagged with a loud exhale. Frustration bubbled beneath the surface like carbonation in a shaken bottle. Why was Tres so invested in tracking Sawyer's every move? The question gnawed at her, an itch she couldn't reach, leaving her restless and on edge.

She tried to shake off the growing unease, almost managing it until she stepped into Catalina's office twenty minutes later and caught sight of Sawyer's expression. Her stomach dropped.

Fear. Pure, undiluted fear flickered across his features before he could mask it.

"What happened?" The words tumbled out faster than she intended. "Why is Tres grilling me about last Friday night?"

Sawyer's boot scuffed against the concrete floor, the sound sharp in the small space. He hesitated, then gripped his cowboy hat between his hands like a lifeline, his knuckles white against the worn edges. His gaze darted everywhere except her face.

"Someone jacked a car in Paradise Valley on Friday night."

The words hit her like a physical blow. Cara's head snapped back, her pulse spiking. "What does that have to do with you?"

Sawyer's mouth opened. Closed. Opened again. Nothing came out, but a strangled sound that might have been the beginning of an explanation.

Something cold and sharp twisted in her chest, stealing her breath. The office suddenly felt too small, the walls pressing in. "Sawyer?"

His Adam's apple bobbed as he swallowed hard, the motion visible in his throat. "Look, Cara, my past..." His voice cracked like he was seventeen again instead of twenty-seven. "I haven't always been the man I am today."

The confession hung between them, heavy as summer storm clouds. Sawyer's jaw tensed, a muscle jumping as he forced himself to continue. "Tres has every right to ask questions."

Cara's mouth fell open, her heart hammering so hard she could feel it in her fingertips. What was he trying to tell her? What did Tres already know that she didn't?

The questions crashed over her in waves, each one more terrifying than the last. Had she been completely wrong about him? Had she let her feelings cloud her judgment so badly that she'd missed the obvious red flags?

Before she could voice any of the chaos spinning through her mind, Catalina Vargas swept into the office, her presence immediately filling the space with warmth and energy. "Cara, *mija*, the supplier dropped off the tile yesterday. You must see it."

Cara forced her facial muscles into something resembling a smile, though it felt more like a grimace. Her chest still felt tight, breath coming in shallow puffs. "Let's look."

Even as she followed Catalina outside, her thoughts remained tethered to Sawyer. His fear on the day she'd taken his picture, warning her it was dangerous to have photos of him. His weird phrasing about people thinking he'd come by the Armani dishonestly. The way he sometimes looked over his shoulder like he expected trouble to find him.

Now this.

The pieces were forming a picture she didn't want to see.

"Does this look like what you ordered?"

Catalina's voice pulled her back to the present. The older woman stood beside several cases of tile arranged in the bright sunlight near the office entrance. The ceramic caught the light, revealing subtle variations in color and texture that hadn't been apparent in the samples.

Cara blinked, forcing herself to focus. She pulled out her

tablet, fingers slightly unsteady as she swiped through screens to find the order specifications. "Yes, this matches the item numbers perfectly."

Catalina's face fell slightly, her shoulders rounding. "Oh."

The disappointment in her voice was unmistakable. Cara's heart squeezed with sympathy, grateful for the distraction from her spiraling thoughts. "You're not loving it?"

"It's more yellow than I expected," Catalina admitted, her fingers tracing the edge of one tile. "In the showroom, it looked more neutral."

Cara offered what she hoped was a reassuring smile. "That's totally normal. Keep in mind, this is in direct sunlight right now. Once it's installed with proper lighting, it'll look much more like the samples you approved."

Catalina's expression remained uncertain, wariness flickering in her dark eyes. "You really think so?"

"I promise," Cara said, meaning it. "Trust the process. When things are fragmented like this—when you're only seeing pieces instead of the entire picture—it's easy to panic. But once everything comes together, you'll see how it all works."

The words left her mouth before she fully processed them, but as soon as she spoke, she realized she wasn't just talking about tile installation. She was talking about Sawyer, about the fragments of his story she'd been collecting like puzzle pieces without understanding how they fit together.

Catalina's face brightened, her smile returning. "Sí, you're right. The same thing happens with life, no? We see only pieces and think we understand the entire story."

The observation hit Cara like a gentle slap of clarity. She'd been doing exactly that with Sawyer by making assumptions based on incomplete information. If she let the uncertainty fester, if she jumped to conclusions before hearing the whole truth, she could destroy the fragile trust they'd been building.

Deep in her bones, she knew he'd proven his character over and over. The way he worked, the way he treated people, the way he'd protected her that night at her parents' party. That had to count for something.

"You're absolutely right," Cara said, feeling some of the tension ease from her shoulders. "Thanks for the reminder."

That resolve lasted exactly four hours and thirty-seven minutes.

After the Vargas brothers demolished the old flooring, filling the air with dust, the sound of sledgehammers banged against concrete. Cara spent the rest of the afternoon overseeing the careful storage of materials, including the tile, the adhesive, the grout, the underlayment. Everything had to be organized and protected from the elements.

She saw little of Sawyer during those hours. He was working on the electrical with Junior, their voices carrying through the walls along with the sounds of drilling and the occasional burst of laughter. The normalcy of it should have been comforting, but instead, it felt like a countdown to something she wasn't ready to face.

By six o'clock, hunger finally drove her to the dining hall. The familiar sounds of conversation and clinking silverware greeted her as she entered, along with the rich aroma of Mexican spices and fresh tortillas. Her stomach growled, reminding her she'd skipped lunch in favor of stress-eating a granola bar.

She'd barely joined the buffet line when Janessa appeared beside her, sliding into place with the fluid grace of someone who'd perfected the art of strategic positioning.

"I seriously can't believe you trust him."

The words were pitched low, meant for Cara's ears only. Cara turned slowly, every muscle in her body tensing. "What are you talking about?"

Janessa angled toward her, moving closer under the guise of reaching for a plate. Her perfume, something floral and expensive, cut through the food aromas. "Sawyer's parole officer checks on him at least once a month."

The plate slipped in Cara's suddenly nerveless fingers. She caught it before it could hit the floor, but her heart felt like it had dropped straight through her chest. "What?"

"More often if he has reason to think something's up," Janessa continued, her voice still conversational, as if they were discussing the weather. "Pretty intense supervision for someone who's supposedly reformed, don't you think?"

Cara's pulse thundered in her ears. The sounds of the dining hall faded to background noise. "Is he — is he in trouble?"

For just a moment, Janessa's mask slipped. Her lips curved into a satisfied smirk, a flash of victory that she quickly smoothed back into neutral concern. Her fingers ghosted over Cara's forearm, the touch familiar and calculated.

"Oh, I'm sure you have nothing to worry about. He seems like a decent enough guy." Then her gaze flicked over Cara's shoulder, targeting someone behind her. "I heard the enchiladas are absolutely incredible tonight."

Before Cara could respond, before she could demand to know how Janessa knew about parole officers and supervision levels, the other woman was gone. She glided away with her plate still empty, leaving Cara standing frozen in the buffet line with her world tilting sideways.

Parole officer. Monthly check-ins. Intensive supervision.

Cara remained frozen in the buffet line, her plate trembling slightly in her hands as she tried to process what Janessa had just revealed. A parole officer. That meant Sawyer was still under supervision, still considered a risk. The questions multiplied faster than she could sort through them.

The words echoed in her head like a broken record, each repetition making her chest tighter.

"Cara!"

Sawyer's voice cut through her spiraling thoughts. She

turned to find him approaching from the back of the line, his expression shifting from friendly to concerned as he registered her face.

"What did Janessa say to you?"

Despite her hunger, Cara let others move ahead of her, stepping toward where he stood. She needed answers, and she needed them now. His eyes were already darkening with wariness, as if he could read the storm brewing in her expression.

She settled her hand on her hip, drawing on every ounce of composure she possessed. "She said your parole officer stops by once a month."

The words hung in the air between them like a challenge.

Sawyer went very still. The casual smile disappeared from his face, replaced by something raw and vulnerable and terrified. His hands tightened around his own plate, knuckles white against the ceramic.

And just like that, every question she'd been pushing aside came rushing back with the force of a dam breaking.

SAWYER'S STOMACH PLUMMETED, the familiar taste of fear flooding his mouth. His chest tightened like someone had wrapped chains around his ribs, making each breath a conscious effort. What else had Janessa told her? How much did she know?

"Can we sit and talk while we eat?"

His voice came out rougher than intended, betraying the panic clawing at his throat. Cara's nod was sharp, precise. Nothing like the easy warmth he'd grown to depend on. The absence of it hit him like a physical blow.

He forced himself to gesture toward the buffet, both of them moving through the motions of selecting food in silence so thick it felt suffocating. The enchiladas that usually made his mouth water looked like cardboard. The rice and beans might as well have been sawdust.

They found a table in the corner, far from the main flow of conversation. The privacy he'd sought now felt like a cage, trapping him with the truth he'd been avoiding. Sawyer bowed his head, offering a brief prayer over the meal, ending with a silent, desperate plea for understanding.

Please, God. Don't let me lose her. Not over this.

When he raised his head, Cara was watching him with an expression he couldn't read. He drew in a shaky breath and jumped off the cliff.

"Remember how I told you I lived on the streets for a few years?"

Her response was flat, guarded. "Yeah."

Each word felt like swallowing glass, but he pushed forward. "I was in a gang."

The confession hit the air like a physical weight. Cara's fork clattered against her plate, sending enchilada sauce splattering across the white ceramic like drops of blood. Her eyes went wide, shocked and hurt and something else—something that looked like betrayal.

Sawyer's heart shattered a little more with each second that passed. Maybe he'd been completely wrong about what they were building together. Maybe he'd read too much into her smiles, her laughter, the way she'd looked at him when she thought he wasn't paying attention.

But stopping now would guarantee he'd lose her completely. So he kept going, even though each word felt like tearing open an old wound.

"That friend I mentioned? Andy? He taught me how to steal cars." His voice dropped to barely above a whisper. "I was good at it. Always been good with my hand. Fixing things, building things. Understanding how engines work."

He stared at a point over her shoulder, unable to meet her eyes. "Turned out I was just as good at taking them apart."

When he finally looked back at her, he was surprised to find her still sitting there. Still listening. Not running for the exit or calling for security. It was more than he'd dared hope for.

"At first, I told myself I was just going along with it to survive. I was hungry, tired of shelter food and sleeping on concrete. The money from that first car..." He shook his head, remembering the intoxicating rush of having cash in his pocket, of being able to buy a real meal. "Stealing became like a drug. The adrenaline, the easy money, the feeling of being good at something."

His hands trembled slightly as he reached for his water glass. "So yeah, I spent five years in prison. And I'm still on parole for a few more months."

Cara's expression had gone carefully blank, her emotions locked away behind a wall he didn't know how to scale. His stomach clenched with dread.

"I'm sorry," he said, the words inadequate but necessary. "I'm sorry I chose that life for as long as I did. Since coming to Vargas Ranch, I've been trying to become someone different. Someone better."

He leaned forward, desperate to make her understand. "Junior's been like a big brother to me, showing me what it means to be a man of honor. Of faith. I'm still figuring out the faith part, but I know I want to live differently. I want to be someone people can trust and respect."

Cara's throat worked as she swallowed. When she spoke, her voice was barely audible. "I thought I knew you."

The words hit him like a physical blow. He reached for her hand instinctively, needing that connection, that proof that they could still bridge this gap.

She pulled away.

The rejection was swift, instinctive, and it cut deeper than any prison sentence ever had. Sawyer's hand hung suspended in the air for a moment before he slowly drew it back, his chest hollow with loss.

"You do know me, Cara." His voice was steady despite the way his heart was fracturing. "The man I am today. The man I'm fighting to stay. I want to live with integrity. I want to be like Junior and Tres—someone others can look up to."

He swallowed hard, pushing through the fear that threatened to close his throat. "Finishing an honest day's work brings me more satisfaction than anything I ever did before. Building something instead of tearing it down, helping instead of hurting. That's who I want to be."

Something flickered in Cara's expression—recognition, maybe, or understanding. "That's why you didn't want me to take your picture that day?"

Sawyer nodded, relief flooding through him at her insight. "I didn't want any reminders of who I used to be. I was afraid if I saw myself that way, I might slip back into old patterns."

Cara drew in a long breath, her shoulders rising and falling as she processed. "The cowboy thing? That's part of the new you, right? The boots, the hat, the whole aesthetic?"

Despite everything, Sawyer felt his mouth quirk up in a ghost of a smile. "Yeah, I guess it is. Sounds kind of ridiculous when you put it like that."

"It's not ridiculous." Cara's voice was softer now, less guarded. "I get wanting to reinvent yourself. It's what I've been trying to do since I moved to Wickenburg."

She met his eyes then, really met them, and he saw something there that made his breath catch. Not forgiveness, not yet, but possibility. Hope.

"I need you to promise me something," she said, her voice steady but her hands trembling slightly around her fork. "Promise me you won't betray my trust. Whatever else you're not telling me, whatever other secrets you're carrying, I need to know I can count on you."

Sawyer's throat constricted. He thought about the deal he'd made with the DA, about the friend he'd testified against to save his own skin. About Wesley Martinez, who'd died in that courtroom so Sawyer Fullerton could be born.

The secrets felt like stones in his chest, each one heavier than the last. But he looked into Cara's eyes—those beautiful, trusting eyes—and heard himself say, "I promise."

The word rang with conviction, even as his conscience screamed at him for the lie. Because he meant it about the future, about the man he was becoming. But the past... the past was a minefield he couldn't navigate without destroying everything they were building.

And a future with Cara Hollis was becoming the most important thing in his world.

17

DAWN PAINTED THE sky in sweeping brushstrokes of coral and gold, the colors so stunning they made Cara's fingers itch for her camera. The urge to abandon her plans and capture the sunrise tugged at her, but there was no time for artistic pursuits today.

She pulled into a parking spot outside *The Lariat*, the gravel crunching under her tires as she came to a stop. After cutting the engine, she sat for a moment, breathing in the warm morning air that would soon give way to the desert's relentless heat. The silence felt sacred somehow, like the calm before a storm.

Inside, she ran her palm along the decades-old bar top, feeling every groove and imperfection worn into the wood by countless elbows and conversations. Each scratch held memories—laughter over birthday celebrations, tears over heartbreak, the quiet healing that happened when people gathered to share their stories. Sunlight streamed through the large windows to her left, illuminating dust motes that danced in the golden beams and highlighting the worn booth seats that had witnessed decades of small-town life.

The thought of tearing it all down sent a pang through her chest, disrupting the peaceful moment. It had been four weeks since Sawyer's confession in the dining hall. Four weeks of working side by side, the first of which had felt like walking on broken glass—every interaction careful, measured, loaded with unspoken questions.

But time had a way of healing even the deepest cuts. Her initial wariness had gradually given way to something deeper, more complex. She'd prayed for wisdom, for discernment. Prayed that she wouldn't be naïve like she'd been with Carson, missing red flags because she wanted so badly to believe in someone who believed in her. Prayed that Sawyer would continue proving himself trustworthy.

And he had. Day after day, in small ways and large ones, he'd shown her the man he was becoming.

Cara sighed, taking in the restaurant's current state—a space balanced on the edge of transformation. Demolition would begin as soon as the crew arrived. Weeks of planning, ordering materials, and mentally preparing for this moment had led to right now. With bittersweet resolve, she scuffed her sneakers across the worn linoleum squares, silently saying goodbye to the dated furnishings that had served their purpose but couldn't survive into the future.

The signature sound of a truck door closing outside made her look up. Through the window, she could see Sawyer leaning against his ancient pickup truck, the morning light catching the faded blue paint and highlighting every dent and rust spot that told the story of its hard-lived life. She wondered how much of it mirrored his life.

Cara unlocked the front door, and the moment it swung open, he flashed her that easy smile—the one that seemed to reach all the way to his eyes and somehow made everything feel possible. The sight of it hit her like a physical force, warm and electric, traveling from her chest down to her toes.

Oh no.

The realization crashed over her with startling clarity. She was falling for him. Not just attracted to him, not just enjoying his company—she was genuinely deeply falling for Sawyer Fullerton, ex-convict and all.

The thought should have terrified her. Instead, it felt like coming home in the strangest possible way.

Sawyer pushed off from his truck with a relaxed confidence that always seemed so effortless, his work boots thudding on the concrete sidewalk as he approached. "Morning, sunshine. I saw the dumpster on the side street."

"Yeah, sorry, we couldn't get it right outside the front door. City wouldn't allow it." Her voice came out slightly breathless, and she hoped he'd attribute it to the dusty air rather than the way her heart was currently doing gymnastics in her chest.

Sawyer flexed his biceps in an exaggerated pose, throwing in a wink that made her stomach flutter. "No worries. It's great for building muscles and getting our steps in for the day."

Cara laughed, the sound coming easier now. "Somehow, I seriously doubt you have any trouble hitting your step goals."

His grin deepened, those ridiculous dimples cutting into his cheeks like they had every right to be that devastating. Before she could continue spiraling over how unfairly attractive he was, the sound of multiple vehicles pulling up announced reinforcements.

Derin Vargas strode through the door first, his brothers Dylan and Devon flanking him, with Adan Franco bringing up the rear. The space immediately felt smaller, filled with the easy confidence and good-natured energy that seemed to follow the Vargas men everywhere.

"I heard you called for some serious muscle," Derin announced, rolling up his sleeves with theatrical flair.

"Hey guys, thanks for coming out," Cara said, already shifting into project manager mode. "Okay, here's the deal. Leave the base of the bar and the counter behind it. The booths need to go in the storage pod outside in the side alley. I'm planning to refinish and reupholster those babies, so treat them nice. New tables are coming, so the existing ones can head straight to the dumpster along with this tragic flooring situation." She met each of their gazes. "If you're not sure about something, just ask."

"You heard the boss lady," Derin said, immediately grabbing the nearest table without hesitation.

The first crack of splintering wood echoed through *The Lariat* as Derin hefted the table toward the door, and with that sound, the real work began. Within minutes, a growing pile of discarded debris accumulated near the entrance — torn booth cushions, broken chair legs, chunks of old linoleum peeling away in layers.

Sawyer and Adan tackled the delicate job of removing the bar top, working with the careful precision needed to preserve the base structure underneath. The Vargas brothers moved through the dining area like a well-oiled machine, years of working together evident in their efficient rhythm. Cara focused on the detail work — stripping old decor from the walls, scraping decades-old lettering off the windows with a razor blade, transforming the space piece by piece.

The air grew thick with dust that caught in the morning sunlight, creating an almost ethereal atmosphere. The sounds of destruction mixed with bursts of laughter and good-natured trash talk between the brothers.

"Watch it, Devon! You're gonna put a hole in the wall," Dylan called out as his younger brother wrestled with a particularly stubborn table.

"Says the guy who once took out half a fence with the tractor," Devon shot back, grinning.

The familiar aroma of coffee began wafting from the kitchen, cutting through the noise and drawing Cara's attention. She hadn't even heard anyone come in through the back entrance.

"Looking good out here," Aunt Greta's voice called from the kitchen doorway.

Cara blinked in surprise, pausing in her window scraping. "What are you doing here?"

"I figured the least I could do was provide lunch and drinks for the crew. There are a few cases of Gatorade and sodas chilling in the walk-in fridge, and I'm just finishing up some sandwiches before I head out." Aunt Greta's eyes sparkled with the kind of warmth that made Cara's chest tight with gratitude.

Cara set down her razor blade and crossed to the kitchen, pressing a kiss to her aunt's cheek. "You didn't have to do that. Thank you for taking care of us."

Aunt Greta placed a gentle hand on Cara's shoulder, her expression growing soft and serious. "Honey, you're like the daughter I wish I'd had. I'm so sorry my brother doesn't recognize how wonderful and talented you are."

The unexpected words hit Cara, making her blink hard against the sudden sting of tears. Her throat constricted with emotion she hadn't seen coming.

"I love you, Cara."

"Love you too, Aunt Greta." The words came out slightly hoarse, and she swallowed hard, tucking the emotion away before it could overwhelm her. "Thanks for everything you've done for me."

"Thank you, sweetheart. I really appreciate everything you've done to keep costs down on this project. I can't wait to see your final design come to life."

After exchanging hugs and promises to call later, Cara poked her head into the dining room to announce the lunch break. The sound of their footsteps echoed in the half-empty space as the men filed toward the kitchen, carefully stepping around the growing mountain of demo debris stacked near the front door. Their conversation shifted from work to food, voices carrying the easy camaraderie of people who genuinely enjoyed each other's company.

In the kitchen, Derin was already halfway through his first sandwich and reaching for a second. "Okay, if we ever had a Wickenburg cooking competition and I was judging, I'd be seriously torn between Aunt Greta and Chef at the ranch."

Cara laughed, pulling a cold Gatorade from the fridge.

"They're both incredible. You guys are spoiled."

"Don't forget Mami," Devon added, speaking around a bite of sandwich. "She might give them both a run for their money."

Sawyer perked up with interest. "Really? I've never had any of Catalina's cooking."

Derin snorted. "That's because we keep her all to ourselves. Can't have the whole town knowing our secret weapon."

Dylan grinned, nodding in agreement. "Smart strategy."

Adan, who'd been quietly demolishing his own sandwich, suddenly became animated. "Oh man, I can totally vouch for that. Nobody — and I mean nobody — makes tamales or enchiladas like Catalina. And her churros?" He pressed a kiss to his fingertips with exaggerated drama. "Especially with that top-secret caramel sauce she makes. It's literally life-changing."

Sawyer's brow furrowed slightly. "Wait, how come you've had Catalina's cooking? I thought it was family-only."

Devon was already pulling out his phone, thumbs flying over the screen. "Dude, now I'm craving churros. I'm totally texting Mami right now."

Adan finally answered Sawyer's question. "My parents have been tight with Tres and Catalina since before I was born. We usually hit up Sunday dinner with them after church. It's like having a second family."

Understanding dawned on Sawyer's face. "Ah, that makes sense."

Derin reached over and clapped a hand on Sawyer's shoulder with enough force to make him wince. Cara had to bite back a laugh at Sawyer's expression.

"Don't worry, cowboy. You ranch guys eat pretty well yourselves, so you're not missing out on too much." Derin threw in a wink for good measure.

Cara gathered herself, realizing her own hunger had finally been satisfied. "Alright, break time's over. This restaurant isn't going to transform itself."

"You heard the lady," Derin said, holding the swinging kitchen door open with a gallant gesture.

Heat rushed to Cara's cheeks as she ducked under his arm, though she couldn't quite figure out why. Derin was undeniably handsome—all the Vargas men were—but she knew his reputation with women. Besides, it was Sawyer's green eyes and angular jawline that made her pulse skip, not Derin's easy charm.

Her gaze automatically sought Sawyer as he and Adan carefully maneuvered the unwieldy bar top toward the exit. Sweat beaded on his forehead and along his neck, catching the afternoon light that streamed through the windows. When he lifted the hem of his t-shirt to wipe his face, she glimpsed the tattoos across his toned abs and lean muscle that came from hard work, not a gym.

Her mouth went dry.

And then he caught her staring.

Their eyes met across the space for one electric moment before Cara quickly pivoted away, heat flooding her face. She'd been too slow, and they both knew it. Pretending she wasn't increasingly aware of him, of the growing connection between them, was becoming more impossible by the day.

"I THINK WE can totally salvage this," Adan said, running his hand along the stripped-down bar base.

Sawyer forced himself to focus on the conversation, though his thoughts kept drifting to the moment he'd caught Cara watching him. The look in her eyes had been... intense. Interested. The kind of look that made his chest tight with possibility.

"What do you think?" Adan prompted again, clearly

waiting for a response.

Sawyer shook his head slightly, refocusing on the bar base now that they'd successfully removed the top without damaging the structure underneath. "Yeah, absolutely. We can sand this down and refinish the parts that won't be covered with the tin tiles."

Adan raised an eyebrow. "Tin tiles? That sounds pretty fancy."

Sawyer couldn't help but smile. "Trust me, when you see Cara's finished design, you'll get how the rustic western elements she's planning will work with the tin. It's going to look incredible."

The confidence in his voice surprised him. Somewhere along the way, he'd started really understanding Cara's vision, seeing how all the pieces would fit together to create something both nostalgic and fresh.

Adan shrugged and called across the room. "Cara, is there anything else you need us to tackle? I'm hoping to make it back to the stables for afternoon feeding."

Cara looked up from where she was carefully removing the last of the window lettering. "No, demo was the primary goal for today. Sawyer and I can start leveling the floor this evening and hopefully get it ready to epoxy tomorrow so we can take a break for Independence Day."

Adan tipped his hat in acknowledgment before heading out. And within minutes, the Vargas brothers had gathered their things and departed as well, leaving Sawyer alone with Cara for the first time all day.

He was relieved to see Derin go, if he was being honest. Something about the way the other man had looked at Cara earlier had rubbed him the wrong way—too appreciative, too familiar.

Cara pulled her hair back into a ponytail, the simple gesture somehow being both practical and incredibly attractive. A few shorter pieces escaped to frame her face, and Sawyer had to resist the urge to reach over and tuck them behind her ear.

"What's that frown for?" she asked, apparently catching his expression.

Sawyer quickly smoothed his features. "Nothing. Just thinking."

"Are you getting tired? Do you need to call it a day?"

"Nah, I'm good. Tres said he'd cover overtime for this project, so I'm not worried about the hours."

Cara's smile widened, and the approval in her expression settled warmly in his chest. "That's awesome."

"Yeah, it'll definitely help with some parts I need for the truck. Just hoping to get her fixed before she completely gives up on me." He rubbed his hands together, surveying their progress while trying not to think too hard about how pathetic his transportation situation probably seemed to someone like Cara.

When she pressed a hand against her lower back and let out a quiet groan, he fought every instinct that wanted to step closer, to work out the tension in her shoulders with his hands. Unfortunately, they weren't at that level yet. Though he was definitely hoping they might get there.

"Ugh," Cara huffed, rolling her shoulders. "I should have asked someone taller to deal with that shelf above the windows."

Sawyer couldn't resist the opening. "Like Derin?"

She snorted, a sound that was both unladylike and completely endearing. "He would literally be last on my list. Don't get me wrong—he's a nice guy and all. It's just that he has a reputation, you know? I wouldn't want to do anything that might encourage him."

Relief flooded through Sawyer, though he tried to keep it off his face. "What about Dylan?"

Cara shook her head with a soft smile. "He's so shy it's actually kind of sweet. Renata told me he's never even been on a date. Can you imagine being twenty-eight and never dating anyone?"

Sawyer chuckled. "That's pretty impressive, actually. What about Devon or Adan?"

He was definitely fishing now, trying to gauge where he stood compared to the other men in her orbit, but he couldn't help himself.

Cara rolled her eyes slightly. "Derin was bossing Devon around all day, keeping him busy with the heavy stuff. And Adan was helping you with the bar demo."

Sawyer took a breath, gathering his courage. "You could have asked me, you know."

"I know I could have." Her voice softened. "But I trusted you with the bar top removal. I knew taking it off without damaging the base would be tricky, and you handled it perfectly."

The praise hit him square in the chest, warm and affirming in a way that still surprised him. After years of being seen as nothing but trouble, having someone believe in his skills, trust him with something important—it meant everything.

The warmth of her approval gave him the courage he needed for the question that had been building all day.

"Do you want to go to the Vargas Fireworks Show with me?"

Cara turned toward him, eyes wide with surprise. "You mean... like a date?"

Sawyer jammed his hands deep into his pockets, feeling his pulse kick up despite his best efforts to stay calm. "That's definitely the idea."

A flush crept up her neck and into her cheeks, and she ducked her head in a way that made his breath catch in his throat. The silence stretched between them, and for a terrifying moment, he wondered if he'd completely misread the situation.

"I'd really like that," she finally said, her voice soft but clear.

Sawyer felt his shoulders relax, the knot of tension in his

chest loosening. "Great. Can I pick you up, or would you rather meet at the ranch?"

She hesitated, and he saw the exact moment she remembered the current state of his truck. "Actually, maybe I could just meet you there? I was thinking about, you know, saving the wear and tear on your truck."

Heat crept up his neck, embarrassment mixing with frustration at his financial situation. Someday—hopefully soon—he'd be able to afford something reliable, something he wouldn't be ashamed to drive a woman like Cara around in. For now, he had to swallow his pride and accept reality.

"Sure," he managed. "That works."

"You wanted to start on the floor tonight?"

Sawyer shook off his disappointment, refocusing on the task at hand. "Yeah, I figured if we can patch and level the concrete tonight, we should be able to epoxy it tomorrow and be done in time for the holiday."

"Let's do this."

They worked side by side as the afternoon light gradually shifted toward evening, settling into an easy rhythm as Sawyer retrieved supplies from his truck and secured the storage pod. Several times, he paused to take a drink of Gatorade, stealing glances at Cara while she worked.

She never complained about the dirty or difficult parts of the job. Never hesitated to dive in completely, whether it was to save her aunt money or simply because she wanted to be part of the process. He liked that about her. Respected it. Wanted to see more of it.

"I was talking to Junior last weekend," Sawyer said as they worked to smooth out a stubborn section of concrete. "I've decided I want to get baptized."

Cara looked up sharply, surprise and something that looked like joy flashing across her features. "Oh wow, really? So you're officially on Team Jesus now?"

Sawyer chuckled, nodding. "Yeah, I guess I am. Junior explained that it's an outward sign of the inner decision I've already made. It feels like the right next step."

Cara reached over and squeezed his forearm gently, her touch warm even through his work shirt. "I'm so happy for you, Sawyer. That's huge."

"I'd really like it if you would come. To the baptism, I mean."

Her smile transformed into something radiant, soft and genuine and full of quiet emotion that hit him like a physical force. "Of course I'll be there. Just tell me when and where."

Sawyer finished leveling the last patch of concrete, then stood and offered Cara his hand. She accepted without hesitation, her palm warm against his as he helped her to her feet.

But he didn't let go right away.

A strand of hair had escaped from her ponytail, falling softly across her cheek. Moving slowly, giving her time to pull away if she wanted, he reached up and gently tucked it behind her ear. Her skin was soft and warm beneath his fingertips, and it took every ounce of self-control he possessed not to let his hand linger there.

"Thanks, Cara."

Her brows drew together slightly. "For what?"

"Everything. For believing in me when I told you about prison. For being such a good friend." He paused, the words feeling inadequate for everything he wanted to say. "For giving me a chance."

The air between them seemed to shimmer with possibility, charged with the weight of everything they weren't quite ready to say out loud. Sawyer held perfectly still, fighting every instinct that wanted to step closer, to test the boundaries of whatever was building between them.

Cara was a forever kind of woman—he'd known that from the beginning. The last thing he wanted was to rush into something that was finally carefully taking shape between them.

The fireworks show. His baptism later in the month.

These would be enough. For now.

18

_____

TWO DAYS LATER, Cara checked the epoxy flooring, stepping carefully across the edge that still felt a little tacky. The finish gleamed under the overhead lights, rich shades of brown and bronze swirling together like polished stone. It had been smart to give it the day to dry—ensuring no accidental footprints before the final touches tomorrow.

She snapped a few pictures, a quiet sense of accomplishment stealing over her. Perfect.

With a pleased nod, she sent the photos to Aunt Greta and her grandparents, then hesitated before forwarding a separate one to Sawyer.

His response came almost immediately.

Wow! Perfect. Looking forward to seeing you tonight.

The words were simple enough, but Cara read them again, her stomach tightening in a way she didn't quite understand. Why did seeing his name make her breath hitch?

She ducked into the kitchen, pushing past her sudden emotions, before slipping out the back door.

Hours later, Cara stood in front of her closet, hopelessly undecided. The temperature would still hover well over a hundred degrees for the fireworks. Desert living.

She held up a lilac sundress with thin straps, one she occasionally wore to church with a cropped cardigan. Not right.

Next, a mauve v-neck summery dress—not quite casual,

not quite formal. She finally tried it on, smoothing her palms down the fabric. It would do.

Still, indecision lingered as she dug out a pair of wedge sandals, then carefully applied makeup, curling the long strands of her hair before twisting them into a clip, leaving a few loose pieces framing her face. When she stepped back, she blinked at her reflection. The look was soft, effortless. Worth the extra effort.

Sliding her phone into her wristlet, she stuffed in her key fob, grateful for the keyless entry to her Porsche SUV.

As Cara drove toward Vargas Guest Ranch and Resort, AC blasting, thoughts tangled in her head. If Sawyer hadn't told her about his past, she never would have guessed. Between Jesus and Junior, he had a solid foundation for turning his life around.

And yet... For some strange, undeniable reason, she wanted to be a part of his new life. More than just the designer and handyman duo.

She sighed, fingers tightening around the steering wheel. Maybe tonight would offer clarity. Maybe it would just make everything more complicated.

Pulling into a parking spot, she cut the engine, smoothing the folds of her skirt. She reached for her phone, then paused.

A cowboy was weaving through the crowd toward her.

Her breathing came quicker, her pulse kicking up. The cowboy version of Sawyer — that was the authentic one. Whatever his past had been, it no longer mattered.

Sawyer leaned down, placing a kiss on her cheek. The simple touch sent warmth spilling down her spine.

"You look amazing," he said, his voice lower than usual, steady but holding something unspoken.

Cara's smile faltered for half a second, catching the sincerity in his eyes. "Thanks."

Sawyer cleared his throat. "I wanted to get you flowers, but I figured they would wilt in your car."

Her heart hitched, the thought unexpectedly sweet. He had thought about her, planned something, even if it wasn't practical.

"Oh, how sweet of you."

He took her hand, his fingers weaving through hers, anchoring them together.

"Hungry? If we hurry, we might beat the worst of the crowd."

Cara squeezed his hand lightly, forcing herself to breathe normally. "Lead on, cowboy."

Inside the dining hall, the mouthwatering aroma of smoked meat filled the air. A true Western BBQ feast spread out across an extended buffet, bigger than any restaurant setup she had ever seen before. Cara blinked at the sheer variety, scanning the trays of pulled pork, brisket, coleslaw, corn on the cob, southwestern baked beans, cornbread. A true feast.

Sawyer tugged her hand, leading her toward the back of the line.

Now, in the light, Cara got a better look at him. Freshly shaved, wearing her favorite cologne. Jorge must have mentioned it after she had taken Sawyer to her parents' party. She forced herself to push that memory aside, refusing to let it dampen the night.

His shirt was new. A solid, bright blue button-up, rougher in texture. Clearly cowboy attire, not the sleek executive shirts her father wore. Same color, though. That shade of blue made Sawyer's green eyes sharper, more vivid, more impossible to ignore.

Even his hat was different, lighter in tone, tan instead of his usual darker shade. Also new?

The dark denim, hugging his waist and thighs, paired with dressier brown boots, peeking out from beneath the cuffs. He looked incredible.

Cara's fingers fanned her face, heat climbing too fast.

Sawyer smirked, mischief flickering behind his green

eyes. "Warm? I'll find us a seat under the AC vent."

She didn't dare admit the reason behind her sudden flush, choosing instead to focus on the food on her plate.

As the dining hall filled within minutes, Cara finally understood why Tres had insisted on pausing construction before the event. This wasn't just a small celebration. It was a major event for the resort.

Sawyer prayed for the meal, then looked at her. "You ever been to this before?"

"First time."

His half-grin appeared with an irresistible thrill in his gaze. "Glad I invited you. Run into any traffic on the way over?"

Cara lifted a shoulder, taking another bite. "It was getting busy. One freeway lane was closed by the Sheriff's Department to allow only event traffic to exit. I didn't know it was so huge."

"Me either."

He leaned back, studying her. "That color looks great on you."

Second compliment. She smiled, that quiet warmth sinking a little deeper with his words.

"Your hair looks nice, too. Is it naturally curly? I thought you've always worn it straight."

Her face warmed again, knowing he had noticed even the smallest details about her. "It's naturally straight. I felt like doing something special since it's our first date."

Sawyer shook his head, smirking. "Second date. I took you out to the steakhouse, remember?"

She rolled her eyes, playful. "I'm not sure I want to count that night."

He waggled his eyebrows. "I do."

She laughed, grabbing her corn on the cob, letting the sweet flavor distract her if only for a moment.

Cara glanced around the crowded dining hall, the buzz of conversation and laughter nearly overtaking the twangy notes of the country music playing overhead. It was all so familiar—friendly faces, the clink of dessert plates, the hum of celebration—but sitting beside Sawyer, the energy felt different. Charged in a way she couldn't quite explain.

When they finished eating, he leaned toward her, his voice low. "Want to head outside before the fireworks start? I know a spot that's a little quieter."

Her heart gave a small lurch. "Sure."

He grabbed two bottles of water from a nearby cooler, handing her one before gently leading her through the crowd and out into the soft desert night. The dry heat wrapped around her like a blanket breathlessly, but she barely noticed. Not with Sawyer's hand brushing hers, not with the thrum of something unspoken pulling her toward wherever he was going.

They skirted the main lawn, passing families unfolding blankets and couples arranging chairs. Beyond the tangle of string lights and cheerful bustle, Sawyer led her through a narrow path framed by prickly pear and desert mesquite. It opened into a quiet courtyard tucked behind the row of casitas—a hidden corner of the resort that most guests didn't even know existed.

A single bench sat beneath a canopy of open sky, stars brightening as the final shades of twilight faded. They sat together in the hush, the echo of the crowd distant now.

Cara tilted her head back just as the first firework streaked high above and burst into gold. "Wow," she whispered.

But she felt his steady gaze more than the shimmer overhead. He didn't speak, and he didn't need to.

And somehow, in that stillness between bursts of color and crowd cheers, Cara knew this night was going to change everything.

THE FIRST FIREWORK cracked overhead, scattering silver sparks across the deep navy sky. Sawyer barely glanced at it. Instead, he watched the glow ripple across Cara's face. Watched her eyes light up with every burst. The soft curve of her smile tugged something loose in his chest. She looked peaceful. Hopeful.

And for once, sitting right here beside her, he felt like he belonged.

They didn't speak at first. They didn't have to.

Another firework blossomed above them in reds and golds, rich against the vast canvas of night. The echoes of the crowd were distant here, hushed by stucco walls and the long sweep of desert between them and the main greenbelt. The little courtyard beside the Sedona Casita — discovered during the renovation, a bench tucked beneath an old ironwood tree, almost lost to time — had become a secret sanctuary. And now it was theirs.

He shifted slightly, their knees brushing. She didn't move away.

Sawyer let out a quiet breath, dragging a hand across the back of his neck. "This place has a way of getting to you. The sky feels bigger here. Like you can breathe."

Cara turned toward him, her features softened by the cascade of light overhead. "I know what you mean."

Just those few words, steady and sure, grounded him. He wanted to bottle this moment with her beside him, the warm quiet between them, the profound weight of being seen and not needing to explain.

Another firework bloomed blue and white, shaped like a falling dandelion.

His chest tightened.

He hadn't planned to come tonight. Crowds made him uneasy. Loud spaces too much like his past. But tonight wasn't loud. Not here. Not with Cara.

This wasn't borrowed joy. It was real.

He glanced at her again, catching the tilt of her chin, the

ease in her posture.

"I'm glad you came," he whispered.

Cara met his gaze, and for a long moment, neither of them looked away. Something passed between them—not electric, not rushed, just... inevitable. Like the tide meeting the shore.

When the finale began, the sky erupted in streaks of brilliance with overlapping bursts that painted the night in color.

Sawyer didn't flinch.

He reached for her hand instead.

And when her fingers curled into his, easy and sure, something inside him settled, deep and certain.

They stayed seated as the cheers faded in the distance as the last of the families packed up their blankets, children yawning and clutching glow sticks. But here, in their quiet sliver of the night, everything felt suspended.

Sawyer glanced around the courtyard—the courtyard he'd nearly walked past during the early days of the reno. Back when the Sedona Casita was more dust than dignity and the path was barely visible under mesquite leaves and scrub. One afternoon, sweaty and starving, he'd wandered behind the building, sandwich in hand, Goldie trotting faithfully at his heels. The old ironwood tree had been there then too, stubborn and crooked and full of shade. And the weathered bench, old but sound, waited like it had been expecting someone.

He'd dropped onto it, unwrapping his sandwich as Goldie flopped onto the cool ground with a dramatic sigh, tongue out, ears twitching.

He smiled at the memory. "I found this bench a while back," he said, giving the slatted wood a small tap. "During the remodel. Goldie and I used to sneak back here for lunch breaks."

Cara smiled, her voice soft and teasing. "So this is where you've been hoarding the best view."

Sawyer laughed under his breath. "Guilty."

Then, a little quieter, "But I always kind of hoped I'd share it with someone. Just didn't know it'd be like this."

She tilted her head, clearly amused. "And you never told me?"

"I had to keep some secrets," he teased, then added with a quiet smile, "but I didn't plan on keeping them forever."

She said nothing right away, just ran her thumb softly across the back of his hand. They sat for a long moment, the night thick with silence and stars.

Then Sawyer spoke again, a little slower this time. "You know, growing up... none of my foster families ever took me to see fireworks. Never. Not even once."

Cara's gaze flicked to him, her fingers tightening slightly around his. "Seriously?"

He nodded, eyes still trained on the stars. "Guess it didn't occur to them. Too much hassle. Or maybe they thought I wouldn't care."

"And did you?" she asked gently.

He exhaled, the truth low in his voice. "I used to sit on the porch sometimes, way off in the distance, and just listen. Couldn't see anything. But I'd imagine what it looked like. Pretend I was there. Pretend I mattered enough for someone to bring me along."

Cara's eyes shimmered even in the dark. She rested her head against his shoulder. Not to fix it, not to fill the quiet, but to meet it with him.

"You matter now," she said.

Sawyer swallowed hard, that old ache rising before her words eased it back down.

"I know," he whispered. "I really do."

He didn't want to move. Didn't want to chase what was already here.

"You ever think about how many lives you've lived?" he asked, his voice low, barely brushing the air between them.

Cara tilted her head toward him, curiosity flickering in

her eyes. "Like metaphorically?"

He smiled faintly. "Yeah. How many versions of your-self you've had to shed just to become someone who fits."

She leaned back, gazing up. "I think I've had two. The me who followed the script. And the me who's rewriting it."

He nodded slowly. "I've had… more than that."

But she didn't push for details. Just turned slightly toward him, eyes open, heart steady. "I like the version I've met."

That unraveled him more than any deep confession could have.

His gaze dropped to their hands, still linked. Still holding.

"I used to think freedom meant getting away from everything," he murmured. "People. Expectations. My past."

"And now?" she asked gently.

He looked up at the stars—vast and unchanging—and for once, they made him feel like there was enough room in the world to just be.

"Now I think it's sitting next to someone who sees who you are right now… and doesn't flinch."

Her lips parted slightly, her gaze locked on his. He felt the shift. Not fear. Not hesitation. Hope.

He didn't kiss her right away.

Instead, he brushed his thumb against hers. A smile tugged at the corner of his mouth, soft and almost uncertain. "You're making it really hard to stick to slow."

Cara's fingers tightened slightly around his, her body leaning just a little closer with unspoken permission woven into the quiet.

Her smile lifted, warm and sure. "Maybe slow's over-rated."

The bench beneath them creaked softly as he turned toward her. The night wrapped close. The distance between them vanished.

He lifted a hand slowly, asking without asking.

She didn't pull away. She met the moment with quiet stillness, no distance, no doubt.

His fingertips found her cheek, trailing down to her jaw. Her skin was warm. Real. Anchoring.

He caught the hush of her breath, the way the starlight kissed the curve of her cheek, and every part of him inched closer.

She leaned in.

So he did too.

Their kiss wasn't searching — it was certain. Unrushed. Full. Like everything they'd both been quietly holding back finally came to rest in this one still point.

She pressed her palm against his shirt. He placed his hand on her back. They breathed in unison.

The connection severed slowly, though his heart entwined with hers in a way he had never expected.

A brief flicker of doubt spread through him.

"I didn't mean to," he whispered.

"I did," she breathed.

He pulled back just a fraction, his gaze dipping to her lips, then back to her eyes. A spark of something familiar slipped in.

"Not even gonna pretend to be surprised. You've been running this show since day one."

She laughed softly, brushing her nose against his. "Maybe. But I didn't do it alone."

And for the first time in a long while, Sawyer didn't feel like a man running from his past. He felt rooted. Steady. Like he'd finally found home.

19

THE SCENT OF clean cotton and lavender hung thick in the small laundry room, warm and dense in the still afternoon air. Cara pulled a freshly laundered towel from the wicker basket, but her hands moved on autopilot—edges aligned with practiced precision while her mind wandered to places that had nothing to do with household chores. The dryer's gentle hum provided a steady backdrop, heat radiating in waves that made the narrow space feel like a cocoon.

Last night clung to her thoughts like morning fog, refusing to burn off despite the blazing Arizona sun outside.

She reached for one of her favorite linen blouses, the soft fabric cool and familiar beneath her fingertips as she tried to focus on the simple, mindless task. The repetition should have grounded her, should have pulled her thoughts back to the present moment. Instead, they drifted like smoke, curling around fragments of starlight and whispered words that had changed everything.

Back to the ranch courtyard. To Sawyer's calloused thumb brushing along her jawline with such gentle certainty, like he'd been thinking about that exact touch for weeks. The way he'd hesitated for just a heartbeat before their first kiss—not uncertain, not rushed, but perfectly, completely right. Like he'd been waiting for that exact moment, that exact permission to cross the line they'd been dancing around for weeks.

Her pulse quickened at the memory, subtle but insistent. She hadn't planned for the kiss, hadn't expected the way all her careful hesitation would melt away the moment his lips found hers beneath the distant glow of fireworks. But when it happened, when he kissed her with that perfect blend of reverence and hunger, she hadn't flinched. She hadn't doubted. She'd just... felt.

And she definitely hadn't been able to sleep afterward.

Heat pooled low in her stomach as she folded the last shirt with hands that weren't quite steady. Even folding laundry felt different now, like moments worth remembering, worth capturing through her lens. She'd spent half the night staring at her bedroom ceiling, replaying the way Sawyer's lips had lingered against hers, how the warmth between them had settled—not like a spark that might burn out, but like the slow, steady burn of something that had been smoldering for a long time. Something that promised to keep burning.

The laundry basket sat empty now, but Cara remained still, her fingers pressed against the stack of folded clothes as if they could anchor her to something solid while her heart raced with possibilities she wasn't quite ready to name out loud.

She exhaled slowly, gathering the warm laundry against her chest. The familiar weight of clean fabric should have felt routine, ordinary. Instead, even simple tasks carried a different energy today, like the kiss had shifted something fundamental in her world, coloring ordinary moments with new meaning and possibility.

Sawyer had always been steady when everything else felt chaotic. But last night—last night, he'd been something more. Something real and unshaken and completely, utterly present.

She carried the clothes to her bedroom, placing them carefully in the dresser drawers before pausing at her closet.

Her fingers trailed along the row of hangers, touching familiar fabrics. Everything looked exactly the same, yet somehow different. The kiss hadn't rewritten their history, but it had definitely shifted what came next.

Her phone buzzed from the kitchen counter, the sound carrying clearly through her small house.

Sawyer: *Any chance I can bribe you with Chinese takeout tonight? I'm already in line at Golden Dragon.*

Cara's lips curved into a smile before she even realized it. She hadn't made plans to see him again this soon—had actually been planning a quiet evening alone to process everything that had happened. But the flutter in her chest had other ideas entirely.

Cara: *Only if you bring extra egg rolls. Like, seriously extra.*

The reply came so fast her phone barely had time to go dark.

Sawyer: *Done. Be there in twenty.*

Twenty minutes. Cara slipped her feet into worn flip-flops and stepped outside, where the late afternoon Arizona heat hit her like a wall, clinging to her skin despite the approaching evening. Sunlight turned the concrete walkway into a shimmering expanse, and the familiar smell of dust and creosote hung heavy in the light breeze that offered no actual relief from the temperature.

She padded toward the mailbox at the end of her driveway, already thinking about what she might say when Sawyer arrived, how they'd navigate this unfamiliar territory they'd stepped into. The metal hinges creaked as she flipped open the lid, rifling through the usual collection of bills and grocery store circulars.

Then her fingers brushed against the stark white cardstock, thick and expensive.

Her stomach dropped before she even saw the names.

A wedding invitation.

Livvy's name shimmered in gold foil script, elegantly scripted alongside Carson's in formal lettering that cost more than most people's monthly grocery budget.

Cara stared at the invitation, waiting for the familiar ache to hit — the sharp, choking pain that had gripped her at her parents' party when Carson had announced his engagement. But it didn't come. Not sharp, not overwhelming. The bitterness that had consumed her that night felt muted now, distant, like it belonged to someone else entirely.

She traced the embossed lettering with one finger, absorbing the sheer finality of it. A rushed wedding, barely four months after the proposal that had blindsided her in front of half of Phoenix's social elite.

She should feel angry. Should feel vindicated or bitter or something sharp-edged. Instead, she felt genuinely concerned.

Cara carried the mail inside, setting the invitation on her granite kitchen counter next to a glass of sweet tea, condensation already beading on the sides in the air conditioning. For a long moment, she simply looked at it, her fingers loosely wrapped around the cool glass, processing emotions she hadn't expected.

Maybe Livvy was completely oblivious to who Carson really was. Maybe she truly believed he'd changed, that he would be faithful to her in ways he'd never been faithful to Cara. Maybe she thought love could transform someone that fundamentally.

Or maybe Livvy didn't care about any of that. Maybe Carson wasn't about love at all. Maybe he was just an escape hatch, a golden ticket out of their parents' suffocating control and endless expectations.

Cara set the glass down and pressed both palms flat against the cool granite, closing her eyes. The solid surface anchored her as she let the prayer rise naturally from her heart, the words coming without conscious thought.

"God, if she's blind to who he really is, please open her eyes before it's too late. And if she sees clearly and chooses this anyway... then give her the strength to endure whatever comes."

The words settled over her like a gentle hand smoothing wrinkled fabric, stretching peace over the jagged remnants of old betrayal. This wasn't her burden to carry anymore. Wasn't her war to fight.

She ran a fingertip along the edge of the invitation one last time, then deliberately folded it shut and slid it into the kitchen drawer beneath the coffee maker. Not thrown away in anger. Not displayed where it could torment her. Just... shelved. Filed away with the rest of her past.

Three firm knocks echoed from her front door.

Cara turned, pulse steady and calm, and pulled it open to find Sawyer standing on her small porch. The setting sun caught the golden stubble along his jaw, and he held a white paper bag in one hand that smelled absolutely incredible. The rich aromas of sesame oil, ginger, and garlic wafted between them, making her stomach growl.

"Chinese," he said simply, lifting the bag slightly with a smile that made her heart skip. "With seriously extra egg rolls, as requested."

Something in the way he looked at her — not probing or demanding explanations, just quietly perceptive — made her throat tighten with unexpected emotion. Like he could sense the subtle shift in her mood without needing her to explain it.

"Perfect timing," she murmured, stepping back to let him in. "Come in before all the cold air escapes."

He entered without hesitation, his presence immediately making her small kitchen feel warmer, more alive. He set the takeout on the counter, and the wonderful aroma of garlic and soy sauce filled the space, mixing with the lingering sweetness of her tea.

Cara pulled two plates from the cupboard, the familiar ceramic cool and smooth against her palms. "Livvy's getting married."

The words came out matter-of-fact, without the pain

she'd expected to accompany them. Sawyer didn't react outwardly, but she felt something in his posture shift, a subtle tightening of attention that told her he was listening.

"Soon?" he asked, his voice carefully neutral.

She nodded, sliding the plates across the granite countertop with a soft ceramic whisper. "Two months."

She didn't elaborate immediately, instead opening the container of beef and broccoli with deliberate movements, letting the comfortable silence settle between them like a held breath. Steam rose from the food in delicate spirals, carrying a rich scent that made her mouth water.

Sawyer moved beside her, unpacking the other containers with quiet efficiency. Not hovering, not pushing for details, just being present in that steady way that somehow made everything feel more manageable.

"I'm not angry anymore," she finally admitted, spooning jasmine rice onto her plate in a perfect mound. "Not the way I was at my parents' party."

Sawyer glanced over, his green eyes steady and patient. "So, what are you feeling?"

She added vegetables to her plate, considering the question seriously. "Concerned, I guess. Maybe a little sad for her."

His brow furrowed slightly, but she saw understanding flicker across his features, like he knew exactly what she meant.

Cara set the serving spoon down, watching steam rise from her plate in slow, ghosting ribbons. "I don't know if she actually believes Carson's changed, or if she just doesn't care that he hasn't."

Sawyer leaned back against the counter, arms crossed loosely over his chest. The position made his shoulders look broader, more defined under his simple t-shirt. "And if it's the second option?"

Cara folded her arms, fingers pressing lightly against her ribs as she considered. "Then Carson isn't about love for her. He's about escape. About freedom from our parents' expectations and control."

Something flickered across Sawyer's face—a tightening around his eyes like her words had hit closer to home than she'd intended. But he didn't argue or deflect. He just nodded with understanding that came from experience.

Cara hesitated before continuing, her voice dropping to something softer, more vulnerable. "I prayed for her. For both of them, actually."

Sawyer's expression didn't change, didn't show even a hint of judgment or surprise. "What did you ask for?"

She drew in a slow breath, appreciating that he didn't question the prayer itself, just wanted to understand her heart. "That if she's blind to who Carson really is, she'll see the truth before it's too late to change course. And if she isn't blind—if she knows exactly what she's getting into—that she'll have the strength to live with her choice."

The words hung in the air between them, heavy with meaning and the weight of hard-earned wisdom.

Sawyer didn't speak for a long moment, just reached for the container of sesame chicken and pulled out a pair of chopsticks. He drummed them once against the cardboard rim, lost in thought.

"Maybe she'll surprise you," he said finally, his voice low and thoughtful. "Maybe she sees more than you think she does."

Cara tilted her head slightly, studying his profile. There was something in his tone—like he was talking about more than just Livvy and Carson. Like he was thinking about second chances and the possibility of real change.

"People can change," she whispered, meaning it. "Sometimes we see who they're becoming before they even realize it themselves."

Sawyer looked up then, one corner of his mouth quirking in a brief, unhurried smile that made her heart flutter. Like he understood exactly what she meant, and maybe even believed it about himself.

Then Cara nudged his arm lightly with her elbow and gestured to their plates. "Come on, let's eat this before it gets cold."

Sawyer huffed a soft chuckle that she felt more than heard. "Yes, ma'am."

And just like that, the conversation shifted into something lighter, easier. The weight of the wedding invitation still lingered somewhere in the back of her mind, but it didn't feel suffocating anymore. It was just another piece of her past, filed away where it belonged.

She'd figure out whether to attend the wedding later. For now, she let herself settle into this moment—good food, easy conversation, and the quiet joy of being with someone who made even complicated emotions feel manageable.

THE GRAVEL CRUNCHED rhythmically under Sawyer's boots as he made his way across the ranch yard toward the bunkhouse, desert heat still radiating up from the ground despite the sun having set an hour ago. The air carried the familiar scents of mesquite and sagebrush, tangled with the lingering traces of sesame oil and ginger that clung to his shirt from dinner at Cara's place.

He kept his hands shoved deep in his pockets, head down, shoulders carrying a tension he couldn't quite shake. His thoughts refused to settle, spinning between the memory of tonight's easy conversation and the way their goodnight kiss had unfolded on her front porch.

Their second kiss. It had slipped into the quiet space between dinner and goodbye, when the porch light caught the copper highlights in her hair and he couldn't bring himself to walk away without knowing what one more taste would feel like. This one had hit harder than their first. Not just the way her lips moved against his, soft and sure like she wasn't asking permission anymore, but the way it stayed with him afterward. Like warmth had taken up permanent residence behind his ribs.

Inside the bunkhouse, the familiar space felt unusually still. No voices drifting from the common area, no sound of boots on wooden floors or the distant murmur of late-night conversations. Just the deep quiet that made everything else seem louder. His own breathing, the settling of old wood, the whisper of his thoughts.

He sank onto the edge of his narrow bunk, running both hands through his hair in a gesture that had become automatic when his mind wouldn't stop spinning.

He'd kissed women before. Plenty of them, back in his old life. But those encounters had been about survival more than connection. Brief moments of distraction from the constant pressure of life on the streets, desperate attempts to scrape up some fragment of human warmth when the world felt like nothing but concrete and cold steel. You don't dream about love when you're sleeping in stolen cars and counting loose change for gas station burritos. You don't believe in it when everyone you've ever trusted has eventually walked away. You just survive around the edges of it, watching other people live the life you've convinced yourself you don't deserve.

But this thing with Cara was completely different. She was different.

The thought stirred something deeper, a memory he usually kept buried so far down he could pretend it didn't exist. Ten years old, standing on Mrs. Patterson's front porch with everything he owned stuffed into a black trash bag, watching her lock the door behind him like he was something dangerous she needed to keep out. She'd called him difficult in her report to the state. Too angry, too defensive, too much trouble for the monthly check they sent her. He'd stood there in jeans that were three inches too short and a faded Teenage Mutant Ninja Turtles t-shirt with holes near the shoulders, clutching a comic book with the cover torn off, while she explained to the social worker that some kids just weren't meant for family life.

The social worker had been twenty-five minutes late picking him up, leaving him sitting on the curb with his trash bag, watching other kids ride bikes in driveways he'd never belong to. Cars had driven past without slowing, normal families heading to normal dinners in normal houses where ten-year-old boys weren't considered too much trouble to love.

That's when he'd learned the fundamental truth that would shape the next seventeen years of his life: people left. Not sometimes. Always. Love was just the word they used right before they walked away, a pretty lie to make the leaving feel less brutal.

He'd built his entire life around that knowledge, constructed walls so high and thick that no one could climb them. Because if you never let anyone close enough to matter, they couldn't destroy you when they inevitably left.

But Cara didn't feel like a promise that could break. She felt like a possibility he'd never dared imagine.

A soft whine from the door pulled him from his thoughts. Goldie rose from her spot near the entrance, stretching with the fluid grace of a dog who'd been waiting patiently for her human to remember she existed. Her tail wagged once, tentatively, as she approached with the careful optimism of a creature who'd learned to read moods and adjust accordingly.

Sawyer scratched behind her ears, and she leaned into him with complete trust, her warm weight grounding him in the present moment. Her dark eyes reflected the soft light from the single lamp, patient and understanding in that way only dogs managed.

"Come on, girl," he murmured, reaching for her leash. "Let's go for a walk."

She rose immediately, moving to his side without hesitation, her entire body radiating quiet joy at the prospect of adventure.

Most nights, they followed the well-worn path that looped around the ranch house and back, a familiar circuit that took exactly twenty-three minutes at a comfortable pace. But tonight felt different. His chest too full, his mind too restless for predictable routes. Instead, he veered off toward the desert, feet following instinct more than intention.

The landscape stretched endlessly around them, vast and quiet under a sky that was deepening from purple to black. Ancient palo verde trees cast long shadows across the sandy ground, their twisted branches reaching like dark fingers against the star-scattered darkness. The air carried the sharp, clean scent of creosote after the day's baking heat, mixing with the earthy smell of cooling stone and the faint sweetness of night-blooming cereus somewhere in the distance.

Goldie stayed close but alert, her paws silent on the packed earth, tongue lolling as she panted softly in the residual heat. Her ears swiveled toward every sound. The skitter of a roadrunner between cacti, the distant call of a coyote somewhere beyond the ridge, the whisper of wind through dried grass. She glanced up at him every few steps, brown eyes reflecting the emerging starlight, as if she could sense the storm of thoughts churning beneath his skin.

Out here, away from any artificial lights, the sky opened up in ways that still caught him off guard after months at the ranch. Endless. Unbroken. A canvas of stars so dense it looked like someone had spilled diamonds across black velvet. Everything felt different under that vastness. Smaller and larger at the same time. The way Cara's laugh seemed to echo in his memory long after she was gone. The way she'd kissed him tonight like she wasn't afraid of the wreckage he'd come from, like she could see past it to something worth keeping.

He'd spent so many years building walls, brick by careful brick, that he'd forgotten what it felt like to want someone on the other side of them. To imagine a future that included more than just surviving day to day.

Goldie brushed against his leg as they turned back toward the housing units, her steady gait matching his, a warm and solid presence in the cooling darkness. But just as they neared the corner of the bunkhouse, voices cut through the desert stillness. Sharp, familiar, and impossible to ignore.

He slowed instinctively, Goldie dropping into a practiced sit at his side, both of them freezing as the words carried clearly in the thin air.

"You actually called his parole officer?" Dalton's voice was low and controlled, but edged with a fury that made Sawyer's stomach clench. "What the were you thinking, Janessa?"

Sawyer went completely still, every muscle in his body tensing. He'd suspected it was her. Had known in his gut that Janessa was behind the increased scrutiny, the questions, the way trouble seemed to follow him despite his careful adherence to every rule. But hearing it confirmed sent ice through his veins.

"I was trying to protect you," Janessa's voice was defensive, pitched higher than usual. "He's a criminal, Dalton. A felon. You have no idea what he's actually capable of."

Of course, she'd try to spin it as protection. Janessa never admitted to wrongdoing unless she was backed into a corner with no escape route.

"You weren't protecting anyone," Dalton shot back, his voice cracking with betrayal. "You were manipulating. Like you always do. You couldn't stand that I finally saw through your games."

"That's not—"

"You lied to me. You used people I care about as chess pieces in whatever twisted game you were playing. Used my name, my reputation like they were yours to spend." His voice broke slightly, raw with pain. "And what about the other guy? Did you think I wouldn't find out about him?"

A long pause stretched between them, filled only by the whisper of wind and the distant sound of cooling metal.

"I—" Janessa started, but the hesitation in her voice said everything Sawyer needed to hear.

He didn't need her to finish the sentence. He knew because he'd seen her with Derin that night and had kept her secret out of some misplaced sense of decency. And she'd tried to destroy him for it anyway.

When Dalton spoke again, his voice had transformed from fury into something rawer, more broken. "I loved you. I was planning to marry you, build a life with you. I defended you to people who tried to warn me." His breath shuddered audibly. "But looking at you now... I don't even recognize who you are. Maybe I never really knew you at all."

The silence that followed was heavy with the weight of things that couldn't be taken back, words that would echo long after they were spoken.

"You're fired," Dalton said finally, his voice flat and final. "Three days to pack your things. Then I want you gone. Don't contact me, don't try to explain. Just... go."

Sawyer took a careful step backward, Goldie rising silently with him, both of them melting into the shadows as Dalton's truck roared to life. The engine growled with barely contained emotion as he peeled away, taillights disappearing down the dusty road toward the Vargas family's ranch house.

Only when the quiet had settled back over the desert did Sawyer allow himself to breathe deeply again. He hadn't realized how tight his chest had been, how the constant tension had burrowed into his shoulders and taken up permanent residence there.

Back inside the bunkhouse, he sank onto his bunk with Goldie pressing close against his legs, her warm weight a comfort he didn't know he needed. For the first time in weeks, maybe months, his shoulders actually dropped, muscles unclenching as relief worked its way through his body like warm honey. The knot between his shoulder blades that had become so familiar he'd stopped noticing it finally began to loosen.

Janessa was done. Finally, completely done. But he'd heard the devastation in Dalton's voice, felt it echo in his own chest with uncomfortable familiarity. Maybe that was the real ache. Recognizing the particular brand of betrayal that came from trusting someone who'd been playing an entirely different game all along.

He rubbed his hand over his face, then let it fall to Goldie's head. She leaned into his touch with complete trust, steady and warm and utterly reliable in a way that humans rarely managed.

Cara's face rose in his memory again. The way she'd looked at him tonight across her kitchen counter, like he wasn't just some ex-con with a past full of bad choices. The way she'd kissed him on her porch like she wasn't afraid of what tomorrow might bring, like she could see something in him worth fighting for.

The world outside hadn't changed. But something inside him definitely had.

For the first time in longer than he could remember, Sawyer wasn't just bracing for the next disaster, wasn't just surviving from one day to the next. With Janessa gone and one less shadow creeping around the edges of his new life, he finally had space to breathe. Space to think about the future without automatically assuming it would be taken away.

Space to hope for something real.

He leaned back against the wall, staring at the ceiling where moonlight filtered through the small window. The bunkhouse was quiet now, the kind of earned quiet that felt like peace. Outside, the crickets had resumed their nightly chorus, their song drifting through the thin walls.

And for the first time since arriving at Vargas Ranch, Sawyer felt like the ground beneath him wasn't about to give way. Like maybe, just maybe, he was finally somewhere he could stay.

20

_____

THE LARIAT PULSED with life, transformed into something that felt both familiar and completely new. Boots scuffed rhythmically against the high-shine epoxy floor that she and Sawyer had poured together, each step creating a soft percussion that mixed with the steady hum of conversation and the warm twang of the steel guitar drifting from speakers overhead. Laughter rose and fell like wind through mesquite branches, weaving together with the rich aromas of freshly pulled espresso shots, grilled paninis, and buttery pastries that seemed to wrap around everything like a welcoming embrace.

Cara stood near the entrance, her hand resting lightly on the smooth surface of the espresso bar—the centerpiece that had sparked so many discussions during the renovation. Golden light spilled from pendant fixtures across lacquered tabletops and rich brown leather booths, casting everything in a warm glow that made the space feel both intimate and vibrantly alive. Behind the counter, the chalkboard menu displayed her own handwriting in careful chalk strokes, each curve and flourish a trace of her personal care. Her photographs lined the walls in clean black frames, no longer looking like afterthoughts but integral pieces of something larger and more meaningful.

This wasn't the old Lariat anymore—that tired diner with worn floors and faded dreams. This was something entirely new, something she and Sawyer had built together through countless conversations, compromises, and shared vision, piece by careful piece.

She let her gaze sweep across the crowd, spotting familiar faces scattered throughout the buzzing space: ranch hands from Vargas Ranch still in their work clothes, locals that Aunt Greta had known for decades, and newcomers drawn in by word-of-mouth and curiosity. The energy was celebratory, electric, crackling with an excitement that came from being part of something special from the very beginning.

It should have felt triumphant. Instead, a quiet ache had settled between her shoulder blades, a tension that came from running on adrenaline for too long. She'd been up since before dawn, making final adjustments to the gallery wall arrangement, coordinating last-minute details with Aunt Greta, solving a thousand tiny problems that seemed to multiply like rabbits. Now that the initial rush was fading, she felt strung as tight as piano wire, her body finally registering the exhaustion she'd been pushing aside for weeks.

"Have you actually tasted that espresso cream filling yet?" Aunt Greta appeared at her elbow like a whirlwind, balancing a tray of perfectly golden lemon tarts with practiced ease. Her rhinestone hair clip caught the warm light. Her face was animated. "I'm telling you, we're going to convert every coffee drinker in a fifty-mile radius!"

Cara managed a genuine smile, feeling some of the tension ease just from her aunt's infectious enthusiasm. "You've seriously created something amazing here."

"We did, honey," Aunt Greta corrected firmly, pressing a tall glass of chilled lemonade into Cara's hands. "You, me, and that ridiculously handsome cowboy who keeps hovering near the espresso machine like he's guarding the crown jewels." She threw in a knowing wink before disappearing back into the crowd with the grace of someone who'd been working rooms like this for decades.

Cara took a long sip of the lemonade, the perfect balance of tart and sweet grounding her in the moment. The coolness spread through her chest, and she felt herself truly absorbing the warmth of the room for the first time all evening. Conversations flowed around her in gentle waves, punctuated by the soft clinks of porcelain mugs and the rhythmic whir of the espresso machine pulling shot after perfect shot. People moved naturally through the space, pausing in front of her photographs with genuine interest, pointing at details, discussing what they saw with an engagement she'd only dreamed about.

She'd always imagined her work displayed in some pristine gallery space—white walls, perfect lighting, hushed reverence. But here, woven into the fabric of daily life, her images lived and breathed within the rhythm of the café. They sparked conversations over coffee, became focal points for first dates, caught the eye of hurried customers waiting for their orders.

They belonged here in a way she hadn't expected, in a way that felt more meaningful than any formal exhibition ever could.

Familiar warmth brushed against her hand before she even saw him approaching. Sawyer appeared at her side with that quiet way he had of moving, his calloused fingers finding hers with the easy certainty of someone who'd earned the right to that casual intimacy.

"It turned out really good, Cara," he said, his voice pitched low and meant just for her, cutting through the ambient noise around them.

She exhaled slowly, her smile small but completely genuine. "Way better than I imagined it would be."

His gaze swept the transformed space with obvious pride, taking in the reclaimed wood they'd chosen together after hours of debate, the tin ceiling tiles he'd suggested that she'd initially resisted, the careful balance of rustic and refined they'd achieved through countless conversations and creative compromises.

"Still think you should have let me convince you on those walnut countertops," he teased, his mouth quirking up at one corner.

Cara huffed a soft laugh, feeling lighter than she had all day. "And lose all that gorgeous character from the original wood? Not a chance."

Sawyer's attention drifted to her photographs, where a small group of customers had gathered, studying the way light caught a horse's flowing mane, the weathered hands of a ranch worker, the vast sweep of desert sky at golden hour. "People aren't just walking past your photos," he observed quietly, his voice carrying a note of wonder. "They're stopping, really looking. They feel something, even if they can't put it into words."

The weight of that observation settled somewhere deep in her chest, warm and satisfying. Her work wasn't just being seen—it was being experienced, felt, absorbed as part of something larger than individual artistic expression.

"It still feels kind of surreal," she admitted, curling her fingers around the cool condensation on her glass.

Sawyer's hand closed gently around her free one, his thumb brushing across her knuckles in a gesture that was becoming beautifully familiar. Not possessive or demanding, just present like an anchor in the swirling energy around them. "You created something seriously worth seeing."

Before she could respond with the gratitude that was rising in her throat, Adan's voice called out from across the room, waving Sawyer over. He lifted her hand, pressed a soft kiss just above her knuckles that sent warmth shooting up her arm, then released her with a gentle squeeze.

"Take a breath," he said, his eyes warm with affection and pride. "Just enjoy this moment."

Cara watched him weave through the crowd toward Adan, the sight of him moving so easily through this space they'd created together, making something warm and content unfurl in her chest like a flower opening to sunlight.

"Cara Hollis?" Mrs. Langston's familiar voice pulled her attention back to the present. The elderly woman approached with her signature floral satchel slung over one shoulder and a half-eaten lemon tart wrapped carefully in a napkin. Her eyes sparkled with genuine delight behind her thick glasses as she gestured toward the gallery wall. "I just finished telling Greta that this place makes me want to curl up with a good book and pretend I'm in some charming Parisian café—only with way better brisket and actual decent coffee." She beamed with infectious joy. "You've pulled off something truly remarkable here, dear. It's not just the food or even the gorgeous ambiance. The whole space tells a story."

"Thank you so much," Cara said, touched by the genuine warmth and enthusiasm in the older woman's voice. "That's exactly what we were hoping to achieve."

Mrs. Langston moved closer to examine a framed print of Dylan Vargas with his horse, their connection almost mystical in the captured moment. The image showed the quiet cowboy in profile, his gentle hand resting on the horse's neck while both seemed lost in their own peaceful world. "This one keeps drawing me back," she whispered, tapping gently near the wood frame. "Every time I think I'll choose another favorite, I end up right back here. It feels so... honest. Like you caught something real."

Cara's heart caught in her throat. Honesty—that's exactly what she'd been chasing in every frame, every careful composition, every moment she'd waited for the perfect light.

"That means absolutely everything to me, Mrs. Langston. Thank you."

"Well, you've certainly earned it. I may need to start clearing some space above my fireplace for a purchase." She patted Cara's hand with maternal warmth before moving toward the dessert counter, already calling out to Aunt Greta for another tart.

Cara's gaze drifted back toward the espresso bar where Sawyer leaned against the polished counter, laughing at something Adan had said while steam rose from the machine behind them. He looked completely at ease, like he belonged exactly where he was—which, she realized with a flutter of happiness, he absolutely did. The sight of him settling so naturally into this space they'd created together made her heart swell with warmth and pride.

Movement near the gallery wall caught her peripheral vision. A woman with a sleek dark braid and a slate-colored blouse stood before one photograph, her posture unnaturally still amid all the celebration and movement around her. Something about her presence felt different from the other guests—more focused, more intent, like she was studying rather than simply admiring. She took a half step closer to the frame, her stillness predatory amid all the celebration around her.

Curiosity drew Cara closer, weaving between clusters of guests until she could see which image held the woman's laser focus: Sawyer leaning against the weathered stucco wall of the ranch casita, one boot braced casually against the stucco, well-worn denim stretched over his bent knee. His simple white V-neck revealed lean muscle earned through honest work, while sunlight caught the sharp angle of his jaw beneath the shadow of his hat brim. Goldie sat contentedly at his feet, his hand resting on her golden head with casual affection. It was one of Cara's absolute favorites—nothing posed or artificial, everything authentic and real.

But the woman wasn't admiring the composition or the interplay of light and shadow that Cara was so proud of. Her gaze was fixed with uncomfortable intensity on something specific. The edge of a tattoo barely visible beneath Sawyer's shirt collar. Dark ink that looked like wing tips, just peeking above the fabric line.

The woman's stare wasn't casual appreciation or artistic interest. It was recognition. Cold, certain recognition.

"That's actually one of my favorite shots," Cara said, keeping her tone conversational and friendly as she approached, though warning bells were already chiming in the back of her mind.

The woman turned with fluid precision, revealing sharp, intelligent features and eyes that seemed to catalog and assess everything in a single calculating glance. "Beautiful work," she said, her voice smooth as polished stone but somehow lacking warmth. "Interesting ink, though. Never thought I'd see that design way out here."

Something cold slid down Cara's spine like ice water. "The tattoo?"

"Very distinctive design," the woman continued, her gaze flicking back to the photograph with uncomfortable intensity. "He works at Vargas Ranch?"

Cara hesitated, instinct screaming at her to be careful even though she couldn't pinpoint exactly why. "He does."

The woman's smile was unreadable, carrying secrets and implications that Cara couldn't guess at. "Small world, isn't it?"

Without another word of explanation, she melted back into the crowd like smoke, leaving Cara standing alone with questions multiplying in her mind. The entire interaction had lasted less than two minutes, but it left her feeling exposed and unsettled, like something important had just shifted without her understanding what or why.

She stared at the photograph again, really examining the tattoo for the first time since she'd taken the shot. Just a hint of dark ink beneath the fabric. Nothing she'd paid any attention to when framing it. But the woman had recognized it immediately, had known exactly what she was looking at.

Cara's gaze sought Sawyer across the bustling room. He was sitting with Junior, relaxed and unaware, studying his hands. Perhaps a serious conversation she shouldn't interrupt. But the woman's words echoed in her mind with growing unease: *Never thought I'd see that here.*

The celebration continued to swirl around her—laughter, conversation, the clink of glasses and the hiss of steam—but something fundamental had changed. A question mark had been dropped into the middle of her perfect evening like a rock into still water, and Cara couldn't shake the growing feeling that whatever it meant, this was just the beginning of something she wasn't prepared for.

SAWYER STEPPED THROUGH the front door of *The Lariat* and stopped dead in his tracks. Just for a moment, just long enough for his chest to tighten with something that felt like awe mixed with disbelief. The warmth of the transformed space wrapped around him like a physical embrace, but his pulse kicked up anyway with a slow, steady press against his ribs as if his body needed that pause to fully absorb what this moment actually meant.

The place was completely, vibrantly alive. Voices threaded through the room in layers, some low and intimate, others bright with celebration and discovery. The soft clinks of ceramic mugs meeting saucers, the gentle scrape of silverware against plates, the rhythmic hiss and gurgle of the espresso machine pulling perfect shots. Fresh coffee scented the air, its bitter richness softened by the butter and vanilla of fresh croissants and sharpened by the smoky aroma of slow-roasted brisket from the kitchen.

He let his gaze sweep across the space with deliberate slowness, taking in every detail he and Cara built together. Lacquered tables gleaming under warm light, wrought-iron chairs that invited lingering conversations, soft yellow walls washed in copper light from the pendant fixtures he'd hung himself. Then his eyes landed on the espresso bar, and his breath caught in his throat.

Tin-paneled. His idea. His passionate argument. His proof that sometimes the right choice wasn't the safe choice.

Five years ago, these same hands had been desperate and dirty, breaking into cars in Phoenix parking lots, looking for easy money. Those hands had taken things that didn't belong to him, had destroyed other people's sense of security for his own temporary survival.

Now those same hands had crafted this. Every careful joint, every precisely fitted panel, every small detail that would probably go unnoticed by most customers, but mattered anyway. He'd helped build something that would hold memories, where people would gather to celebrate milestones and ordinary moments alike. Not just a business, but a constant in people's lives.

The crooked, broken path that had been his existence for so many years—the streets, the gang, that final crime which still haunted his sleep—had somehow led him here. Learning construction skills in prison workshops. Cara's unwavering belief in his potential when he couldn't see it himself. Junior's patient guidance. All of it had converged to create this moment, this place, this proof that transformation was actually possible.

He exhaled slowly, letting the magnitude of that realization settle deep in his heart, then started moving through the crowd with purpose. Nodding at familiar faces from the ranch, offering firm handshakes and genuine smiles to neighbors he was still getting to know. The energy was better than good. It was electric with possibility and community.

Sawyer found Cara near the gallery wall, a tall glass of lemonade in her hand, pride and exhaustion warring visibly in her expression. She looked beautiful and overwhelmed and completely in her element all at once. He approached without hesitation, brushing his fingers against hers in quiet greeting, feeling the tension in her shoulders ease visibly at the sight of him.

"It turned out great, Cara," he said, pitching his voice low, so it was meant just for her ears.

Her smile was small but radiant. "Way better than I ever imagined it could be."

Their exchange was brief but meaningful. Nothing heavy or dramatic, just acknowledgment of what they'd accomplished together through months of planning and weeks of intensive work. He could see her gaze drift toward the framed photographs, watching people stop and actually study her work instead of just walking past. The realization was clearly landing that her art wasn't just decoration anymore. It had become part of the rhythm and soul of this place.

Without really thinking about it, he lifted her hand and pressed a soft kiss just above her knuckles—a moment of quiet connection and appreciation before Adan's voice cut through the ambient noise, waving him over.

Sawyer made his way through the crowd, falling into easy conversation with Adan about the evening's turnout, sharing jokes about the installation headaches they'd survived, and basking in the deep satisfaction of seeing their collective work come together so beautifully.

The front door chimed again, and Sawyer straightened instinctively, his attention drawn by the familiar sound of a walker's rhythmic tapping against the polished floor. Junior entered slowly but steadily, navigating the bustling space with the careful determination that had carried him through decades of ranch life. Sawyer crossed the room immediately to meet him halfway, falling into step beside the older man without making a show of offering support.

"I can manage just fine," Junior said, his tone gruff but not unkind, the independence in his voice as strong as ever.

"I know you can," Sawyer replied simply, helping him settle into a booth with a clear view of the entire transformed space.

Junior took his time looking around, his weathered eyes absorbing every carefully chosen detail. The tin panels on the espresso bar that had sparked so much discussion. The precise joints in the woodwork that spoke to quality crafts-manship. The way the warm lighting fell just right across tables and walls, creating an atmosphere that felt both wel-coming and sophisticated. His gnarled hands traced the smooth edge of the table, feeling the satin finish they'd ap-plied with such care.

"You know what I see when I look around this place?" Junior's voice was quiet, reverent in a way that made Saw-yer's chest tighten. "You didn't just help them build a res-taurant. You gave them something that's going to last. Something that matters."

He looked up then, his eyes bright with emotion despite his advancing age. "Five years ago, you were stealing cars and running with a gang that would have gotten you killed, eventually. Today, you built this place where families are going to make memories for decades to come."

Sawyer shifted uncomfortably, unsure how to respond to the praise that felt both deserved and overwhelming.

Junior leaned forward slightly, his voice taking on the steady cadence of someone sharing hard-won wisdom. "Psalm 17, verses four and five," he said, and Sawyer in-stinctively met his gaze. "By the word of Your lips, I have avoided the ways of the violent. My steps have held fast to Your paths; my feet have not slipped."

Sawyer exhaled slowly. He'd seen those words painted in elegant script on the dining hall wall at the ranch hun-dreds of times, had read them during countless meals. But hearing them spoken here, in this place he'd helped create with his own hands, they carried entirely new weight and meaning.

Junior's gaze held firm, unwavering. "It's not just about avoiding a fight or staying out of trouble. It's about walking steady when it would be so much easier to fall back into what you knew, what felt familiar, even if it was destroying you."

Sawyer looked down at his hands—calloused from honest work, steady despite the storms they'd weathered, capable of creating instead of just taking.

"You've walked that path every single day, son. With every choice you made, every temptation you turned away from, every morning you got up and chose to be better than you were the day before." Junior's gesture encompassed the entire café. "And this—this beautiful place—is proof that a man can be completely remade. Not just forgiven for what he's done, but transformed into someone new."

The words settled deep in Sawyer's chest, heavier and more precious than any praise he'd ever received in his life.

"I still think about slipping sometimes," Sawyer admitted quietly, the confession feeling both vulnerable and necessary. "About how easy it would be to go back."

"Good," Junior said without the slightest hesitation. "That means you're still paying attention, still taking your commitment seriously. But you haven't lost your footing once from where I'm sitting." His voice softened with paternal affection. "I trust you completely, Sawyer. And I don't say that lightly about anyone."

The words landed solid as stone, settling into a place in Sawyer's heart he hadn't known was empty. He nodded once, his throat tight with emotion that felt entirely right and good. Junior reached for his coffee and settled back in the booth as if he hadn't just handed Sawyer something more valuable than gold.

Then something shifted in the atmosphere, subtle but unmistakable. A prickle at the base of Sawyer's neck, that old street instinct for danger that had kept him alive through years of sketchy situations. He scanned the crowd with practiced casualness, his gaze sweeping until he found the source of his unease—a woman near the gallery wall. Dark braid, professional slate-colored blouse, posture too sharp and focused for a casual evening out. She was studying one particular photograph with laser intensity, and her stillness felt dangerous.

His photograph.

But her expression wasn't appreciation or artistic interest. It was recognition, cold and certain.

"I should probably check on Cara," he murmured to Junior, already rising from the booth, every instinct screaming that something was wrong.

By the time he reached the gallery wall, weaving through clusters of celebrating guests, the woman had vanished, melting back into the crowd like smoke, leaving no trace except the chill of unease she'd left behind.

"Who was that woman?" he asked Cara, keeping his voice carefully even despite the ice forming in his chest.

Cara turned toward him, concern already flickering in her expressive eyes. "The one looking at your picture? She asked about the photo, specifically about your tattoo. Whether you worked at Vargas Ranch." She searched his face with growing worry. "Why? Do you know her?"

Sawyer's gaze snapped to the framed photograph, and his blood turned to ice water in his veins.

There it was, just barely visible beneath his shirt collar, peeking above the V-neck like a whisper of his past he'd thought was buried forever. Dark ink formed jagged wings. The phoenix tattoo that marked him as a member of Phoenix Rising—the crew he'd run with before prison, before everything changed, before he'd learned what it meant to choose a different path.

He hadn't even realized it showed in the photograph. Hadn't thought about it when Cara was taking the shot, too focused on her smile and the way the afternoon light caught her hair. But someone had seen it. Someone who knew exactly what those wings meant, what crew they represented, what kind of man had earned the right to wear that particular mark.

If Sierra's people had tracked him here, if they'd found him despite all his precautions...

"Sawyer?" Cara's voice seemed to come from very far away, muffled by the roar of blood in his ears. "What's wrong? You look like you've seen a ghost."

His chest tightened as the implications crashed over him in waves. If the woman had recognized the gang tattoo, if she knew what crew it represented and what it meant, then his carefully constructed new life wasn't as secure as he'd believed. Phoenix Rising was looking for him. Someone had found him. Someone knew exactly where he was.

He scanned the crowd again, this time looking for faces that didn't belong, bodies positioned for quick exits, shadows that seemed out of place. Nothing appeared immediately threatening, but that didn't matter now. The damage was already done. His location was compromised, his cover blown.

The warmth of *The Lariat*, the pride in what he'd built, Junior's words about being remade—all of it felt suddenly fragile, like something beautiful that could be shattered with a single wrong move.

"It's nothing," he lied, forcing his voice to stay steady and calm. "Probably just someone who liked the photography."

But even as the words left his mouth, Sawyer knew he was wrong. The woman's stare had been too focused, too knowing, too dangerous. She hadn't been admiring Cara's artistic vision or the composition of the shot.

She'd been hunting. And now she knew exactly where to find him.

21

CARA PAUSED IN the doorway of *The Lariat*, struck by how different the space felt from the grand opening two weeks ago. The initial excitement had settled into something steadier, like the rhythm of a place that had found its groove. Regulars occupied their favorite spots, newspapers spread beside half-empty coffee cups. A mother wiped sticky fingers while her toddler pointed at the photographs on the wall, babbling something that sounded like *horsie*. The lunch rush was winding down, leaving behind the comfortable hum of a community gathering place.

She watched an elderly man near the window studying her landscape photograph of the Hassayampa River Preserve, his weathered hands wrapped around a mug of coffee. He wasn't analyzing composition or technique. He was remembering something, his eyes soft with nostalgia. At another table, two women leaned over their phones, one pointing at the framed image of Dylan on a trail ride. "I swear that's the trail we rode last month," she was saying.

This wasn't the carefully orchestrated energy of opening night. Her photographs had become part of the living, breathing heart of the bistro—not just decoration, but conversation starters, memory triggers, pieces of a larger story.

"Cara, honey!" Aunt Greta appeared at her elbow, practically glowing with pride. "Look at this place. I can't get people to leave!" She gestured toward the bustling dining area. "And it's all because of what you and Sawyer created."

Her heart swelled with quiet satisfaction. "It turned out better than I imagined."

"Oh, it's more than that." Aunt Greta lowered her voice conspiratorially. "Mrs. Langston came in yesterday asking if she could commission a custom photograph for her living room. She wants something with the same feeling as the Dylan piece, but featuring her late husband's favorite riding trail."

"Really?" Cara's pulse quickened. Not because of the money, but because of what it meant. Mrs. Langston didn't want art to look at. She wanted art to live with.

"And that's not all." Aunt Greta's eyes sparkled. "The Hendersons want to know if you do kitchen renovations. The Morettis are asking about their guest bathroom. Word is spreading, honey."

Cara nodded, absorbing the implications. In a traditional gallery, these same images would have felt cold, sterile. Here, they made people feel something, remember something, want something.

The high school Habitat project flashed through her memory. The way the mother had cried when she saw the simple prints and pottery Cara had bought with her father's credit card. Not because they were expensive or impressive, but because they made a house feel like a home.

"You know," Cara said slowly, the realization crystallizing as she spoke, "I used to dream about having my own gallery. Pristine white walls, perfect lighting, people studying my work like it was in a museum."

Aunt Greta angled her head, listening.

"But this?" Cara gestured around the bustling café. "This is so much better. My photographs aren't just being seen — they're being lived with. They're part of someone's lunch conversation, part of a family's afternoon together. Reliving fond memories with loved ones. They matter in a completely different way."

"Art that serves," Aunt Greta whispered. "Art that blesses."

"Exactly." Cara felt something shift inside her chest, a door opening to possibilities she hadn't even considered. "I don't want a sterile gallery. I want to create spaces where art and life intersect. Where beauty serves purpose."

The front door chimed, and Sawyer appeared, slightly windblown from circling the block. His eyes found hers immediately, that familiar warmth spreading through her at the sight of him.

"Had to park three blocks away," he said, approaching with an easy grin. "This place is officially a Wickenburg institution."

He reached her side, his hand settling naturally at the small of her back as he leaned down to press a soft kiss to her temple. The simple gesture sent warmth cascading through her, a reminder of how natural they'd become together.

Aunt Greta beamed. "And it's only been two weeks!"

"Speaking of which," Cara said, turning to her aunt, "what can we get for lunch? We need to head back to work on the dining hall this afternoon."

"Two specials coming right up. And Cara?" Aunt Greta touched her arm gently. "I'm proud of you. Of both of you. You've given this old place new life."

As her aunt bustled away, Sawyer's hand found hers, fingers intertwining with practiced ease. "You look thoughtful. Good thoughtful or worried thoughtful?"

"Good thoughtful." She squeezed his fingers. "I've been thinking about the future. About what comes next."

"And?"

"I think I know what I want to build."

Their lunch conversation had started simply enough. Cara shared her revelation about art serving life rather than existing in isolation. But as they talked, something bigger began to take shape.

"Interior design with integrated photography," Sawyer mused, biting into his turkey sandwich. "Custom pieces for each space you create."

"Not just photography. All of it." Cara's excitement was building, her words coming faster. "Furniture, lighting, art—everything working together to tell a story. To make a space feel alive."

Sawyer leaned back, studying her. "That's ambitious. You'd need significant capital to really do it right. Quality materials, a proper studio space, maybe even a showroom."

Cara hesitated, then took a breath. The trust fund. She'd mentioned it once, briefly, when explaining why she couldn't just live off her family's money. But she'd never told him the actual amount.

"I have resources I haven't used," she said carefully.

"Your family's money?"

"My trust fund." The words felt strange in her mouth. "It became fully accessible when I turned twenty-five. No conditions, no oversight. Just... available."

Sawyer's fork paused halfway to his mouth. "How much are we talking about?"

Cara swallowed. "Twelve million dollars."

The fork clattered against his plate.

"Twelve..." He blinked, clearly trying to process. "Million?"

"I know it's hard to understand why I haven't touched it. But it felt like accepting their control, like admitting I couldn't make it on my own." She twisted her napkin in her lap. "Every time I thought about using it, I heard my mother's voice, telling me I'd never amount to anything without their money."

Sawyer was quiet for a long moment, his green eyes studying her face. "Twelve million dollars, and you chose to live in a duplex and drive a six-year-old SUV."

"I wanted to prove I could make it without—"

"No." His voice was soft, but certain. "You wanted to

prove you were worthy of being loved for who you are, not what you have." He reached across the table, fingers intertwining with hers. "Well, mission accomplished."

The simple truth of it made her throat tight. "Sawyer..."

"I fell in love with a woman who gets paint in her hair and argues with me about tile patterns. Who brings me Chinese takeout and trusts me with her dreams." His thumb traced across her knuckles. "The money doesn't change that. It just means we can dream bigger."

Her breath caught. He'd said it so casually, woven into the conversation like it was a given. Like loving her was as natural as breathing.

"Besides," Sawyer continued, a small smile playing at his lips, "if you're going to revolutionize interior design in Arizona, you might as well do it right."

"We," Cara corrected softly, giving voice to her growing feelings for him. The dream would feel incomplete and empty if he weren't a part of it. "If we're going to do it right."

Sawyer's smile widened, something tender and wondering in his expression. "We," he repeated, like he was testing how the word felt. "I like the sound of that. Not just for business."

Heat bloomed in her cheeks. "What else?"

"Everything." The word was simple, honest. "I want to build everything with you, Cara."

"I can't build spaces like the casitas without someone who understands construction, who can bring the vision to life. I need a partner who—" She stopped, heat rising to her cheeks as she realized how that sounded. "I mean, professionally. If you're interested. In working together."

Something shifted in Sawyer's expression that had nothing to do with her impromptu job offer. "I'm very interested in working with you, Cara. In whatever capacity you'll have me."

The weight of his words, the way he looked at her when

he said them, made her pulse quicken. This wasn't just about business anymore, and they both knew it.

"Good," she managed. "Because I have some ideas about what we could create together."

THE DRIVE BACK to the ranch felt different somehow. Not just the comfortable silence that had become second nature between them, but something charged, full of possibility. Cara's hands gestured as she talked about her vision—custom homes, boutique hotels, restaurants like *The Lariat* but bigger, bolder. Her excitement was infectious, painting pictures of a future that seemed both ambitious and entirely achievable.

Twelve million dollars.

Sawyer gripped the steering wheel a little tighter, trying to process the magnitude of what she'd shared. He'd known she came from money, but this... this was generational wealth. Money that opened every door, removed every obstacle.

And she'd been living in a modest duplex, driving a six-year-old SUV, fighting for every design contract.

The trust fund revelation should have scared him. Should have reminded him of the gulf between their worlds. Instead, it filled him with something like pride. Cara had chosen to build her own life, to prove herself on her own terms. The money hadn't shaped her; her character had.

"Renewal Designs," she blurted.

"What?"

"That's what we could call it. The business. Renewal Designs." She turned to him, eyes bright. "Taking something worn or broken and making it beautiful again. Making it serve its purpose better than before."

Renewal. The word resonated through his soul, carrying

echoes of his own transformation. "I like it."

"Good. Because I think we could build something amazing together."

Together. The word hung in the air between them, loaded with meaning that went far beyond business partnerships.

As they pulled into the ranch, Sawyer felt something settle in his heart. Not just the satisfaction of good work or even the excitement of new possibilities. It was deeper than that. More permanent.

He loved Cara Hollis. Not just attracted to her, not just enjoying her company. Love. The kind that made a man think about forever, about building a life together, about commitment that went beyond shared projects and professional dreams.

The realization should have scared him. Six months ago, he'd been an ex-con with no future, no prospects, no reason to believe anyone would ever see past his mistakes. Now he imagined a lifetime with a woman who could have chosen anyone. Who had every advantage. Who trusted him not just with her business dreams, but with her heart.

They parked behind the dining hall, and Cara gathered her tablet and measuring tape. "Ready to make this place beautiful?"

"Always," he said, and meant it.

Inside, they fell into their familiar rhythm — Cara directing, Sawyer executing, both of them building something together. But today felt different. Every shared glance, every moment their hands brushed passing tools, every small laugh over some shared joke — it all carried the weight of what was growing between them.

As Sawyer sanded the new wooden mantel they'd installed yesterday, he thought about the future in concrete terms. Not just the next project or the next month, but years. Decades. A lifetime of working beside Cara, of building beautiful things together, of coming home to each other every night.

The thought no longer scared him. It felt inevitable, like gravity or sunrise. Something fundamental and right.

But as he reached for another piece of sandpaper, something prickled at the back of his neck. The feeling of being watched. He glanced toward the windows, scanning the visible grounds, but saw nothing unusual. Just ranch hands going about their afternoon tasks, horses grazing in the distance.

Still, the feeling persisted. Like eyes tracking his movements, cataloging his routines. Someone who knew what to look for. Someone from his past.

He shook it off, focusing instead on the rhythm of the sandpaper against wood, on Cara's quiet humming as she worked. Whatever it was—probably nothing—it couldn't touch what they were building here. This was real. This was permanent. This was home.

But the unease lingered, a shadow at the edge of an otherwise perfect afternoon.

22

———————

THE SCENT OF spicy tacos hung in the air. The dining hall pulsed with low conversation, the scrape of silverware, the quiet rhythm of shared meals and familiar faces. Adan leaned back in his chair, swapping stories with two of the ranch hands, their voices blending into the steady hum of the room.

Sawyer sat across from Cara at their usual table, boots hooked over the rung of his chair, his plate mostly cleared. It had been two rigorous weeks of remodeling the dining hall. They finished the last touches an hour ago, just in time for lunch service.

And on the far wall was Cara's last mark.

The Vargas family motto, hand-painted in bold, neat strokes. Verses from Psalms below it. Words meant to settle into the hearts of whoever passed through these doors — guests, ranch hands, men like him.

"By the word of Your lips, I have avoided the ways of the violent; my steps have held fast to Your paths, my feet have not slipped."

Sawyer's gaze lingered there, the words rooting deeply in his soul. A reminder, a declaration, a choice. His parole had officially ended last week. Jerry's last visit had been brief, almost anticlimactic. A signature on paperwork, a handshake, and then real freedom, not just the supervised kind.

"Think it'll make a difference?" Cara's voice was quiet, uncertain.

Sawyer shifted his weight, rolling his shoulder where the week's labor had settled deep. "Already has."

She huffed a breath, shaking her head. "The café's done. This place is done. And now..."

She didn't finish the thought. He understood. The end of one chapter, the beginning of another.

"About that," Sawyer said, reaching across the table to cover her hand with his. "I talked to Tres yesterday. About transitioning some of my time here to helping you launch Renewal Designs."

Cara's eyes brightened, hope flickering in their depths. "And?"

"He's supportive. Said the ranch will always need maintenance work, but he understands I want to build something with you." His thumb traced across her knuckles. "We can start small—take on projects while I still handle repairs here. Test the waters."

"Really?" Her smile was radiant, transforming her entire face. "You're serious about this? About us building a business together?"

"I'm serious about building everything with you," he said, meaning every word. "Business, life, future—all of it."

The weight of his words settled between them, warm and certain. Cara's fingers tightened around his, and for a moment, the busy dining hall faded into background noise.

"There's a long list of repairs waiting at the resort too," Sawyer added with a grin. "Can't say I'll be bored while we're getting Renewal Designs off the ground."

Cara scoffed, shaking her head. "You? Bored?"

He smirked, but before he could answer, something prickled at the base of his neck. His breath pulled tight. Something had shifted—small, subtle, just enough to scrape against his instincts.

"You good?" Cara's voice was low, measured, concern

creasing her brow.

Sawyer scanned the room. Servers moved between tables. Ranch hands laughed at something Adan said. The steady flow of a normal summer afternoon.

Then he saw her.

A flicker of motion near the serving station. Dark braid. Rigid posture. Too familiar.

Sawyer straightened, chair legs scraping the floor, muscles bracing before his mind fully caught up.

She turned.

Sierra.

Not just watching. Waiting.

She advanced — smooth, unhurried, deliberate. Pressing into his space with that controlled grace she always had — until she wasn't controlled anymore.

Sawyer stood, slow and measured. Every instinct warned him she wanted this moment, had planned it.

She stopped a few feet away, eyes locked on him like she was staring at something unfinished, something she wasn't done wrecking.

"Took me a while to find you, Wesley."

The name hit like a weapon.

Sawyer clenched his jaw, didn't move. Didn't react. But something inside him coiled tight.

She tilted her head, laughing low, mocking bitterly, like she had already won.

"What? No warm welcome?"

Sawyer exhaled slowly, steadying himself against the weight of her presence. Against the rage boiling in his veins.

"I don't forget betrayal." Her voice sharpened, cutting clean through the noise of the dining hall. "Angelo made you. You were nothing before him. Nothing."

The past pressed in hard, but Sierra wasn't finished.

She leaned in, eyes glinting sharply. "Did you forget the meaning of your tattoo, Wesley?"

Phoenix Rising.

Sierra laughed again—sharp, cutting.

"What's funny is I didn't even have to work that hard to find you." She shifted, glancing toward Cara. "Your girlfriend's parents' party. I saw you then. I know you saw me."

Sawyer's stomach dropped. She had been there. He remembered.

"And your girlfriend?" She gave Cara a slow once-over, eyes gleaming with something too sharp. "She confirmed you lived here."

Then Sierra's attention snapped to Cara—an unspoken decision, a slow pivot toward destruction.

The blade appeared in her hand like it had always been there.

Cara's eyes went wide, glass-bright with shock, her breath caught behind her ribs. Her throat bobbed against steel, pulse hammering visibly at the base of her neck.

Sawyer's world collapsed into a single moment. He saw the exact spot where Cara's skin met steel, saw the precision in Sierra's hand, saw how little pressure would be enough.

Sierra smiled—slow, deliberate, savoring it.

"See, Wesley?" Her voice was low, mocking, but her grip was steady, blade sure. "This is what happens when you forget where you came from."

Sawyer's fingers flexed at his sides. No sudden moves. No missteps.

"You don't get to walk away." Sierra's grip tightened, just enough for Cara to stiffen. "You don't get to change your name and pretend you never owed him—never owed me."

Sawyer's world narrowed. His voice came low, controlled—dangerous in its steadiness.

"Let. Her. Go."

Sierra's smile twisted, amusement laced with rage.

The blade pressed in, just enough to steal Cara's breath.

Sawyer's jaw locked—his body ready, bracing. Holding steady for just one more second.

Then he closed the distance.

THE DINING HALL had been steady, warm, familiar — until it wasn't.

Cara glanced across the table at Sawyer, her lips curving slightly. The final renovations were complete, her painted motto settling into the wall like it had always belonged there. Something they'd built together, stroke by stroke, decision by decision. She liked the rhythm of working beside him, the way he strengthened her vision instead of reshaping it.

Their plans for Renewal Designs felt more real now, more possible. A future built together, project by project.

What came next wasn't clear yet, but for the first time in a long time, that didn't scare her.

Then something shifted.

Sawyer's shoulders tensed — just slightly, but enough to strip the warmth from the space. His exhale was too controlled, too sharp.

"Sierra."

The name dropped between them like a brick. Not a question. Not a warning. Just recognition — reluctant, heavy, unavoidable.

Cara's fork paused halfway to her mouth. The afternoon light streaming through the windows suddenly felt too bright, too harsh. Around them, conversations faltered, chairs scraped against the floor.

She followed Sawyer's gaze to the woman near the serving station. Not just standing — lurking. Watching. The same woman from the party who'd stared at Sawyer's tattoo like she was reading a map.

The woman smiled, but it wasn't warm. It was the smile of someone who'd finally cornered their prey.

"Took me a while to find you, Wesley."

The name hit Cara like a physical blow. Wesley? She turned to Sawyer, searching his face for confusion, for denial, for anything that would make this make sense.

He didn't look confused.

He looked trapped.

"Sawyer?" Cara's voice came out smaller than she intended.

He still wouldn't meet her eyes, and that terrified her more than the stranger's words.

The woman—Sierra—stepped closer, her presence filling the space between them like poisonous gas. "You think you get to just move on? Walk around free while Angelo rots in a cell?"

Angelo. Cara's mind raced, trying to place the name, but it meant nothing to her. Apparently, it meant everything to Sawyer.

"All he ever did was protect us," Sierra continued, her voice rising just enough to carry across the now-silent dining hall. "All he ever did was make sure we had something."

Us. The word stung. Sierra and Sawyer had been an 'us' once. Cara could see it in the way Sierra looked at him—not just angry, but betrayed. Heartbroken.

"You think Angelo meant to kill him?" Sierra's laugh was bitter. "It was an accident, and you know it."

Cara's breath caught. Kill him. An accident. She felt like she was watching a movie in a foreign language, catching fragments but missing the crucial plot.

"And you sat in that courtroom and let them bury him."

Courtroom. The pieces clicked into place with sickening clarity. Sawyer had testified. Against someone named Angelo. Someone who'd killed someone else by accident.

"You testified against your own brotherhood," Sierra pressed on, her voice dropping to something almost intimate, almost loving. "Against the man who made you. Against the family that gave you a name—gave you power."

Brotherhood. Family. Power. Words that painted a picture Cara didn't want to see. She studied Sawyer's face — the tension in his jaw, the way his fingers gripped the table's edge. Still, he said nothing.

"Say something, Wesley." Sierra's head tilted, amused. "Tell her I'm lying."

Cara held her breath, waiting. Praying. For him to laugh, to deny it, to tell Sierra she was wrong.

The silence stretched between them like a chasm.

"Sawyer?" Cara whispered. "Please."

But he couldn't even look at her.

Sierra's laughter was low and cruel. "Phoenix Rising was built on loyalty. Built on blood. But you —" She shook her head, almost pitying. "You traded blood and loyalty for a name that opens doors. For a life that's bought and paid for."

The accusation hit Cara like ice water. Twelve million dollars. Her name. Had Sawyer known who she was before they met? Had he sought her out, used her for her family's wealth?

But no — that couldn't be true. She remembered their first meeting, the way he'd flinched at the price of her camera lens, how he'd seemed genuinely overwhelmed by her world. He hadn't known her then.

Had he?

The doubt crept in anyway, poisoning every memory. Every moment of connection, every whispered declaration of love, every time she'd pulled him deeper into her life, every door she'd unknowingly opened for him.

"You don't get to walk away," Sierra said, and suddenly she was moving, her hand clamping around Cara's arm like a vise. "You don't get to change your name and pretend you never owed him — never owed me."

Pain shot through Cara's arm as Sierra's fingers dug in. She jerked back, but Sierra's grip was iron. The dining hall was silent now, everyone watching, but no one moving to help.

Sawyer's entire body went rigid, but he still didn't speak. That silence—it wasn't calm. It was the stillness of a coiled spring, taut and ready to snap.

Then Cara felt it—cold metal against her throat.

The blade was sharp, precise, biting into her skin just enough to make its point clear. Her breath hitched, her world shrinking to the feel of steel and the wild hammering of her heart.

"Now you'll listen," Sierra whispered against her ear. "Now you'll pay attention to what your precious Wesley really is."

But Cara already was listening. She was watching Sawyer's face transform, seeing something dangerous and unfamiliar slide into place behind his eyes. This wasn't the man who'd helped her paint scriptures on the wall.

This was Wesley.

And Wesley was someone who knew exactly how to handle a knife at a woman's throat.

He moved like lightning, and Cara's world exploded into chaos.

23

SAWYER LUNGED WITHOUT hesitation, without thought. Just pure instinct and a desperate need to protect what mattered most.

The blade sliced through his forearm like it was nothing, cutting through fabric and biting deep into flesh with surgical precision. Fire spread immediate and sharp from the wound, but the pain barely registered. Sierra still had the knife. Still stood too close to Cara. Nothing else mattered.

He struck fast and hard, but Sierra twisted away like a cornered animal, her breath coming in wild gasps. The scent of sweat and adrenaline hung thick in the air between them, mixing with the metallic tang of his own blood.

"Cara!" The name tore out of his throat, raw and desperate, his voice cracking with fear he couldn't contain. "Are you hurt? Tell me you're okay!"

Silence stretched for what felt like an eternity, his heart hammering so hard against his ribs he thought it might burst.

Then Drake's voice cut through the chaos, steady and reassuring. "She's fine, Sawyer. She's safe. Focus on what you're doing."

Sawyer forced himself to breathe, to push past the fire spreading down his arm and the terror clawing at his chest. Sierra swung the knife again, reckless and desperate, but he was ready. He caught her wrist, feeling bones shift under his grip as he forced her arm back with everything he had.

She fought him with pure fury, every muscle in her body straining against his hold, thrashing like a wild thing caught in a trap. But he was bigger, stronger, and fueled by something more powerful than rage.

He wasn't losing. Not now. Not ever. Not when Cara's life hung in the balance.

The knife hit the tile floor with a sharp metallic crack, skittering away across the smooth surface until it came to rest near an overturned chair.

Sound erupted around him like a dam breaking. Chairs scraping against tile, boots slamming against the floor, voices shouting warnings and instructions in overlapping chaos.

"Tomas!" Sierra spat the name like a curse, her voice hoarse from struggling.

The second gang member moved fast, trying to reach the discarded weapon, but Derin intercepted him with a bone-jarring collision that sent both men sprawling. Dylan immediately stepped in to help contain the threat, their teamwork seamless from years of working together.

Sierra was still fighting in Sawyer's grip, her breath hot and desperate against his skin as she struggled uselessly against his hold.

"He made you!" she spat, her voice venomous with rage and something that might have been grief. "You betrayed Angelo! You destroyed everything we built!"

Her words hit deeper than the blade had, cutting into old wounds he'd thought were healed.

"You think this is over?" Her voice turned mocking, desperate, but edged with a certainty that made his blood run cold. "You think they'll just let you disappear? Let you play house with your pretty little girlfriend?"

Then the ranch hands moved in like a well-oiled machine, gripping Sierra's shoulders and forcing her down to the ground with controlled but implacable strength. Her body shook against their hold, against the defeat that was settling over her like a heavy blanket, against the truth that was finally pressing in.

She would not win. Not this time. Not ever.

The fight finally drained from her limbs, leaving her limp and defeated on the cold tile.

Adan's voice cut through the afternoon chaos, steady and authoritative as he spoke into his phone. "This is Adan Franco at Vargas Ranch. We need officers out here immediately. We have two suspects in custody and one injury."

The fight was over. Sierra was restrained, Tomas was subdued, but Sawyer couldn't seem to move. The burning in his arm was sharper now, pulsing in rhythm with his hammering heartbeat, pain spreading slow and deep through muscle and nerve.

Devon Vargas appeared at his side with a first aid kit, already assessing the damage with practiced efficiency. "Sit down. Now."

Sawyer didn't argue. His legs felt unsteady anyway, adrenaline beginning to ebb and leave him shaky. He barely felt the sting of antiseptic as Devon cleaned the wound, too focused on scanning the room for threats that were no longer there.

The dining hall felt different now. Less chaotic, the immediate tension slowly bled away like air from a punctured tire. Sierra had gone quiet, her face set in lines of defiance that couldn't quite hide her defeat. Not panicked anymore. Not pleading. Just watching with the flat stare of someone who'd already accepted what came next.

Someone exhaled sharply near the overturned tables. Someone else muttered, "Thank goodness it's done."

But Sawyer knew it wasn't done. Not for him. Not for Cara. Sierra's words echoed in his head like a prophecy: *You think they'll let you go just like that?*

He turned toward Cara with his heart in his throat.

She hadn't moved from where she'd fallen when Sierra grabbed her. She sat frozen in the same spot, eyes wide and unfocused, breathing shallow and too fast. Her arms were wrapped tight across her chest like she was still bracing for impact, like she hadn't found solid ground yet and wasn't sure she ever would again.

Sawyer's lungs constricted with something deeper than physical pain. The weight of everything left unsaid, everything that had been revealed, pressed down on him like a crushing weight. His hands were still clenched into fists, fingers locked from a fight that was already over, but his body didn't believe it yet.

The warmth at his arm felt heavier now, blood soaking through the gauze Devon had applied. But none of it mattered. Not the pain radiating down to his fingertips, not the exhaustion pressing into his bones like lead, not even the way his pulse still pounded against his ribs like he was still in danger.

Hours ago, he'd told her he wanted to build everything with her. A business, a future, a life worth living. Now he wasn't sure she'd let him build anything at all.

Because Cara was looking at him, really looking, and for the first time since he'd known her, he had absolutely no idea what she saw when she looked at his face.

What she thought. What she felt. Whether she could ever forgive him for the secrets he'd kept.

That realization hit harder than any knife could. This wasn't like the physical fight he'd just won through strength and determination. This was infinitely worse, because it was out of his control entirely. If Cara couldn't trust him after this, if she looked at him and saw something she couldn't accept, then none of it had mattered.

Not the fight. Not the victory. Not the way he'd put everything on the line to protect her.

Cara could end everything with a single look, a single decision, a single word.

And he was completely helpless to stop it.

THE CHAIR BENEATH Cara felt too solid, too real, like the only steady thing in a world that had just tilted sideways. Devon's voice drifted from somewhere nearby, calm and reassuring as he worked on Sawyer's arm, but the words barely registered over the sound of her own pulse thundering in her ears.

Her fingers had drifted to her throat without her realizing it, pressing into the skin where Sierra's blade had rested just minutes ago. The flesh felt tender, hypersensitive, like it remembered the cold kiss of steel even though no blood had been drawn. Had someone really just held a knife to her throat? Had that actually happened, or was this some kind of nightmare she couldn't wake up from?

Sierra's voice echoed in her head with crystalline clarity: *You think this is over? You think they'll let you go just like that?*

The words settled deep in her chest, carving out spaces for every future shadow, every glance over her shoulder, every moment of wondering if she was truly safe.

Her hands were shaking. When had that started? She clasped them together in her lap, trying to stop the tremor, but it just seemed to spread up her arms and into her shoulders. The delayed shock was hitting now, her body finally processing what her mind had been too terrified to absorb in the moment.

Red and blue lights flickered through the windows near the barn doors, casting strange shadows across the dining hall walls. Voices exchanged low, official orders as Sierra was forced toward the patrol car, her wrists secured behind her back. Cara could see it all happening in her peripheral vision, but it felt distant, surreal, like watching a movie of someone else's life.

She was too focused on Sawyer.

He sat just a few feet away, Devon wrapping fresh

gauze around his forearm with practiced efficiency. Blood had soaked through the first bandage, dark red against the white fabric. His breathing was uneven, whether from pain or adrenaline or something else entirely, she couldn't tell.

But it was his eyes that held her captive. Waiting, searching her face with an intensity that made her chest tight.

Angelo. The name Sierra had thrown at them like a weapon, like a grenade designed to destroy everything they'd built together. Sawyer had never mentioned that name. Not when he'd told her about foster care, about his struggles on the streets, about his time in prison. Not when they'd planned Renewal Designs together just hours ago, their future spreading out before them like a beautiful map. Not when he'd promised to build everything with her, his voice warm with certainty and hope.

He'd kept it locked away, and Sierra had ripped it out in the cruelest way possible.

For the first time since she'd known him, Cara wasn't sure if she really knew him at all.

The thought terrified her more than the knife had.

"She wasn't completely wrong."

Sawyer's voice cut through her spiraling thoughts, hitting harder than Sierra's threats ever could. Not sharp, not defensive, not angry. Just truth, raw and unprotected, offered up like a sacrifice.

Cara's breath caught in her throat. The attack had knocked the wind out of her, but this was different. Colder. More real. More final.

"I never wanted Angelo's name in this, in my new life." His voice was steady, controlled, but she could see the cost of that control in the tight lines around his eyes. "I didn't betray him for money or revenge or any of the reasons Sierra probably told you. I saved myself. That's the truth."

He paused, and something vulnerable flickered across his expression, like a door opening just a crack. "I just need to know if you can believe that. If you can believe me."

The silence pressed against her skin, heavier than the moments before the fight had even started. She should speak, should say something, anything, but the words felt stuck in her throat.

"What does that even mean?" Her voice barely sounded like her own, thin and shaky in a way that made her hate how weak she sounded. "You didn't betray him, but you saved yourself? I don't understand what you're trying to tell me."

Sawyer's jaw tightened, a muscle jumping beneath his skin, but he didn't look away from her face. Didn't try to dodge or deflect or minimize what was coming.

"I never wanted you to know this part." He exhaled slowly, like the words physically hurt before they even left his mouth. "The real reason I testified against Angelo. The reason everything fell apart."

The dining hall felt too small suddenly, walls pressing in from all sides, but Cara couldn't move. Couldn't breathe properly. Could only wait for him to destroy whatever was left of the man she thought she'd fallen in love with.

"It was supposed to be simple. Just another car." His voice roughened at the edges, taking on the cadence of someone reliving a nightmare. "Angelo and I had stolen cars together before. Too many to count. It was what we did, how we survived. But that night..."

The words came slowly, carefully, like he was afraid they might cut him if he spoke too fast. The owner had come back too soon, appearing in the parking garage just as they were getting the engine started. Angelo had reached for a gun that Sawyer hadn't even known he was carrying. Sawyer had tried to talk him down, had begged him to just run, to get out while they still could.

"We could've just run. Should have run. I told him that, kept saying it, but Angelo..." Sawyer's voice broke slightly. "He wasn't thinking straight. Something had snapped in him. The gun went off."

Cara's stomach clenched, nausea rising in her throat.

"Single shot to the chest. The guy went down, and there was so much blood. We ran, but the damage was already done. He died in the hospital three hours later."

The words hung in the air between them like an accusation, like a confession, like the end of everything.

"Sierra wasn't there that night," Sawyer continued, and something like bitter shock colored his voice. "She acted like she lived it, like she saw everything, but she wasn't there. No one else was. Just me. Just Angelo. Just a dying man whose only crime was coming back to his own car."

That hit Cara like a physical blow. Sierra had acted like she'd witnessed everything, had spoken with the authority of someone who'd been there. But it had all been fabrication, manipulation designed to cause maximum damage. Just like her accusation about Sawyer targeting Cara for her money. Another lie crafted to destroy.

Sawyer had been alone with the weight of what happened. Alone with Angelo and a dying stranger and the knowledge that everything had gone wrong in the space of a heartbeat.

"Angelo refused to confess," Sawyer's words came faster now, like he needed to get them all out before he lost his nerve. "Even with the guy dead, even knowing we were both going down for murder, he wouldn't admit to pulling the trigger. The DA offered me a deal. Testify about what really happened, tell the truth about who fired the gun, and I'd only serve time for the car thefts."

He met her eyes directly, unflinching. "So I did. I told them exactly what happened. That Angelo shot him, that I tried to stop it, that I never wanted anyone to get hurt."

The confession landed between them with the weight of a gravestone.

This was the truth Sawyer had never told her. The secret he'd carried alone. The reason he'd changed his name, why he lived in fear of his past catching up with him, why Sierra's appearance had terrified him so completely.

And Cara had absolutely no idea what to do with any of it.

Her chest felt tight, like someone had wrapped steel bands around her ribs and was slowly tightening them. She wanted to say something, anything, but every word felt inadequate. This wasn't just new information she needed to process. This was fundamental. This changed everything about who she thought Sawyer was, about the foundation their relationship was built on.

Not that she didn't know how to respond. It was something deeper, more troubling. Sawyer's voice hadn't broken completely, his posture hadn't collapsed, but something in his eyes was raw and wrecked and desperate, and it made it impossible to look away.

She wanted her Sawyer back. The gentle handyman with the golden retriever who made her laugh. The thoughtful cowboy who brought her Chinese food and listened to her talk about her dreams. The man who'd been baptized just weeks ago, who talked about building a future together with such quiet certainty.

His past had muddied the image of the man she thought she knew, like throwing stones into clear water. The ripples were still spreading, distorting everything she'd believed about him.

She wasn't sure how to get him back, how to reconcile the two versions of Sawyer that now existed in her mind.

But she desperately wanted to try.

24

RED AND BLUE lights pulsed against the weathered barn walls, fracturing the evening shadows into sharp, jagged pieces that danced across the ground. Officers moved with quiet efficiency, securing Tomas with practiced movements and guiding Sierra toward the patrol car with controlled professionalism that made the entire scene feel surreal.

It should have felt like closure. Like the end of something dark and dangerous that had been hunting them. But it didn't.

Sawyer's breath came slower now, each inhale dragging through bone-deep exhaustion, pulling against the persistent ache radiating from his bandaged arm. The pain sat beneath everything else like a dull drumbeat, secondary to the crushing weight pressing against his ribs, to the way Cara still hadn't really looked at him since the fight ended.

She sat in the same spot where she'd fallen during the attack, fingers curled protectively against her arms, holding herself together like she was afraid she might fall apart if she let go. Still bracing for something that lingered between them, heavy and unresolved.

The quiet wrapped around them like a second skin, thick with everything that hadn't been said, everything that couldn't be taken back.

"You should get some rest," Sawyer said, barely recognizing his own voice. It sounded rough, worn thin, edged with something heavier than physical fatigue.

Cara didn't respond right away. Didn't move from her careful position. Didn't look at him the way he desperately needed her to — like he was still the man she'd fallen in love with instead of some stranger wearing Sawyer's face.

"I can take you home," he offered quietly, hating how uncertain he sounded.

A flicker of something crossed her features. Just enough for him to see her blink slowly, forcing herself back into the present moment, back to the reality of police cars and bandages and decisions that couldn't be avoided.

"You need stitches first." Her voice was steady but distant, like she was speaking to him from across a vast canyon. Not sharp or demanding, just stating a fact with a detached practicality that hurt more than anger would have.

The observation hit him harder than it should have — not because of what she said, but because of how she said it. Even now, even after everything she'd learned about his past, the instinct to care about his wellbeing was still there. Bruised, maybe. Uncertain. But still there.

"Yeah," he managed, his voice barely holding any weight at all. "I know."

"Take me home first," she said, and this time there was no hesitation in her voice. Just quiet determination.

Cara pressed her car keys into his palm without ceremony, the metal warm from her skin, solid and steady in his grip. Her fingers grazed his knuckles for just a second — too brief, barely there, but it sent a jolt of something like hope through his chest.

Sawyer curled his hand around the keys, gripping them just tight enough to feel their weight, to anchor himself to this one slight gesture of trust when everything else felt like it was crumbling.

The drive back to her house stretched longer than it should have, time twisting and warping around the silence that sat between them like a live wire. The adrenaline had completely faded now, leaving the ache in his arm to settle deep beneath his skin, pulsing in rhythm with his heartbeat.

Cara didn't speak. Neither did he. But this wasn't the easy silence they'd shared so many times before, the kind filled with quiet understanding. This silence settled between them, already shaped by words that couldn't be taken back and truths too heavy to ignore.

Sierra's voice still crawled through his mind like poison, taunting him with everything Cara had heard, everything she'd been forced to process in a few brutal minutes. The way Sierra had wielded his past like a weapon, using it to destroy the one thing that mattered most to him.

When he pulled into her driveway, Cara unbuckled her seatbelt before the engine had even settled into silence. No hesitation, no pause to look at him or offer some kind of re-assurance. She just stepped out into the warm evening air like she couldn't wait to put distance between them.

Sawyer followed anyway, because the thought of leaving her at the door without seeing her safely inside felt impossible. Because some instincts ran deeper than uncertainty or fear.

The neighborhood was settling into its evening rhythm. The air had cooled significantly, bringing with it the familiar aroma of someone grilling dinner on a backyard patio. Somewhere beyond her house, a dog barked once, followed by the distant hum of a car passing on the main road. Normal sounds. Life continuing as if nothing had changed.

Cara reached for her front door handle, then stopped. She held out her hand without looking back at him, palm up, waiting.

He dropped the keys into her palm, the brief contact of metal against warm skin sending another slight shock through his system. Then she was turning the lock with steady fingers, pushing the door open into the familiar warmth of her home.

She handed the keys back to him, still not meeting his

eyes, still maintaining that careful distance that felt like a chasm.

"Drive yourself to the hospital," she said, her voice even and controlled. "Get those stitches taken care of."

She turned toward her open door, fingers clutching the frame like she needed the solid weight of it beneath her palm to keep herself grounded.

Sawyer didn't move, didn't argue, didn't push for more than she was ready to give. But the need was there, burning in his chest—to touch her, to close the space between them, to say something that would remind them both that tonight hadn't shattered everything beyond repair.

Instead, he let the moment stay where it was. Let her walk inside to safety and solitude. Let himself linger just long enough for the ache to settle into his bones before turning back toward her SUV.

The hospital felt like another world entirely—bright fluorescent lights, sterile white walls, the artificial atmosphere of a place designed to fix what was broken. The stitches were quick and impersonal, twelve neat sutures to close the gash Sierra's knife had left behind. Done before he'd even had time to fully process how deep the cut had actually gone.

While the nurse worked with efficient precision, Sawyer stared at the ceiling tiles and tried not to think about what Cara might be doing right now. Was she replaying Sierra's words, analyzing every revelation for signs of deception? Was she questioning every moment they'd shared, every truth he'd told her, every kiss they'd exchanged? Was she trying to decide whether Wesley Martinez was someone she could live with, someone she could love?

If the future they'd planned just hours ago—Renewal Designs, building a life together, all those careful dreams—was already slipping away like sand through her fingers.

His mind refused to settle, thoughts chasing each other

in endless circles. Maybe it never would settle again. Maybe this was just what loving someone felt like when you'd kept secrets that could destroy everything.

Hours crawled by with methodical, unwelcome precision. His stomach eventually reminded him that it had been far too long since he'd eaten—not sharp hunger, but a quiet, persistent pull. Another reminder that the world kept moving forward, even when everything else felt suspended in amber.

So he stopped at *The Lariat* on his way back, the place they'd worked on together, where her photographs still hung on the walls. Picked up something simple. Burgers and fries, comfort food that wouldn't demand too much but would tell her, without words, that he was still here. Still choosing her, even if she wasn't ready to choose him back.

The drive to her house wasn't rushed or hesitant—just movement forward, carrying the uncertainty that had taken up permanent residence in his chest.

By the time he pulled into her driveway again, the porch light was still on, casting a warm yellow glow across the front steps. A beacon in the darkness that felt like an invitation, or maybe just a coincidence.

Sawyer sat in the car for a moment, feeling the weight of the takeout bag in his grip, gathering the courage to find out which one it was.

THE WORLD WAS wrapped in gentle quiet when Cara's consciousness gradually surfaced from the depths of exhausted sleep. Too quiet, like the world was holding its breath. Dim light from the kitchen cast soft, familiar shadows across her living room ceiling, and the throw blanket someone had draped over her legs was twisted from hours of restless, dream-filled sleep.

She hadn't meant to fall asleep on the couch. Hadn't planned for sleep at all, really. Her mind had been too full, too chaotic, spinning through everything that had happened like a broken record. But exhaustion had been stronger than anxiety, pulling her under despite the questions that refused to stop circling.

The warmth came first, drawing her gently back toward full awareness. A careful pressure against her arm, fingers tracing light patterns along her skin. Not demanding or urgent, just there. Present. Real.

Her breath hitched, not in fear or shock this time, but in the overwhelming weight of everything crashing back at once. The attack. Sierra's revelations. The way Sawyer had looked at her in the dining hall, like he was waiting for her to decide his entire future with a single glance.

She blinked slowly, vision swimming through the low light as her eyes adjusted, and then she saw him clearly. Sawyer sat beside her on the couch, his presence filling the space with something that felt like safety and uncertainty all tangled together. His touch was anchored and sure, like he belonged exactly where he was.

Cara sat up without thinking, her body moving before logic could interfere, before the questions could catch up with the emotions, before doubt could stop the overwhelming need for something solid and real. She pressed into him, arms curling tight around his shoulders, forehead finding the familiar curve where his neck met his collarbone.

Her breath came uneven, caught somewhere between relief and disbelief. He was here. He'd come back. Despite everything Sierra had revealed, despite the way she'd frozen up and couldn't give him the reassurance he'd needed, he was still here.

"Did that really happen?" The words escaped as barely more than a whisper, fractured and raw. "All of it?"

Sawyer didn't answer with words. Didn't try to explain or rationalize or make sense of the senseless. He just held her, his palm pressed firm and steady against her back, fingers curling gently against the soft fabric of her shirt. Grounding her. Anchoring her to this moment instead of the nightmare that had preceded it.

Minutes passed, or maybe just seconds. Time felt suspended, wrapped in the quiet hum of the refrigerator and the distant rustle of wind against the windows. The familiar sounds of her house, her life, her world that was slowly reassembling itself around this new reality.

Then, finally, his voice cut through the silence. Normal, familiar, achingly gentle. "I brought dinner."

Her chest tightened, but not painfully. More like something loosening, opening up. A reminder that the world hadn't stopped spinning, that tonight hadn't taken everything, that there was still profound safety in the way Sawyer said those simple words.

"Burgers," he added, shifting slightly so he could meet her gaze. "From *The Lariat*. Figured comfort food was probably the way to go."

The soft overhead light cast a warm, golden glow across her small dining table, settling over the takeout bag he'd placed there like an offering. She uncurled herself from his embrace slowly, reluctantly, and moved to sit across from him. Her fingers found the edges of the paper wrapper, not unwrapping it yet, just holding onto something tangible while the weight in her chest continued to shift and rearrange itself.

Sawyer settled into the chair across from her, hands resting flat against the table's surface. His breathing came measured and calm. No urgency in the way he moved, no pressure to fill the silence or rush her toward forgiveness. He just let the space exist, patient.

Then, quietly, he bowed his head. His voice came low and genuine. Not rehearsed or performed, just deeply real. A simple prayer of thanks for the meal, for protection during the attack, for both of them being alive and whole and sitting here together.

The breath caught sharp and unexpected in Cara's throat.

Wasn't this proof? Him bringing dinner when she'd given him every reason to walk away. Driving her home when she'd barely been able to look at him. Not pushing her for trust or demanding that she reconcile everything she'd learned tonight. Just sitting here in her kitchen, choosing to be present, choosing her in every quiet way that mattered.

She exhaled slowly, fingers tracing the edge of the wrapper as understanding began to settle inside her chest like puzzle pieces finally clicking into place.

"Wesley wouldn't have come back," she said, the words escaping before she'd fully formed the thought. "The man Sierra described, the one from all those years ago. He wouldn't have brought dinner. He wouldn't have prayed over it. He wouldn't have..."

She swallowed hard, lifting her eyes to meet his. "You're not him anymore, Sawyer. You haven't been for a long time."

Sawyer's jaw tightened slightly. Not defensively, just absorbing the weight of what she was saying. Processing it. The silence stretched between them, but it felt different now. Comfortable instead of charged.

"I see you," she continued, her throat tight with the weight of everything she finally understood. "I see the man you are now, the man you've become through all that pain and growth and choice. The man I trust completely. No more conditions. No more wondering if there are other secrets waiting to destroy us."

She reached across the table, covering his hand with hers. "I see the man I love."

Sawyer went very still, barely breathing, like he was afraid that moving might shatter whatever fragile peace they'd found.

"I was scared," Cara admitted, her voice soft but steady.

"Not of you, but of losing the version of you I'd fallen in love with. Sierra made it sound like that person was just an act, just another con. But sitting here now, watching you pray over takeout burgers..."

A small smile tugged at the corner of her mouth. "This is who you really are. This gentleness, this care, this faith you've found. It's not fake. It's the most real thing about you."

Sawyer's hand turned beneath hers, fingers intertwining with careful reverence. "I was terrified you'd look at me and only see Wesley. See the worst thing I've ever done."

"I see both," Cara said honestly. "I see where you came from and where you are now. The journey between them. And that journey, that choice to become someone better, that's what I love most about you."

His thumb brushed across her knuckles, and she felt the last pieces of doubt fade into nothing, replaced by something stronger and more certain than anything she'd ever felt before.

They were going to be okay. Different than before, maybe. Changed by what they'd survived tonight. But together, and that was all that mattered.

25

THE WORDS STILL hung in the air between them, settling into the quiet like they belonged there. "I trust you." Simple, certain, no conditions or doubt or second-guessing. Cara saw him—not just the parts he wanted her to see, but all of him—and chose to believe in who he was now.

Sawyer should have felt relief. And he did. But something deeper clawed at the edges of his chest, something he hadn't let himself feel in a long time.

He set his burger down, the paper crinkling beneath his fingers, and exhaled slowly. "I need to say something."

Cara didn't speak. Just watched, listened, waited.

So he said it.

"Phoenix Rising felt like family. At least, I thought it was. I thought they saw me, that they accepted me." His throat tightened. "But it wasn't real. It was control, manipulation. And Angelo—I never really knew him. I thought I did, thought we were close, but during the trial I realized I didn't know him at all. I had no idea he had a gun that night."

The words came harder now, pulled from somewhere deep. "I never wanted any of it. Never chose that life thinking it would lead there. I just wanted—" He stopped, felt the weight of the truth pressing against his ribs. "I just wanted to belong."

Cara's breathing was slow and careful. She didn't move,

didn't tell him to stop, didn't tell him it wasn't his fault. She let him say it, let him breathe through it, let him finally lay it down.

Sawyer blinked, forcing the air deeper into his lungs. "And then I came here. Junior took me in, taught me things no one else had, treated me like I mattered. And you—" His gaze met hers, held steady. "You trusted me. Accepted me. Saw me."

The next words came quieter, settling deep between them like they had been waiting to be spoken. "And the only thing I thought was missing was love."

He pushed his chair back, heartbeat loud against the silence. "But it wasn't missing. Not anymore. Not at all." The truth felt solid now, unshakeable. "I love you, Cara."

The air shifted, pulled tight. Cara pushed back from the table, chair legs scraping softly against the floor—not in hesitation or doubt, but in something deeper, something deliberate. She moved before he had time to think, before he had time to brace, before he had time to fear that she wouldn't feel the same.

She paused, her fingers pressing briefly against the table's edge, making her choice. Then she settled onto his lap, warmth pressing against him.

"Me too," she whispered. "I've wanted the same thing—to be really known, accepted, loved. Aunt Greta has been that for me—someone to look up to, someone who loves me like a daughter. And so has my Savior." Her touch was reverent, a quiet confession in itself. "And so have you."

The breath left Sawyer's lungs slow and deep, full of something heavier than relief. Something absolute, something earned.

Then her lips met his—soft, certain, unquestioning.

And finally, he knew. He was loved. By a brotherhood of real friends at Vargas Ranch, by Junior, by God, by Cara. Maybe those verses Cara had painted that morning on the dining hall wall had been meant for him all along. His feet hadn't slipped. He was still the new man God had made him to be. He had avoided the ways of Sierra's violence, the path that once seemed inevitable.

God's word had redirected him, had kept him anchored, had led him here—to this table, to this love, to Cara. It was the path he walked now. It was Cara's path, too.

The understanding settled between them, heavy but certain. Love had never been missing—not from Junior, not from Vargas Ranch, not from God, not from Cara. It had been there all along, waiting for him to recognize it, to accept it, to believe he was worthy of it.

Sawyer exhaled, long and complete. "We do not deviate from the Lord's plan." The conviction in his voice surprised even himself. This wasn't something he was trying to live by anymore—this was something already written into every cell of his being.

Her fingers rested gently against his jaw, her touch soft and reverent. "We don't," she whispered.

His forehead pressed lightly against hers. "Then we keep walking it together."

Cara's lips curved into something barely there—not just a smile, but something deeper, something full of promise. Something that spoke of tomorrows and next weeks and all the quiet moments they'd build together, one day at a time. Renewal Designs. A life built side by side. Everything they'd dreamed of just hours ago, now more certain than ever.

Sawyer kissed her again—soft, unhurried, anchored. Not hesitant, not searching. Just home.

Epilogue

DALTON VARGAS OPENED the front door, the familiar creak barely audible over the sound of laughter from the porch.

Sawyer and Cara stood there—newly married, faces bright with the quiet glow of happiness that came from knowing you had finally found your place, your person. The kind of happiness Dalton had once believed he'd had.

He'd been a fool.

Dalton forced a smile, nodding as he stepped aside to welcome them in. His house now. His parents' house. The house that should have been his fresh start, should have been for his bride.

For Janessa.

The familiar ache spread through his chest, but he pushed it down, kept the smile in place. "Married life looks good on you both."

"Ay, si!" Mami bustled in from the kitchen, her warm voice wrapping around the words like they weren't just conversation but confirmation that love could thrive here. She beamed at Cara, hands held out in welcome. "And the casitas! *Dios mío*, the guests cannot stop talking about them. You have such vision, *hija*. The casitas, the dining hall—everything you two have touched has come alive again."

Dalton's chest tightened, but not entirely from pain.

They'd done good work—exceptional work. The resort had never looked better, and bookings were already up for next season. At least something good had come from his spectacular failure with Janessa.

"You make the house beautiful too," Mami continued, her eyes flickering briefly toward the hallway leading to the owner's suite. The space she kept insisting would be ready for when Dalton found someone new.

He wouldn't. Not after what his desperation for a wife had nearly cost his family.

Sawyer glanced around the house, then smirked at something only he seemed to find amusing.

Cara caught the look. "What?"

"Just remembering how Goldie pawed you that first day."

Her eyes rolled, but her smile was pure affection. "Well, I'm still not convinced you should have brought your dog to the worksite."

"Hey, Goldie's been invaluable quality control on every project since," Sawyer defended with mock seriousness.

"Quality control," Cara repeated dryly. "Is that what we're calling it when she steals sandwiches and tracks mud through fresh paint?" She nudged his arm with her elbow. "And worksites aren't the only inappropriate places for Goldie. You really shouldn't let her snuggle in bed."

"She gets cold," Sawyer protested, but his grin gave him away.

The easy banter between them, the comfortable way they fit together—it was real in a way that made Dalton's throat tighten. This was what he'd thought he'd had with Janessa. What he'd been so desperate to have that he'd ignored every red flag, every manipulation, every sign that she saw dollar signs where he saw forever.

He'd nearly signed over portions of the ranch to prove his commitment to her. Thank goodness his grandfather had insisted on waiting until after the wedding. If Dalton hadn't paid attention to the rumors—if he hadn't overheard her laughing about how easy it was to string along the "lonely cowboy"—

"Good to see Renewal Designs thriving," Dalton said, forcing his tone light, pushing the memories down where they belonged. "Even if it means I have to book you in advance now."

Sawyer chuckled, squeezing Cara's fingers. "I think I got an upgrade."

The shuffle of footsteps drew their attention as his grandfather approached, leaning heavily on his walker but steady, voice carrying its usual weight. "I thought I heard your voice."

Sawyer stepped forward without hesitation, wrapping his arms around the older man in a careful but firm embrace.

"Glad to have you working on the family home, Sawyer. Coming full circle from where it all started."

Junior grinned, tapping Sawyer's shoulder with a proud nod. "What's this new company called, anyway?"

Sawyer glanced at Cara, a quiet exchange passing between them—something knowing, something unspoken. When he turned back, his voice carried certainty. "Renewal Designs."

Dalton inhaled slowly, letting the name settle. Not just renovation, not just interior work. Renewal. Sawyer had spent years trying to rebuild his life—now he offered that same transformation to others. The irony wasn't lost on Dalton. Some people got second chances. Some people found redemption.

Some people just got left with the wreckage of their own poor judgment.

Cara squeezed her husband's hand. "We believe in restoration—inside and out."

Junior's gaze lingered on Sawyer, his nod slow but weighted with something deeper than approval. "Then you're walking the right path."

The right path. Sawyer had found his. Dalton had thought he'd found his too, right up until he'd discovered hard evidence that Janessa had cheated on him. How she planned to convince her "sweet, lonely fiancé" to sell his family's land.

Mami launched into animated descriptions of future projects, leading them toward the kitchen—the heart of the home, she always said. Dalton followed, forcing himself to focus on their success rather than his failure. Cara and Sawyer deserved their happiness. They'd earned it through honesty, hard work, and genuine love.

Everything Dalton had thought he'd had with Janessa had been a lie. He'd just been too blind to see it.

His gaze drifted toward the hallway, toward the owner's suite that waited for him like an obligation. Mami kept talking about when he'd find someone new, when he'd fill that space with love and laughter.

Never again. He'd learned his lesson about trusting his heart. About confusing desperation with love. About putting the ranch—his family's legacy—at risk for a woman who'd never seen him as anything more than a means to an end.

Sawyer had found renewal.

Dalton had found the truth: some hearts weren't meant to heal. Some mistakes taught you to never make them again.

He pressed his palm against the counter, grounding himself. At least the ranch was safe. At least he'd learned before it was too late.

That would have to be enough.

Read Dalton's story in Falling for a Real Cowboy (Vargas Ranch Book 1).

From the Author

────────

WHEN I WAS editing this story, I had one of those magical author moments. I suddenly realized I'd accidentally written a role-reversal Cinderella tale! There was Jorge, playing fairy godmother with all his theatrical flair, transforming Sawyer from paint-stained handyman to Prince Charming in an Armani suit. Cara became both the prince choosing her unlikely partner and the one orchestrating the magic. Even the borrowed finery that becomes permanent felt like a twist on the classic fairy tale.

But then I realized there was an even deeper layer I hadn't consciously planned. While Jorge was Sawyer's fairy godmother for one transformative evening, Junior Vargas was his fairy godmother for life. Jorge gave him a new suit. Junior led him to a new heart. Jorge prepared him for a party. Junior prepared him for a completely new existence. Jorge's magic worked from the outside in, but Junior's worked from the soul outward.

I also love how Sawyer's name change echoes the Biblical tradition of God giving His people new names when He calls them to new purposes: Abram became Abraham, Jacob became Israel, and Saul became Paul. Wesley becoming Sawyer wasn't just about escaping his past; it was about embracing the man God created him to be.

And Cara had her own fairy godmother story too. Aunt Greta helped transform her from a broken, emotionally neglected woman into someone overflowing with forgiveness and grace. But unlike traditional fairy tales where transformation means rising in station, Cara's journey was about rising in authenticity and kindness—choosing to love deeply despite the wounds from her past, choosing to see worth in others that society might overlook.

The real fairy tale wasn't about fitting into high society or winning the girl (though those are lovely bonuses!). It was about two people discovering they were worthy of redemption, love, and belonging—not because of what they wore or how they looked, but because of who God created them to be.

Sometimes the best stories write themselves when we're not looking, and apparently my subconscious was determined to show that every broken heart deserves not just its fairy tale moment, but its own spiritual transformation. I hope you enjoyed watching both Sawyer and Cara discover that the most important makeover isn't the one that gets you through the door—it's the one that changes your heart forever.

If you're curious to see how God transforms another broken heart, keep reading the series. Up next? Dalton's sworn-off-love attitude may just melt when he finally meets the right woman with a godly heart and snarky humor. Find out how in *Falling for a Real Cowboy*.

Blessings,

Karen Baney

About the Author

Karen Baney is passionate about writing stories full of flawed characters. She enjoys weaving together stories of second chances, redemption, and overcoming personal trials. As a transplant to Arizona, she loves researching the state's history and finding ways to seamlessly incorporate real history and real settings into her novels. In addition to writing and speaking, Karen works as a Software Development Manager for a Christian ministry.

Her faith plays an important role both in her life and in her writing. Karen and her husband, Jim, make their home in Gilbert, Arizona, with their two dogs, Bella and Daisy. Both Jim and Karen are active at Rock Point Church in Queen Creek, Arizona.

Discover faith-laced stories with characters who feel like lifelong friends.

Visit www.karenbaney.com to discover more historical romance series set in the American West. Follow Karen's writing journey and get behind-the-scenes glimpses of her research adventures on social media.

Facebook: @AuthorKarenBaney
X: @karen_baney
Instagram: @AuthorKarenBaney
BookBub: Follow Karen Baney for new release alerts

Books By Karen Baney

<u>Contemporary Romance</u>

Vargas Ranch Series:
Love is in the air at the Vargas Guest Ranch & Resort near Wickenburg, Arizona. Meet the Vargas family—five swoon-worthy brothers and their cousins who live by their family motto: "We do not deviate from the Lord's plan." These rugged cowboys run a successful working ranch and luxury resort while navigating the rollercoaster of finding true love.

Falling for a Fake Cowboy
Falling for a Real Cowboy
Honeymoon with a Real Cowboy
Falling for a Shy Cowboy
Falling for a Bossy Cowboy
Falling for a Smart Cowboy
Falling for a Humbug Cowboy
Falling for a Devoted Cowgirl
Falling for a Pregnant Cowgirl
Falling for a Cowboy's Legacy

Steadfast Love Series:
The *Steadfast Love* series follows a close-knit group of friends as they navigate the beautiful mess of modern life in the Phoenix area—workplace drama, complicated families, and love that shows up when they least expect it. These contemporary romances blend emotional depth with authentic faith, reminding us that even when life unravels, God's love never does.

The Heart I Rescue (prequel)
The Air I Breathe

Historical Western Romance

Prescott Pioneers Series:
Step back in time to the wild, untamed Arizona Territory where survival depends on grit, faith, and the courage to start over. Follow three pioneer families—the Andersons, Colters, and Larsons—as they risk everything for the promise of a new life in a land that demands both strength and hope.

A Dream Unfolding
A Heart Renewed
A Life Restored
A Hope Revealed
Hidden Prospects

Desert Manna Series:
Sometimes the most beautiful love stories bloom in the desert. Set in the growing frontier town of Prescott during the early 1870s, these tender romances follow women rebuilding their lives after heartbreak and the unexpected men who help them discover that second chances at love are worth the risk. Set in Prescott, Arizona between 1871 - 1873.

Beauty for Ashes
Joy for Mourning
Oaks of Justice

Colter Sons Series:
Power, legacy, and forbidden love collide in this sweeping family saga set in the Arizona Territory. The Colter ranch empire has weathered decades of frontier life, but now family secrets and buried betrayals threaten to destroy everything. As five brothers—and one resilient sister—navigate the treacherous waters of love, loss, and redemption, they

must decide what's worth fighting for. Set in Prescott and other locations within the Arizona Territory in 1887 - 1906.

The Reluctant Cattleman
The Roaming Adventurer
The Railroad Magnate
The Resourceful Stockman
The Restless Wrangler
The Resilient Bride

Larson Sisters Series
Meet the next generation! These delightful novellas follow the three daughters of Adam and Julia Larson from the *Prescott Pioneers Series* as they navigate love, courtship, and finding their own happily ever afters in territorial Arizona in 1886 – 1894.

In Love at Christmas
In Love with the Rancher
In Love with the Horse Trainer

Desert Life Media

———

Desert Life Media: *There Is Life in The Desert*

Entertainment-first Christian fiction set in the Southwest, featuring redemption, family, and faith

Publishing clean, wholesome, and uplifting fiction since 2010

———

desertlifemedia.com

www.ingramcontent.com/pod-product-compliance
Lightning Source LLC
Chambersburg PA
CBHW071854220626
47052CB00002B/111